D1316523

Roseheath

Also by KATHERINE TROY:

FARRAMONDE

Roseheath

by KATHERINE TROY

DAVID McKAY COMPANY, INC.

New York

ROSEHEATH

Library of Congress Catalog Card Number: 78-80473

MANUFACTURED IN THE UNITED STATES OF AMERICA

VAN REES PRESS • NEW YORK

CHAPTER

1

I AWOKE from a dream. In it, my cousin Oliver had said:

"It's a piece of monstrous injustice. Of course Grandmother was out of her mind and the will must be contested. Why, you little upstart, you don't even belong to our family. And here you are, inheriting Roseheath."

"But you know I want you to think of the house as yours; your home for always. I want you to stay—" My dream voice had been a high thin wail. I added in tears, "Oh, Oliver, I'm sorry..."

And he, so controlled, so reserved, had struck me. The blow, which must have been some movement of my own arm, woke me up. I lay trembling with shock, half wondering, in my swinging sleep state, whether the conversation had actually taken place some time before I had gone to bed.

The white-faced, censorious Oliver of my dream had spoken the truth. I did not belong to the Wyncourt family. I possessed their name only by the grace and favor, and love, of my adoptive parents—Grandmother Isabella Wyncourt's son and daughter-in-law.

I had no real right to Roseheath, this ancient house standing near the vast brooding caves that cut into the Mendip Hills. I had no right, unless love in itself was a right. And I loved every dove-gray stone of my elegant Somerset home.

My past had never mattered to me before. My parents had told me when I was still a child how they had brought me to Roseheath when I was less than a year old.

Father had said, "Your mother picked you up out of a cot and said to the nurse in charge, 'If you don't let me have her, I shall steal her,' and asked your name." The nurse said that they were calling me "Chérie."

"Oh, she can't go through life with that," my mother had said. "We'll call her Suzanne."

My real mother and father could be somewhere in the world, but they were less to me than the people in Magnon Down, our village that clung to the hillside and looked south toward enchanted Glastonbury and the Isle of Apples.

During my childhood, the house was full of laughter. My parents could even charm that old matriarch, Grandmother Isabella Wyncourt. Only Oliver, who had lived at Roseheath all his life, had never quite approved of them.

He had said, "They live as if there's no tomorrow, cramming everything into today. They'll burn themselves out."

Perhaps they did. Their life together was the "shining palace built upon the sand." And, like that, it did not last.

I was a schoolgirl when they died within two years of one another. My father had worked in the family business, the Wyncourt Glass Works, of which Oliver was chairman. For a hundred and fifty years, the low russet brick buildings had stood on the outskirts of Amesdale. The cut crystal, the engraved glass, the famous Jewel Glass—peridot green and tourmaline—were exported all over the world.

After my parents' death, there was just my grandmother, my cousin Oliver, and I in the great house.

A few years ago, Oliver had managed to persuade Grandmother to let him divide the house in two right down the middle of the fine wide staircase and the great hall. After that, the only access we had to one another was through a door in the hall. Oliver had explained that he needed to

2

entertain and it would be embarrassing for his guests if they wandered into the part of the house where Grandmother and I lived. The reason he gave was, I knew, the best that had occurred to him—he wasn't very imaginative. Had he suggested it a few years earlier, my grandmother would have refused to have the door erected. But she had aged suddenly since my parents' death, as if a light in her tough, dogmatic heart had gone out. Not that she had mourned them in any plaintive, self-pitying way. She had set her lips, and her fierce eyes had defied any show of sentiment. But she had not objected to the door, where once she would have forbidden such a travesty to her lovely home. She said to me when she told me that Oliver had suggested it:

"What does it matter? He is so dull. He has always bored me."

I knew that his intention was to secure himself against any encroachment he feared might come from a difficult and self-willed old woman. I doubted if it ever occurred to Oliver that he bored her.

I lay in the bed that was like a carved wooden island in my lofty room and my mind skipped back ten days.

My grandmother had been sitting with the companion who came daily and stayed in the evenings when I was out playing tennis in the summer, dancing or just sitting around with friends drinking coffee and putting the world to rights on winter evenings. The companion was a quiet little woman from the village who lived with her sister, who was the postmistress. She always looked like an early Victorian governess dressed up in clothes out of her period, and I knew that she was both awed by Grandmother and admiring of her.

When I returned on that humid Thursday night only ten days ago, Grandmother was muttering angrily at something on television that irritated her.

Ethel Channing, the companion, was fussing around her.

3

"Now you have a nice snooze, dear. You really mustn't get worked up like this over a silly old play."

"I shall get as worked up as I like," my grandmother had retorted. "And don't use that terrible word 'snooze.' It sounds like a swarm of bees buzzing around me. Oh, dear, there's no air tonight..."

Grandmother, however, did close her eyes. A few minutes later she gave a little sigh and died.

It was hard to believe that she was gone from the house. Such was her personality.

Tomorrow, I told myself, now fully awakened from my nightmare, *tomorrow it will be different.* None of this would seem strange any more. A full week would have passed since the funeral, and I should have accepted it.

The moonlight poured through the tall windows of my bedroom. For the past ten nights I had not drawn the curtains when I went to bed, wanting the companionship of the things outside this house where I was so suddenly alone. I had lain listening to the occasional sounds that broke the stillness of the countryside—the cry of an owl, the distant barking of a dog, even the rustle of the trees in the late summer wind. I needed assurance that familiar things were not far away. And light, I had needed that, too, even if it were just the dead, opaque glow of the moon.

I pulled myself up on the pillow. I loved color, but the room was colorless. The leaf-green walls, the sun-yellow curtains were blanched by the moonlight.

It was absurd to feel this enveloping loneliness when there were two other people in the house—Oliver and his housekeeper, Danielle Goddard. But the door between the two wings was locked, and we were as detached in our homes as strangers in a city street.

It was nearly three years since Fay, Oliver's wife, had left him. There had been no divorce. I never knew why.

4

Perhaps Fay hoped that one day Oliver would ask her to come back. At the time of the break-up of their marriage, he had seemed merely annoyed that he had lost a hostess for for his business entertaining; his real feelings were apparently uninvolved.

Oliver had immediately engaged a housekeeper. She was what he wanted, a reserved, attractive woman, perfectly able to cope with entertaining on a formal scale. Danielle Goddard was a widow, and she had been with him now for three years. I often wondered why she stayed.

I had once said this to my other cousin, Magda, and she had laughed. "My dear, must you be so blind? Danielle has ambitions. She intends to be the second Mrs. Wyncourt when Oliver has finally divorced Fay for desertion. That's why he has made no move—time is on his side. And that is why Danielle stays."

The room was full of pre-dawn, that cool, remote, primeval sensation. But my pillow was hot with the fretting distress of my dream.

I lifted my hair, holding it on top of my head, and felt the air cool on my neck.

Somewhere outside the room, a floorboard creaked. Immediately my heart began its familiar racing. I dropped my hand from my hair and braced myself, watching the door. The creak came again. I strained forward, listening for footsteps. Then suddenly all the tension went out of me, and I took a deep gulp of air.

I did not believe in ghosts. Nobody was coming along the passage, nobody was going to open the door and wake me with some fantastic story about the house being on fire, or thieves in a downstairs room. Not any more . . . never, never again. The nights when I had been roughly awakened out of sleep by my grandmother's angry delusions were over. She could no longer shake me awake with her terrifying tales nor rail at me for not listening to her. But her dominance

5

died hard. It was curious that her mind was so clear and alert during the day and only misted over with senility in the quiet hours of the night.

I put out a finger and twisted the bedside clock toward me. The luminous hands pointed to a quarter to five. Almost morning.

I got up and pulled on a green robe and went to the window. Chill air drifted through the cracks in the ancient frames. I crossed my arms, shivering a little, not so much with the dawn chill as with shaking myself out of the nightmare.

I opened the window and leaned out, looking along the façade of the house.

It stood grayly luminous in the fading sky, a classically seventeenth-century Palladian mansion. I could just see the curling details of the capitals of the Corinthian columns that framed the doorway, the tall windows, the carved stone pediment. Roseheath was nobly beautiful, and I was as proud of it as if it had been my own ancestors who had built it.

Through the trees to my left, I could just see the white corner wall of Amber Court, the only house near Roseheath. My other cousin, Magda, lived there.

Underneath his cool manner, I felt that Oliver must hate me for being mistress of Roseheath. What did Magda feel? Did she hate me, too? And Sarne, her husband?

I leaned my chin on my hands. We were all so strangely linked, like the silks woven into a tapestry. And superimposed over the whole pattern was the question mark. Why had Grandmother left the house to me? For not only was I no true relative, but I doubted very much if she had liked me any more than she had liked Magda or Oliver. The only explanation that had come to my stunned mind since I had learned the contents of the will was that all her life this intelligent, impatient woman had been a *malicieuse*. She had enjoyed upsetting complacency, shattering foregone conclusions. She must have known that both Magda and Oliver had speculated as to which of them would inherit Roseheath, and so leaving it to me must have been a piece of calculated mischief.

I turned my head and looked toward the moors. I could just see the tops of the great Mandrake Caves, like asses' ears and giants' teeth against the oyster tint of pre-dawn.

Mandrake was the largest of the great group of caves that dominated the moors. Only very daring and experienced potholers had ever climbed down to the thick waters three hundred feet below and swum to the incredible underground caverns beyond. I had seen color photographs of the beauty of those nearly inaccessible caves with their glittering pink stalactites and green waterfalls, the brilliant glint of quartz. They had been described as the most beautiful caves in England, and the most deadly, their approach being "hell through which the traveler must go to find the glory beyond."

Psychiatrists would probably have told me that by reliving a terror, I would be free of it. It hadn't happened that way with me. I was as afraid of the caves now as I had always been.

I was only seven when I had wandered on to the moors and into the caves and become lost in the maze of passages. Black bats had fluttered about me, and gulleys of water trickled between the harsh rocks to make slippery paths for my frantic flying feet. The vast underground lake glimmered in the half light through the cave entrance. I could manage to avoid falling into that, but as I had run in panic back and forth along the narrow scalloped rock walls, I could not see the sharp edges that tore at my legs and tripped me so that I kept falling on my face. My terrified voice echoing, the lisp of the invisible water, the distant disturbance of bats made a cacophony of sound that, had I realized it, would have drowned the voices of any rescuers.

7

It was three hours before men from the village found me huddled against a wet rock, exhausted and soaked. If they had asked me my name as they picked me up and carried me to safety, I doubt if I could have told them.

For a long time after that, I believed in the tales told by the older villagers of evil spirits, of lorelei, who lured human beings into the vast depths of the caves and then destroyed them. The crystalline trickle of the water, the flutter of the bats had been, to me, the sirens' songs.

Three years ago, hating and dreading what I was about to do, I went deliberately to the caves again. I went because Sarne Eskinholm wanted to see them. He had been sent to England for four months from his home in Stockholm to learn English and was staying with Maurice Trent, the Wyncourt lawyer. Sarne came often to Roseheath, because Grandmother and Oliver were impressed by him. They thought him highly intelligent and brilliantly creative. To me, he was a young god with his tallness, his bright corn-gold hair and his eyes that were dark gray with yellow lights.

I was nearly nineteen, he was twenty-five, and I fell in love with him deeply and hopelessly.

For the first three months of his stay, he had treated me with only a vague interest, sometimes taking me to a cinema in Amesdale "because I need to study English." Sometimes he dined at Roseheath with Grandmother and Oliver and me.

Then, on an early spring day, he said he wanted to see the caves. Someone must have told him of my fear of them, because when I said, "I'll take you," he had looked down at me, laughing. "Be careful what you suggest. The caves are full of sirens and things that go bump in the night—I found that expression in a novel I'm reading—and you were frightened there once. Oh no, *you* mustn't take me."

I said heatedly, "I was only—a child then. I'm grown up now—"

8

"Grown up?" he had teased me, looking at the too-simple country dress I wore, looking also at my unpowdered face, my unrouged lips, my dark hair. "Oh, but in my country we would call you *skolflicka*. It means a schoolgirl. That's all you are." And he had put out his hand and touched my cheek. "An enchanting one, but still—"

"Not any more," I had protested, "and *I'll* take you to the caves. I will. I—"

"All right. You shall."

"This evening," I had said, "just before sunset. You've no idea how lovely the moors are then."

So we had gone to the caves. Grandmother had warned, "Don't try to go too far in. Now remember, always keep in sight of the opening and come out before it's dark, or you'll never find your way."

"I just want to show Sarne the underground lake."

I knew she wasn't happy about our going, but I, too, had a strong will and I was ready to fight furiously for the right to show Sarne that I was no longer afraid of the Mandrake Caves, to show him that I was fearless. I needed desperately to look good in his eyes. But inside myself, I felt the old terror rise as we walked together out of the small gate at the end of the copse and on to the moors.

So, I led him across the grass and heather and into Mandrake. The lake that lay thirty feet below us guarded what was called the Chamber of Aphrodite.

But when Sarne knelt down and peered over into the water, I cried, "Don't do that! If you fell—"

He looked up and back over his shoulder at me, laughing. "Then I'd keep afloat until you got someone to rescue me." He leaned deliberately out, reaching down to touch a piece of green quartz that glittered in front of our flashlight.

"Sarne, come back..." For the life of me I couldn't keep the high hysterical note out of my voice.

He gave me another look, unsmiling this time, and rose.

9

He said, "Goodness, you *are* frightened, aren't you? I shall call you 'Rabbit.' A scared little rabbit with beautiful long dark hair."

The last bit of his sentence didn't soften the mockery in his voice. I turned and walked back toward the entrance of the cave. The sun rested on a blood-red horizon that illuminated the whole moorland.

"Suzanne," Sarne called to me. I turned and found him sitting on a boulder outside the cave.

"Come here."

I went to him and he reached out and drew me down to his side. He put his hands around my throat and tilted my head. "You have a rosy face," he said. And as I closed my eyes against the brilliant crimson light, he kissed me.

My heart danced and leaped and then nearly stopped. His mouth was almost rough on mine; his hands gripped my shoulder, pulling me to him. I didn't mind his ungentleness; I wanted him to want me fiercely, to prove that it was no casual, brotherly affection. I wanted Sarne to love me. I heard him whisper, "We must meet again, darling. Soon—soon . . . !"

"Jason . . . *Jason* . . ."

I knew the voice that broke through the silence of that roseate moment. Sarne heard it, too, and started away from me.

My cousin Magda was walking toward us over the moors, calling her great dog, which had bounded ahead. I did not know whether she had seen us before we broke apart. In fact, I hoped she had. I wanted her—I wanted the whole world—to know that Sarne and I loved one another.

It was my first sight of Magda for nearly six months, for she had been in Italy studying dress designing. I sat quite still by Sarne's side thinking, "She's more beautiful than ever"; and I envied the assurance with which she walked, the proud beauty of her face, the flaming red-gold of her hair.

By my side, Sarne neither moved nor spoke. He just watched the girl, obviously not quite certain whether I knew her or not.

I said, "It's my cousin, Magda Wyncourt."

We rose slowly, like dream people. I said, without enthusiasm, resenting the way in which she had deliberately broken into our private moment, "Hullo. When did you get back?"

"This morning. After a bumpy flight through a storm. But I'm here. And—?" she turned her brilliant gaze to Sarne.

I introduced them. She said quickly, "I called at Roseheath on my way, and Grandmother told me you were out here. She's a bit anxious, Suzanne. She says she knows how scared you are of the caves and how easily you could get yourself, and Sarne—I may call you Sarne, mayn't I?—lost."

Sarne looked at his watch. "I didn't realize how late it was. I have to go back to the Trents' to dinner."

Magda said, "I shall be there, too," and turned to call her dog. The evening was spoiled for Sarne and me. I whispered, "Tomorrow ... at the same time ... tomorrow, here ..."

Magda turned and leashed Jason. "Come, Suzanne. I'm quite certain you've got mountains of homework."

I said angrily, "Of course I haven't. I'm at the College of Arts now. I'm an adult."

I was still too bemused to know what I had expected of this evening. Perhaps that we would have had dinner together. Instead, he was going back to the Trents' house and Magda would be there. I was, however, too happy to feel jealousy. Magda was beautiful and sophisticated, but she was too late. This was the beginning of a love affair. Suzanne Wyncourt ... Mrs. Sarne Eskinholm ...

Grandmother watched me closely that night. I could not

keep my happiness from her, and I told her, "Sarne loves me."

"Goodness, girl, what are you talking about?"

"Love," I said.

"Puppy love, my dear, like puppy fat, soon dies away. You're only a schoolchild . . ."

"I'm nearly nineteen. And Shakespeare's Juliet was years younger than I am."

"You see," she exclaimed. "You're mixing the romance of literature with real life. Of course Sarne doesn't love you. He doesn't even know his own mind yet. At his age, men are just feeling their power over women; it's a testing time." She told me to go and wash myself and come in to dinner. I didn't care. Tomorrow evening I would see Sarne again.

I went the next evening, running across the strip of moorland, to the caves; to Sarne.

He wasn't waiting for me at the entrance. It was a cold evening with a threat of rain. I thought he might be sheltering inside, and I went in, calling him.

There was a sound somewhere deeper into the space. "Sarne?"

The sound came again, distorted, hitting the cave sides and bounding back. Someone was calling my name. "Suzanne . . . Suzanne . . ."

The old fear of the cave leaped up to mix with my joy. The voice was so strange, so disembodied, yet it was Sarne calling me, teasing me because he knew of my fear of Mandrake.

I called back, "All—right. I—know—you're—somewhere. But don't tease me, Sarne. Please—don't. I'm not in the least brave." It took a long time to speak those words, slowly and clearly, so that the echo did not distort. When I had finished, I waited.

For some moments there was no sound. Then I heard the

laugh. Then the harsh whisper again. "Come and find me, darling."

I thought wildly, *I'll find you. I'll damn well find you* . . . And I began to run deeper into the cave. I flew down a passage from where I thought the laughter had come. "Sarne . . ."

Silence. And then the laugh again. A black winged thing fluttered across my face; I hit a protruding rock and stumbled.

Sarne . . .

I cried, "I *must* find you. I *must* find someone—"

When the echo had died down the voice came again . . . "Suzanne . . ."

I knew then that whoever was in the cave had no scruples about frightening me. There was more than a touch of cruelty in the deliberate evasion, the taunting. A wild thought seized me in a panic grip. I could be killed here. I could be flung into the underground lake. My fears trebled, quadrupled, and I relived the appalling experience of my old childish terror. I turned to escape and found that I could no longer see the glow of sunset at the cave entrance. Somehow or other I had wandered too deeply into the cave passages. I was lost again.

For the second time, villagers came to find me and took me home. This time my hysterical tears were not only for my terror of the caves, but also because I was certain that it had been Sarne who had scared me, had gone there to mock and laugh and leave me in Mandrake's blackness. What had Grandmother said? That young men tried out their powers over women. So Sarne had tested the emotions of this English girl he quite liked. And I had been too eager and so, bored, he had to disentangle himself and had chosen the sadistic method of playing a terrifying trick on me.

When I returned to Roseheath, it was Grandmother's scolding that shook me out of my uncontrollable terror.

"What were you thinking of, going to the caves alone?

13

I've never known anyone so unutterably stupid. You know you're easily scared."

"I'm not. I'm not. There was a voice—"

"Nonsense. Bats' wings or water seeping through. Really, Suzanne—"

"Anyway, I went there to meet someone."

"Who?"

"Sarne."

She said icily, "I never thought that you were stupid, Suzanne. I suppose it is that you're still so adolescent. Running after a man..."

"He—came to me. You don't understand. When two people are in love—"

Her small, bright eyes had regarded me with mockery. "Sarne—wanting *you*? My dear child, I know his type. When he was born, the fates gave him the love of power to heat his blood, not the love of women. When he marries, it will be for ambition, not for love. He is what we want for Wyncourt's one day, when he has had more experience. But he is not for you..."

I fled from her to my room and locked the door.

But Grandmother was merciless—or perhaps she had seen it as being one of those "cruel to be kind" gestures. For when I came home from the College of Art and Technology the next night, she told me that Magda had called to see her that afternoon.

"I told her about your panic last night," she said. "We're worried, Suzanne. You really must keep more calm."

"Would *you* be calm if you thought you were lost in caves where men had died—"

"You should never have gone there in the first place. Anyway, you won't go again. Because Sarne won't be there for you. Tomorrow he and Magda are going together to the Manor Ball."

I stared at her. "I don't believe it."

14

But I knew it was true. Magda went every year. I was never asked.

When I next saw him, I gave Sarne a frozen "Hullo" and turned my back on him. But my love was an utterly helpless thing. I longed for him to come to me and say "I'm sorry, Suzanne, that I teased you in the caves. Forgive me." I dreamed that he would then kiss me and tell me that I was more important to him than Magda. Of course, he never did. I tried to hate him, but I only made myself more miserable.

He never came to Roseheath again. I knew that he wanted to avoid me.

Two months later he went back to Sweden. Magda drove him to London Airport. She came back radiant, announcing to Grandmother, Oliver, and me, "He doesn't know it yet, but I'm going to marry Sarne Eskinholm."

In those days, I was a little afraid of Magda as one is afraid of someone older, more sophisticated. I longed to shout at her that Sarne had loved me until she had come along; that perhaps when he returned—as it was arranged that he should—to work at Wyncourt's, I would no longer be an adolescent. And what had attracted him to me before she broke into our lives might attract him again. But I knew that Magda would only laugh at me if I said these things. So, I kept quiet.

CHAPTER

2

FOR three years I heard nothing of Sarne. Then he returned to Amesdale to a job Oliver offered him at Wyncourt's. Sarne's father had put money into the business, which was struggling for survival. I heard what the workers said. "That Swede has bought his way into Wyncourt's." Less than three months after his return, he married Magda. It was summertime and I took a sudden holiday so that, at the time of the wedding, I was many miles away in southern Spain, swimming and sunbathing with friends and trying not to think of the old Saxon church at Amesdale and the round stained glass window through which the sunlight would filter onto my beautiful cousin and Sarne Eskinholm. I tried to think of him as cruel, because he had deliberately terrified me in the Mandrake Caves. But I learned, bitterly, that one did not love the good in people. One loved . . . It was as simple and terrible as that.

If Magda had stayed away from England just another two weeks, I wondered whether our fates would have been different, whether Sarne would have married me. But Magda *had* come and our magic was broken.

So, leaning on the window ledge in that dawn, I stared out at the tops of the caves, and remembered.

From the east, where the light began to glow, came a soft wind. It whispered round me, playing in my hair, caressing, its singing in the leaves of the trees like a siren's voice.

I turned in obedience to that lure of the south wind and peeled off my nightgown and reached for my slacks. I slid a green sweater over my head and shook my hair free.

Then I went downstairs and out into the dewy dawn. I walked down the paths between the beds of delphiniums and roses toward the silver birch copse. The wind came with me, tossing the leaves. At the end of the copse was the small gate that led to the moors. I pushed it open and stepped from the ordered world of Roseheath onto the lonely moorland that stretched in patches of emerald and purple and gray to the horizon.

The air was like cold crystal; the stillness was of a world not yet awakened. In the distance, to my left, I saw the caves.

I had walked almost without realizing it toward them. But suddenly I veered right, away from the gorgons that guarded Mandrake's unearthly beauty. I was alone in this dawn world, and the thought was as exciting as if I had discovered a new earth. There was no one ...

And then I saw the man. He was standing with his back to me, outlined against the flamingo sky. Neither feature nor coloring was visible, yet I could have described him as well as I could have described myself.

Blonde hair; short, straight features; a brooding darkness of the eyes; power in the mouth and chin. A man of temper and temperament. Sarne Eskinholm.

The sun had just appeared over the horizon, and a shaft of it struck his hair, turning it to bright gold.

A gust of wind blew my hair across my eyes. It was so deliberate that I could have made an unconscious movement and done it myself. *Cover your face* ... An unaware movement of self-preservation. For I loved Sarne far too much and too deeply, and my feelings for him were dangerously near the surface of self-control. Pride and common sense helped me to keep my secret from everyone. Yet there was always the fear that one day the thin veneer would crack and awakened emotions and longing flesh would break through.

I flung back my hair with impatient hands and, holding it against my head, watched Sarne.

He stood so still that he could have been made of dark stone. I longed to know what his thoughts were; I dreaded for him to see me, yet I longed for him to turn my way. My fiendish imagination pictured the moment when he might turn. I played with the thought like a child playing with an enchanted dream. He would walk toward me, his hands held out to me as mine were to him. I enlarged on my fantasy, imagining him calling my name. "Suzanne . . . Suzanne." And then his hands thrusting through my hair, pulling me with a wild force toward him and making love to me in this primeval, dawn world . . .

Reality jerked me back into reason. It was better if he didn't see me. I was still far enough away from him to escape back to the house. Yet I stayed. I went quickly and as silently as I could through the rough grass to the Mandrake Cave and sat on a mossy boulder at the entrance and watched him.

What restlessness had brought him out at this hour? A quarrel with Magda? A tormented realization that their marriage was a mistake?

It was common knowledge that they had, for some time, lived their own lives, gone their own ways. There was no longer love between them if, indeed, there ever had been. As Grandmother had said, "Sarne has all the attributes that Magda wants. He is handsome, ambitious, and the kind of man who attracts hard-headed women. It must satisfy her colossal vanity that she has won him over the heads of all the other women who have ever tried to marry him." (For instance, one Suzanne Wyncourt, whom Sarne had once held as if he loved her...) And Oliver had said of Sarne, "He has married Magda for the shares she holds in Wyncourt's. He has one god, success... And success means control of the business. But that's something he'll never have while I'm alive."

The sun rose slowly out of the heather-green horizon, and Sarne turned unexpectedly.

I crouched back into the shadow of the wall, not wanting him to see that I was watching him.

But he cried, across the distance between us, "Suzanne!" and came toward me in great, seemingly slow, strides.

I said as calmly as I could, "Hullo, Sarne."

He sat down beside me on the boulder. "What brings you out so early?"

"It's lovely and peaceful," I said. "We keep wrong hours. We should wake at dawn and go to sleep at dusk like the birds."

"And live like vegetables." He turned suddenly and fixed me with his gray-gold eyes. "Why did you flinch when I sat down beside you?"

"I didn't. I just...well, I suppose I wasn't too keen on you seeing me here, in case you might think I was...spying on you."

He burst into quiet laughter. "And who am I to imagine you should spy on me? Oh, Suzanne."

I turned my face away, feeling childish and hurt.

"If you want to know," Sarne said, "I came out because, as you have said, the dawn is peaceful. It always promises a new day, new beginnings, fresh hopes—although, God knows, it breaks that promise every time."

"Perhaps you don't really want to achieve peace."

He answered angrily, "You talk as if it were a quality we can manufacture at will. Well, we can't. We are too reliant on each other. It's the old adage about no man being an island."

19

I hugged my knees and stared down at the tossing grass. How right he was! How little I could know peace when I lived here in his orbit; when every time I saw him with Magda it was like tigers' claws at my heart.

He said, looking out at the empty world and seeming to talk more to himself than to me, "Or perhaps I am using the wrong word for being here. Perhaps I was trying to escape."

"From—?"

"Say it. From what?"

"Then—what?"

There was a sudden tension about us both. Sarne moved a little from me and looked behind him. "Are you still afraid of the caves?"

I had been waiting for an answer. Instead, I got a reminder. A cold shiver went through me. The caves were something we could not talk about. I said, "You haven't answered my question. What do you want to escape from?"

"I changed the subject. Doesn't that show you that I'm not telling?" He put out a hand and traced the line of a rock.

"All right," I said. "But *I'm* answering your question. Yes, I'm still afraid of the cave."

I looked the way Sarne was looking, toward Roseheath. I said, "You like that house, don't you?"

"Yes. I like your beautiful Roseheath."

I felt that, although we looked at the house, our thoughts were very different. I had an odd idea that he was not even connecting me with Roseheath; that if I got up and left him, he would scarcely notice that I had gone. By staying here with him, I might even be like the last guest at a party: outstaying a welcome.

But it was he who broke the silence. "Dear God, another day!" He tossed the fragments of his cigarette on to the ground.

I said, "You take on too much. You're doing a marvelous job at Wyncourt's, but—"

"I take on too much. Heaven be my witness, you've no idea how right you are!"

With an involuntary movement I reached out a hand. "You didn't come out here to listen to the dawn chorus or watch the sunrise."

"No. I didn't. I have no liking for getting to bed at two o'clock and rising again at a quarter past four."

"So something is worrying you and you can't sleep."

He didn't answer me. But I felt his arm stiffen under my hand. I moved it to my lap. The morning was cold and I shivered. I felt certain that there had been another violent quarrel with Magda in the early hours of the morning. Perhaps it was his fault, perhaps hers. I wasn't concerned with that. All I knew was that this man who had tormented me in the caves on that second evening four years ago was hopelessly and obsessively in my blood.

If he had said, "Come away with me. Be a tramp, a vagabond, a beachcomber," I would have gone. I'd have given up Roseheath for him.

The birds had long ago finished singing, staking their claim on a particular tree branch. Everything was silent, and the wind was gentle. Not even a distant dog barked.

"Sleep and I," Sarne said as if my last words had only just reached him, "are like two people who were once friends and now can no longer find mutual ground."

"The hazard of a successful man," I said. "Or an ambitious one. Too much on your mind."

"I seek peace and can't find it." He ran his hands over his face. "Violence. That's what's in the place where peace should be." He drew in his breath in one great gulp. "And what will they say when the managing director of Wyncourt Glass Works is thrown into prison?"

From anyone else, the sentence would have provoked the

faint impatient laughter of disbelief. Coming from a man like Sarne, who was not given to joking or excessive statement, it had the terrifying ring of portent.

My voice came, sharp with fear. "Don't talk like that. Why should anyone throw you in jail? Or do you go round the great houses stealing the family silver?" I tried to lighten the tone of my voice.

I felt his shoulders jerk as if my voice had brought him out of some Stygian depths to the reality of place and time. He said, on laughter that had no joy in it, "Oh, in trying to pull the business out of the quagmire, I've stepped on too many toes. The only way to stop me would be to throw me in jail."

I let a moment pass, then said, "That isn't what you really mean."

He turned and looked at me. "All right, so that's not what I meant."

We met each other's eyes belligerently.

I looked away, rubbing the palm of my hand over the cold face of the rock, needing the shock of the pin pricks of jagged edges as a diversion.

I said, "If I could help. If talking would make things a bit easier . . . they tell me I'm a good listener."

He rose and looked down at me, his tall broad frame shutting out the brightest part of the eastern sky. "Remember your children's story books, Suzanne. Remember Pandora's Box. She was curious and she lifted the lid . . ."

"And out came evil. But—"

But what evil? What tormented him? What shadowed Amber Court? I began to tremble and got up.

"I can't begin to understand you when you talk in riddles."

"That's just as well." He put out his hands and seized my arms. "Sometimes a man flounders in his own hell—and he has to be very strong to swim out of it."

"Still riddles—"

"Go home, Suzanne."

I felt a pulse beating in my throat. The red sunrise seemed to flood the moors in front of my eyes; I was trembling, and without knowing that I had moved, I leaned toward Sarne. His hands moved with a violence to my shoulders and he held me close to him. I didn't take my eyes from his face. A heart beat violently, his or mine—I was too close to him to know which.

"What the devil did you come out here for? What do you want? Oh, don't answer, I know. You saw a pretty sunrise, so you came out to look at it. I came for a different reason. I saw hell—and I came to escape. And so we met. God, Suzanne, get away from me."

"And ... if ... I ... don't?"

"I shall make love to you." He lifted my hair and put it to his lips. Then he let it drop heavily back on to my shoulders.

I laid my forehead against his coat. "If you aren't happy, is it wrong ... to take happiness?"

He thrust me from him with such violence that I stumbled against the boulder. "I want no siren tricks from you. If I made love to you now, it would mean nothing. Nothing, do you hear, except a normal man's hunger. Do you want that? Do you? Because, as God is my witness, I don't."

I turned and fled. I ran over the pathless moors toward Roseheath, stumbled through the birch copse, across the dew-wet lawn, and pushed open the front door.

I reached my room and flung myself across the bed. At some time or other during the next hour I must have fallen asleep in my uncomfortable position, for when I opened my eyes again it was eight o'clock.

CHAPTER

3

I ROSE and dressed, still in a haze of doubt as to whether my dawn meeting with Sarne had been real or a too vivid dream.

When Oliver had put in the door that divided the two wings of the house, the wide sweeping staircase had also had to be halved. Sometimes, as I walked down I could hear his footsteps stepping abreast of me on the other side of the paneled division.

There was a smell of coffee and toast coming from the kitchen. For many years, Mrs. Joanna had come to cook and clean for us. In the heyday of Roseheath, Grandmother had had three indoor servants. Now, there was only Mrs. Joanna. Most of the rooms were closed and dust sheets hid the sheen of old furniture.

Mrs. Jo, as she loved to be called, was almost square. Her hair was dark and naturally curly, and she loved bright clothes. She was honest and even-tempered, and although she was known as the biggest gossip in Magnon Down, she was never malicious. She just loved to tell all to everyone.

The only other mobile inmate of my south wing came to meet me as I entered the kitchen.

His splendid name was Ming of Trebizond, and he sprang, like all Siamese cats, from ancestors who had been presented to England eighty-seven years ago by the King of Siam. Ming was a seal point with a creamy oatmeal coat and

24

Oriental eyes like sapphire stars. He loved me, but not because I fed him and gave him my attention—Siamese cats do not love for gain.

He padded over the floor toward me, and the little bell at his throat made light music. We called it his "temple" bell. He yowled a morning greeting at me and I picked him up and felt the strong muscles ripple under my hand. It was the one thing my grandmother and I had in common, our love of cats.

Mrs. Jo slapped bacon into the pan.

"Oh, no," I said. "You know I don't eat breakfast."

"You've had a trying time this past few days with your granny dying, and you've got to be fed up. I'm not letting you go to work on an empty stomach."

The bacon had begun to smell good, so I didn't argue.

"It's cool this morning." I looked out of the window at the lavender mist clinging to the oaks.

"The swallows were flying high last night. That means another fine day," she said.

"But it was a red dawn," I said, without interest. "That means rain."

She wheeled round. "How do you know it was a red dawn?"

"I . . . I was . . . awake."

"Then you shouldn't have been. Young people like you need their sleep."

Young people like me . . . I avoided her kind, probing gaze and took my tray into the small morning room, thinking of Sarne. For him, I was a woman, he was a man, and the urge had been there to make love to me. For me, it wasn't like that. There was nothing superficial in my feeling for him. It came from a depth inside me, not just emotional, not merely physical—a helpless thing beyond all reasoning.

Grandmother had been right. Magda could destroy him, perhaps was destroying him with that power some women had over men. It was not their beauty alone, but some magnetism. The same magnetism that Sarne had for me.

Those who knew the world might say, "Oh, snap out of it. Go and get yourself a job somewhere else." It was the answer. And yet I couldn't do it. I thought as I ate my bacon, "And now I am more deeply tied here. I have Roseheath and that is a trust I can't ignore."

Excitement and depression washed like waves over me. I heard Mrs. Jo singing in the kitchen, and I envied her simplicity. I was quite certain she had never been torn by emotions. She had met a solid, unimaginative cowman and married him. She had had three children, brought them up to fear the Lord, and now, a widow in her late middle age, was devoting her life to me. She was as uncomplicated as the flowers in the fields, as calm as the hills beyond Glastonbury.

When I had poured my second cup of coffee, I carried it out on to the terrace and stood with my back to the stone balustrade and looked at the house.

The sunlight was trying to break through, making hazy bruises of the shadows. The grounds of Roseheath were mostly trees and lawns. Gardeners were hard to come by. Tom McGully had worked with us for ten years, and at one time there was an under-gardener to help him. Now he coped alone, and so the flower beds were kept to a minimum. They glowed in the flowing, spun-gold light, crescents and circles of crimson and yellow and violet, the color that the bees seemed to love best.

I finished my coffee and paused, looking up at the house. During the last few years of her life Grandmother had become suspicious of strangers. Roseheath was hers, and nothing Oliver could say could persuade her to have the outside of the house restored.

"I will not have strangers climbing around and peering in

my rooms. The house, as it is, will last my lifetime. When I am dead, you can have your workmen."

The outside walls, long neglected, were criss-crossed all over with faint lines so that they looked as though millions of petrified spiders clung to the stone.

Roseheath . . . My father had told me that three hundred years ago a monastery had stood on this site, taking the overflow of monks from Glastonbury. Legend had it that the last Abbot had been called Father Rose and that that was how the place received its name. I reached out and touched the wall and loved the feel of it.

A car revved up outside. At a quarter to nine every weekday, Oliver gave me a lift to Wyncourt's, where I worked as a designer. I had my own small car, but that had always been left for Tom to drive my grandmother around if she wanted to go out, and I was still given a lift by Oliver.

Tom had just arrived as I left the house. His face was like dark creased copper; his light eyes were brilliant with health.

"Them Ophelia roses are fine, Miss Wyncourt. Do you want some for the house?"

"Yes, please."

"And you, Mr. Wyncourt?" he turned to Oliver.

"You must ask Mrs. Goddard." He looked toward the terrace as he spoke.

Danielle was standing, resting her hands on the stone balustrade, watching us. Slim and not very tall, she wore a green dress that matched the color of the lawn; her short, curly hair was almost white, in strange contrast to the youth of her face. I never knew her age. She could be anything from thirty to forty-five, the youthful figure and smooth skin making her seem the former; the white hair and grave, enigmatical face, the latter.

I waved to her and she lifted her hand slightly in recognition. In spite of the fact that only a door divided us, Oliver's housekeeper and I had never become very close.

There was a formality that was certainly not of my doing. I was not sure if it was that she did not want my friendship, or that Oliver did not wish us to be closer.

Tom had the car door open for me, and I got in.

Oliver was already behind the wheel. He said stiffly, "Good morning, Suzanne," like a polite acquaintance.

We sat in silence as he drove down the long avenue of oak trees. The mist had not quite cleared, and the arches between the trees had a kind of unreal enchantment that fitted my mood.

After we had driven two miles along the main road, the hills opened out and I saw the city of Amesdale with the twin towers of the cathedral, the spires of the churches, the dome of the City Hall all lying softly opalescent in the morning.

Quite suddenly Oliver broke the silence. "We'll have to have a talk about the house."

I looked at him, my heart sinking, remembering the dream.

He had the ascetic face that belonged to a monk or a certain type of artist, long, lean, without humor. It occurred to me that I had never heard Oliver laugh. Even his smile was reluctant.

I said cautiously, "What about the house?"

"How are you going to live alone there?"

"If you mean, how am I going to cope with the whole house, I don't want to do that. I thought, I hoped, you would stay. Oliver, you will, won't you?"

He steered the car round a slow-moving farm cart, and I waited, my hands linked and taut.

He took too long to answer. I went on. "It has always been your home; you like living there. What Grandmother has done need not make any difference."

"You are asking me to become your tenant."

"Oliver, no. I'm asking you to look on Roseheath as your

28

home, just as it's always been. There's such loads of room there, and we live separately. Please stay."

"And when you marry . . . ?"

I gave a sudden, jerky laugh. "If I ever do, how on earth do you think I'd want more room than I've got? I'd have to have twenty children to fill Roseheath. And I'm not going to beget an army." I turned to him again. His thin, blue-veined hands guided the wheel of the car; his expression was withdrawn. I added, wildly, "After all, if anything happens to me, the house will be yours. You know that. Not even any . . . any husband I might have, or any children, would have prior right if . . . if I died. I am not really a Wyncourt—I couldn't leave the house away from the family and—and if I married, I know my husband would be the kind of man who wouldn't want me to."

"Fine, generous words," he said coldly. "But they stand to be proved."

He was right, of course. By the terms of the will, if anything happened to me, Roseheath must go to Oliver. *If anything happened to me . . .* How easy, with youth and health burning in me, to talk glibly about death; like thinking of an active volcano when one has never lived in the shadow of one.

We joined the stream of traffic pouring into Amesdale and stopped at the red lights.

I said, "I feel badly about Magda, too. It's possible that she might have hoped to inherit the house."

"You can put that out of your mind," he said icily. "She has plenty of shares in Wyncourt's, and she has Amber Court. Magda's all right. And she has no feeling for Roseheath, anyway." The powerful car crawled in its line of traffic. "Thank heaven we bought up Grandmother's shares in Wyncourt's some years ago and made her an allowance, otherwise I'm quite sure she'd have died in debt."

29

"You make her sound like an inveterate gambler, and she wasn't—"

"She was always a spendthrift. Buying that sable coat when she had a perfectly good mink; flying to Paris at the age of eighty to order model gowns she didn't need."

"She looked marvelous in them—she always carried herself so beautifully."

Oliver said impatiently, "Wyncourt's was in a bad way at the time."

"But she sold all her jewels to save the firm. Give her credit for that."

"Those vulgar emeralds given her by someone—she would never tell us who—"

"A secret lover," I said brightly. "After all, why not? Grandfather had his little secrets, too."

Oliver said without amusement, "They talk about our permissive society, but it's no worse than what went on in Edwardian days."

"High old times at Roseheath," I said lightly. "What those walls could tell . . . Anyway," I went on, "when Sarne joined the firm and pulled it together, Grandmother didn't moan that she wanted her jewels replaced; she—"

"*Sarne—pulled—the—firm—together?* Really, Suzanne, I think that was a combined effort that we could have achieved without his help."

I didn't argue, because I didn't want to think about Sarne. I switched my thoughts quickly. "Why did Grandmother do it? Oliver, why did she leave the house to me?"

"I'd have thought you could have worked that one out for yourself."

"The obvious answer would be because I was her favorite. But I wasn't. I think she found us all . . . tiresome in some way or other."

"She was a Wyncourt woman," he said. "They're all alike.

30

They love themselves. That's why she did what she did and then, in her will—like a debt paid—she left you Roseheath."

"I don't know what you're talking about."

"Compensation," he said.

"You mean for being—adopted? Oh, no. Grandmother knew I had no feelings about that. I was picked up from that orphanage out of love—that's quite something, you know."

"I'm not talking about adoption."

"Then you'd better tell me why Grandmother should think I needed to be compensated."

"For Sarne."

My heart gave a lurch. I said in complete bewilderment, "Why? *Why?*"

"He was attracted to you, wasn't he, when he first came to England? Magda saw you together on the moors the evening of the day she returned from Italy. And Grandmother had already guessed. You were dreamy and starry-eyed—it didn't take much perceptiveness to know why."

He swung into a one-way street and headed for the Wyncourt Works.

"Go on," I said through stiff lips.

He said in his clipped, hard voice, "Since you've got Roseheath, you may as well know why. It's now old history, anyway."

"Then can I have the rest of it? You've got as far as 'compensation' and ... and 'Sarne' ..."

"After that evening when you got lost for the second time in the caves Grandmother had a talk with Sarne. She told him that as a family we were worried about you. You were a hysteric; that was why they watched you so carefully, why you had been educated locally and not sent away to boarding school. She told him that she was worried because you could very easily get worse—even unbalanced."

I gasped twice before answering. Then my words came

31

jerkily, as if I hadn't enough breath to maintain a whole smooth sentence. "I . . . a hysteric? I . . . having to be educated in Amesdale because . . . I had to be . . . watched? But it's not true. I was educated there because I wanted to be able to come home every day. And the . . . the only times I could be called hysterical were when I was lost in the caves. Try it yourself sometime. It's . . . terrifying."

"I'm sure it must be, but—"

" 'But' nothing," I shouted furiously. "I can't, I just *won't*, believe that any of you really thought me unbalanced. So why did Grandmother say those wicked things about me to Sarne?"

"Because she wanted her own way. And Magda told him the same story. Sarne was young and ambitious. A hysterical wife—even if he ever thought of you as a wife—would not be in his plans for himself."

I whispered, "Why? Oliver, *why* did they say such things about me?"

"It's so simple. Grandmother wanted you at Roseheath. She knew she could not look to me for companionship, nor to Magda. So, there was only you. She wanted you with her to the end of her life. And what a Wyncourt woman wants, she gets. So she had to kill any budding romance between you and Sarne. She read his character perfectly. He was not the type of man to live under a matriarchal roof; he wouldn't be subservient to her. And he was ambitious; he didn't want a wife who might harass him with her neurotics. He was also young and a comparative stranger to our family. To him, Grandmother was a wise old woman, and whatever was between you was fresh enough to be nipped in the bud."

"It's hard to believe! It's so unutterably cruel. So scheming—"

"Of course. But they were like that, Grandmother and Magda—from the moment she saw him, Magda wanted him."

32

"If I'd known, I could have gone to Sarne and made him understand."

"But you weren't the type to run after a man. They knew that, too. 'Suzanne is proud,' Grandmother said once to me."

"And *you* knew, and you didn't help me. You let them say these things about me."

"It wasn't my affair."

Oh, but it was, I thought. Oliver didn't want to be saddled with Grandmother either. I said aloud, bitterly, "And Sarne believed it all!"

"A young man in a strange country and only at the beginning of being interested in a girl. It would very likely have come to nothing, anyway. Grandmother said that, too, to try and self-justify. Sarne was testing himself, indulging in a few light affairs. That was probably all it was so far as you were concerned, so I shouldn't let it upset you too much. It's over and done with."

Over and done with, when every time I saw Magda and Sarne together I was gripped by the claws of hurt and longing.

I cried, "And it suited you, too, to have Sarne believe me unbalanced. Three of you working against me for your own ends! 'Someone has to keep Grandmother company, so let it be Suzanne.' Oh, I know how you argued. 'She's a self-willed old woman. Anyone who lives with her will have to be subservient. So, let it be Suzanne. She should earn her right to have our name.'"

"You never seemed to mind living with Grandmother."

"Of course I didn't mind," I stormed at him. "I was grateful to her for looking after me; I would never have left her alone, as you and Magda would have done. But I thought she understood me. I thought she'd have known that if Sarne and I came together, she would always have had a place with us."

"She would never have left Roseheath. And even if Sarne

had wanted to marry you—which I doubt—he would never have lived in someone else's house. Grandmother dominated. But so does Sarne. And you know, you're turning a few kisses into a marriage. That's silly. I suppose it's a case of distance lending enchantment to the affair."

My heart was pumping up in my throat in sheer anger. My Wyncourt father and mother had taken me in, had loved me. But after their deaths, the time came for payment.

Oliver must have sensed my resentment, for his head flashed round. "You must take it from me, Suzanne. What happened was for the best. Sarne would never have made you happy, even if he had wanted to marry you, which, as I say, I doubt. Young men like to experiment, test their powers. It was probably no more than that."

It was more than that, for me, at least. But nothing would induce me to tell Oliver so.

I sat back in the big car, hands clasped, and wondered what would happen next time I saw Sarne. How would he behave? After this morning's dawn, how could our relationship ever again be outwardly easy? It would always be between us now that he had so nearly been my lover. But Sarne was a sophisticated man; I had run from him, so he would in all probability shrug his shoulders and look elsewhere. Who was I to blame him? If Magda had been different... If she had loved him, I might have found it easier to hate Sarne for wanting me without loving me. As it was...

I realized that Oliver was speaking. His words broke through my thoughts. "... they're two of a kind, Magda and Sarne. It's evens which one of them will destroy the other."

The way he spoke, savoring the words like rare wine, sent cold shivers down me. Oliver had hated Magda ever since his wife had left him. He blamed Magda for the break-up of his marriage, although Grandmother had once said that Oliver was born to be a failed husband. Ever since they had been children, Magda and Oliver had quarreled, and when

34

he found that Fay spent a lot of her time with Magda at Amber Court, he tried to stop her visits there.

It was soon after this that Fay left Roseheath with a mountain of suitcases and her white poodle, Dubonnet.

Magda had been quite unsurprised by the break-up of their marriage.

"My dear Oliver, you don't want a wife, you want a house-keeper who will share your bed occasionally."

I could remember his bitterness and Magda's amusement even now, as I watched the familiar scene from the car window. Soon we would turn right to the Wyncourt Glass Works and my office, my drawing table, my wide window that looked toward the city.

The luxury of a room to myself was not due to any lofty position I held, nor to my own desire for solitude. Oliver had decided that it befitted a Wyncourt, and I knew that it was better that way because the staff would always feel frustrated if the 'boss's cousin' worked cheek by jowl with them. I could now see the russet roofs of the Wyncourt Works merged beautifully with the landscape, their walls softened by a hundred and fifty years of wind and sun and rain.

After I left art school, Oliver had insisted that if I was to join the business, I must learn something about every branch of it. For days I had watched the master craftsmen with their great lungs maneuvering the liquid glass at the end of the blowing iron. I had stood by the conveyor belts watching the glass slide into the ovens and the miracle of crystal begin. I had had to learn the rudiments of using the engraver's cop-per wheel. Color, texture, design—I had to know something of them all.

We swung into the drive and stopped at the executive building. The doorman came and greeted us and took charge of the Humber.

In the wide central hall were showcases of exquisite glass,

ancient and modern; scalloped bowls and slender vases, some opaque glass sculpture; ruby and sapphire and topaz gleaming under the concealed lighting.

Oliver followed me into my office and bent over my drawing board looking at the design. "That's good."

I said, "I took it from 'The Sacrifice to Apollo' in the Louvre. There's a wonderful reproduction of it in a book in the Works library. It's for Kris to work on." Kris was our chief engraver, whom Sarne had brought over from Denmark.

"I'd say you'll have to simplify it. It's a bit elaborate for a glass engraving."

"I was afraid of that," I said ruefully. "I'll ask Sarne—"

"You'll do nothing of the kind. You'll discuss it with Kris."

"Sarne has to make decisions so far as design is concerned, and he likes to see them first."

"I'm damned sure he does," Oliver said angrily, "but it so happens that my decision can override anything Sarne Eskinholm decides. I say that design of yours is too complicated for work on glass. As it is now, the detail will obscure the line."

Oliver was right, of course.

At the door he said, "If I am to stay at Roseheath I will share the expense of its upkeep."

"That's kind—"

He cut me short. "It will suit us both," he said.

When he left, I hung up my coat, put my handbag in the bottom drawer of my desk, and found that one thought obscured everything else. How Oliver hated Sarne . . .

CHAPTER

4

THERE were few lights on when I left the Works that night. I had stayed late, simplifying the design Kris was waiting to work on the following day.

Oliver had left early, probably to meet a client over a drink, and I realized that I was just in time to catch the six o'clock bus. I whipped up my coat and bag and, ignoring the lift, ran down the stairs.

When I reached the hall, I heard a car door slam and guessed it could be Sarne, who often worked late. Not wanting to see him, I stayed where I was, staring at the jeweled glitter of the glass in the showcases. Although too shy to face him, I had a burning longing to know how he would react when we did meet again.

And how would *I* react? How would *I* carry off the situation? I thought in despair, "I can never be casual with him again," and I heard the thought like a breath on the quiet air of the hall.

I went to the closed door and dragged it open. As I did so, I saw that it was six o'clock. I would miss that bus if, for once, it was punctual. I closed the door and ran down the steps and hurtled, full tilt, into Sarne.

He put out his hands and asked, laughing, "Hey, where's the fire?"

The laughter was so natural that it should have eased the

tension, but it didn't. I said, making my body taut under his restraining hands, "I can just make the bus if I run."

"With my car here? Come on, get in."

The briskness of his voice was both relief and pain. I told myself that Sarne was being subtle, that his casual manner was meant as a message to me. "Don't build wild thoughts about our meeting on the moors. I am susceptible to dawn magic, and it would have been the same with any other woman." Was that the message behind the easy-going order to get in the car? So I must be casual, too, treating the moorland meeting as if it were as unreal as the memory of a dream.

"I saw the lights on in your office and waited for you," Sarne said. "Magda wants me to bring you home for drinks. Adrienne is staying for the weekend. And Hugh."

"Thank you." I threw my coat on the back seat. "I'm going to bring my own car to work in future. I can't rely on Oliver giving me a lift home, and the bus is always crowded."

Sarne drove a dark red Rover, purring at sixty along the road that led to the moors and our two isolated houses. He asked, "You have decided to keep Roseheath?"

"Of course."

"It's a big house for one—"

"Mrs. Jo is coming to live there and look after me. And I hope Oliver will stay. You see, I don't want to possess—"

Sarne cut in quietly, "You don't have to explain your actions to me. If remaining at Roseheath is what you want, then you must stay."

"I love it. I want it so much."

"And Justin?"

"What about Justin?"

He laughed. "All right. So he doesn't come into the argument."

"That's right, he doesn't." I sounded cross. It was a cover, really, to hide all the emotions that stung me whenever

38

Sarne mentioned Justin Norton's name. It was an unbearable irony that the man against whom I was continually waging a secret emotional war inside myself talked about the man whom I was perfectly free to love and couldn't.

I knew that Sarne, like everyone else, believed that my fate was nicely sealed. As soon as Justin Norton had established himself as a sculptor, we would marry. I was certain of no such thing.

"How is Justin?"

"He's coming down for the weekend."

"Oh, good."

If I had retorted, "It's not good at all," I might start an argument. What was I going to do with my life? Be a career woman? Practice and study until the time when I was competent to work straight onto glass? A top engraver? To a time when there would be an occasional brief paragraph about me in some glossy magazine, my photograph along with four or five others headed "Top Women in Industrial Design" ... "And the third photograph is of Suzanne Wyncourt of the famous glass works in Somerset. Miss Wyncourt is unmarried, dedicated, she tells me, to her career."

This trend in my thoughts invariably led to restlessness. I turned my head and noticed suddenly that Sarne was taking the longer of the two roads home. I wondered if it was because he had wanted sufficient time to talk about Roseheath. Had Magda asked him to find out if I intended to stay there? Or if I was prepared to sell the house? Had they discussed it, perhaps for once in agreement with one another? "A young girl like that inheriting a mansion; a girl without even a drop of Wyncourt blood..."

Magda had never wanted the house. But suppose Sarne wanted it? Suppose they had made a pact with each other, that Magda would agree to live at Roseheath on some condition that suited herself...

39

But two people would have to die before Roseheath went to the Eskinholms.

"You're driving a long way round," I said. "Won't Magda be wondering where we've got to?"

"After a day in the office, it's good to get the moorland air. And, no, Magda won't worry. She'll be too busy with her guests."

His hand over mine, light though it was, became a torch to the stake, the immediate flame. I should know by now that it was more difficult to control love for someone who gave back friendly affection than someone utterly indifferent. The lightest touch—an affectionate gesture—and the forbidden love could spill over in confusion, embarrassing both.

"Oh, damn!"

"What's the matter?"

"Just a thought."

(A thought about you. This morning on the moors you knew, didn't you, that you could have taken me to the cave and made love to me. You saw, didn't you, that look of instinctive surrender on my face before I turned and ran from you back to Roseheath?)

But Sarne was behaving as if our dawn meeting had never happened. I stared out the side window and moved a fraction closer to the car door, away from him. I could just see the outline of the caves. I shut my eyes, keeping my face turned away from Sarne.

Magda's Chinese cook, Mai Chang, was in the hall. There was nothing inscrutable about her. She smiled broadly and did her funny little bow of obsequious welcome.

The living room was alight with flame and white and yellow.

There were only two people in the room. Magda came toward me like a gracious hostess greeting a welcome guest.

There is often a pattern resembling a ballet about a group of people in a room, some standing around a fireplace, some seated, the rest moving—all of it in slow motion while they talk, lift drinks, glance at their reflections in a mirror. It only lacked music, and sometimes there was that, too.

Although I loved people and my mother had called me gregarious, I had never felt part of the circle that gathered at Amber Court. I was always conscious of being a looker-on. It was as if I wore a magic ring which I turned as I stepped over the threshold of Magda's drawing room, so that I became invisible to those around me. Perhaps I was oversensitive. The Wyncourt personality had always dominated me—old Isabella, Oliver, Magda.

I had said once to Justin, "I have a feeling that if any of us were injured and there had to be a blood transfusion, mine and the Wyncourts' would be incompatible."

Magda loved hot, exciting colors and chose to live among them: flame and clear yellow and coral.

Hugh Gayer, Magda's friend, was talking about an auction sale at a country house he was attending the next day. He was an antique dealer, and judging by his clothes and his beautiful car, he did very well out of buying and selling. Somerset had more than its share of fine houses where the heads of the great families died leaving their children and their grandchildren heavy death duties and furniture that richer but less ancient families coveted and paid highly for.

Hugh lived in Bath, but whenever he had to attend a sale in our part of the county, he always stayed at Amber Court, often for days on end.

I didn't like him, nor, quite obviously, did Sarne. I often wondered why he allowed Magda to invite him so frequently.

I watched him now, describing the Louis Quinze console, the William and Mary cabinet he was bidding for at the auction. Hugh was handsome in an unspectacular way. It was said that he went to a hairdresser once a week to have his light-brown hair waved; it was also said that, since he loved good living, he was already, at thirty, developing a paunch which he carefully concealed by a belt. He had a habit I loathed in all people, of moving his eyes without turning his head.

Oliver had once said, "I've never understood how Magda can stand Hugh Gayer. She's not interested in antiques, and there are times when I've caught her looking at him as if she despised him. But she probably likes his empty social gossip."

I saw Hugh now, sliding his eyes round toward the exquisite peridot-and-diamond ring worn by Magda's other guest, Adrienne Wand. Of all the people who came regularly to Amber Court, I might have liked Adrienne the best, had I ever got to know her well enough. But she was very reserved, and here again, her friendship with Magda seemed a curious one. Adrienne was not in the least like Magda's other friends. She was quiet and, I felt, sensitive. On the other hand, there must have been a toughness in her, for she was an extremely successful woman in her own field. She was a gemmologist and an expert on French eighteenth-century and Georgian jewelry.

Tonight she looked plain. Not that anyone could have thought her beautiful. She had nearly black hair, worn strained back from her face as if to luxuriate in her uneven features. Her nose was long, her mouth thin and humorous, and she always accentuated it with rose and silver lipstick. Her eyes were slanted very slightly like Ming's. She was tall and dressed usually in the jewel colors that suited her—sapphire and amber and jade.

Again, it was Oliver who supplied the explanation of their friendship. "Adrienne is an expert on old jewelry. Anyone connected with things of personal adornment will attract Magda. That's why Adrienne is always a welcome guest."

"But from her point of view? She comes so often," I said. "And they can have very little in common."

"Mai Chang," he said.

Magda's super Chinese cook. I said unbelievingly, "Just for food? But she's rich enough to eat whatever she likes without having to come to Amber Court to get it."

He looked vague and put out. "Well then, it could be that she comes because of Sarne."

I had said quickly, "Oh, no. I'm sure they—"

"They, what?"

I was silent. I couldn't say, "Sarne isn't the kind to have affairs with women." I couldn't say it because I wasn't all that certain.

Hugh's voice brought me out of my secret thoughts.

"...and the console table will probably fetch five-hundred guineas ..."

"Five hundred guineas," said Magda and stretched her lovely arms, her deep voice thrilling, "would buy me that pink topaz bracelet I saw in Bond Street last time I was in London."

Lying between us, sleek head on his paws, was Magda's red setter, Jason—the dog that four years ago had rushed up to Sarne and me and betrayed our shadowed whereabouts on the moors.

I bent and stroked him. As I rose, Sarne handed me a martini. My artist's eye was so momentarily fascinated by the light glittering on the delicately engraved crystal that I took the glass clumsily and our fingers accidentally touched. I jerked the glass away, and some of the drink spilt on my dress.

Sarne said quickly, "I'm so sorry."

"It was my fault." I fumbled in my handbag for a tissue, furious at my awkwardness. I felt all their eyes on me, amused or bored that I was so clumsy. Or, I went cold inside. Were they aware of our touching hands, and had they drawn the obvious conclusion about me? Would they discuss it later with Magda, all of them laughing? "Suzanne is in love with you, Sarne. You'd better watch out." And Magda, utterly secure, holding her husband by her beauty and her alternating moods of passion and indifference, would laugh. It seemed that men loved most those women who advanced and retreated, teasing them by uncertainty. Fundamentally, men were hunters. My grandmother had once quoted, "What's won is done." So perhaps women like Magda made certain they were never wholly won.

I had no idea at what moment I realized that Adrienne and Sarne were missing. I think it could have been when I saw Magda with her head raised, looking toward the dark garden. I knew that she was only pretending to listen to what Hugh was saying, that her thoughts were somewhere else. She looked neither pleased nor angry, only proud, her smile secret and knowing.

I wanted to go home. The week had been distressing, and I was in no mood for even this which was in no sense a party, but just a group of a few people meeting for a drink.

To my surprise Magda, who was usually casual about such things, came into the hall with me.

She said, "If Sarne were here, he would have walked home with you."

"It doesn't matter in the least."

She paused by the carved table and adjusted a few displaced roses. "You've probably noticed that when Adrienne is around, she and Sarne tend to ... er ... wander." She used the hesitation and the last word deliberately, and she looked at me half over her shoulder with narrow, amused eyes.

"They've probably gone out for some air after being cooped up in the city all day," I said.

She laughed and picked up some fallen white petals

44

and cupped them in her hand. "Oh, the cooping up, if that's what you like to call it, comes when work is over. They—" She stopped suddenly, obviously changing her mind about telling me. Then she said in her bright society voice, "I'll call Hugh. He'll walk home with you."

"Please don't," I said quickly and gave a small, false laugh. "I don't need an escort. If I take the short cut through the side gate, I only have to cross the road and I'm home." I opened the door and ran down the steps waving a hand as I went.

The lights of the house streamed out, illuminating the first part of my walk across the lawn to the small side gate in the yew hedge that hid Amber Court from the road. To my right I saw the glimmer of the swimming pool and beyond it the curve of the main drive that ended at the wrought-iron gates and the small gardener's lodge.

There were so many shadowy corners in Magda's garden, clipped arches leading to the lupin garden, the rose walk; an alcove where a stone naiad stood; a white wrought-iron seat in a secluded corner. Places where two people could hide and be alone . . . Adrienne and Sarne were somewhere together, and Magda knew. And didn't care? Or was that an act of pride for my benefit? *Dear heaven, don't let me look round and see them . . . Don't let me hear their voices . . . their soft laughter. It isn't true, of course. Sarne doesn't philander. Sarne wouldn't . . .* As if I had a special file on Sarne's behavior.

I began to run and reached the small white gate out of breath, shaking and angry with myself for minding. I stood at the roadside waiting for two cars to pass. One car slowed down as the headlamps picked me out in my light coat and white face. I dodged behind it and ran toward the tall poplars that formed an arch over the drive of Roseheath.

45

CHAPTER

5

MRS. JO had laid a place for me in the morning room. Ming sat on my grandmother's Queen Anne bureau, prim and elegant, tail curved around sable satin feet. I was late home, and he was too displeased at my lateness to bother to get down and welcome me.

There was a letter from Justin on the table. I read it while I ate grapefruit.

At the end of the garden at Roseheath was a hut that Grandmother had allowed him to use as a weekend studio.

He wrote to remind me that he would be coming down on Friday, but that I wasn't to make any fuss. He knew I would be upset by my grandmother's death, and he wouldn't even come near the house. He would bed down in the hut. He had a sleeping bag, and he'd roll up in that at night. He was in a hurry to finish the small wooden sculpture he was working on during the weekends he came to stay with us. I wasn't even to bother about getting his meals. Though of course, I knew perfectly well, didn't I, that he was waiting like a caged lion to see me again?

Mrs. Jo took away the grapefruit skin and set some cold chicken and salad in front of me.

I said, "Mr. Norton is coming down tomorrow."

"Well, now, isn't that fine? I'll get a room ready."

"He says he'll sleep in the hut."

46

She said, shocked, "But you can't let him do that. The roof leaks, and if it rains—"

"I wouldn't dream of letting him. We'll fix him a room in the house."

She hovered, saying, "I hope you're happy that he's coming."

"Oh yes. Yes, of course."

"You could do a lot worse," she said and reached over and put the salad dressing within my reach. "Though it's a pity he's got that beard."

I knew she was prepared to stand and discuss the merits and demerits of Justin Norton. She would have loved to be able to tell the villagers that Suzanne Wyncourt was going to marry that sculptor chap and there'd be children again running about the house, and that's what it needs. But I only laughed and unfolded the letter, wanting to re-read it.

In its heyday sixty or seventy years ago, the hut had been a playhouse for the Wyncourt children. It stood on the far side of the copse where the boundary of Roseheath land met the moors. It was built of logs and consisted of two rooms. When Oliver and Magda and I were children, my father had had electric light and a heater installed there. The largest room had two windows, and one looked out over the moors toward the caves. My grandmother, who had liked Justin and had been flattered when he had carved her angular old head in elm wood, had heard him complain one hot summer day that his studio in Amesdale was impossible. It was a converted garage in a noisy mews. She had suggested that if he liked to use the hut on weekends as a studio, he would be welcome to it. Justin had been delighted.

His larger works would have to be done at the Amesdale studio, and as he taught three times a week at the College of Art there, only his weekends would be absolutely free. At Roseheath he would be able to work on small sculptures. His carving of my grandmother still stood on the chest in her bedroom. The room with its three tall windows was largely as it had been for two generations; the same furniture, the same paintings in their heavy gilt frames, the same four-poster where the greatest Wyncourt of them all, Isabella, had slept, begotten children, and died.

The train of thought took me from Justin to Grandmother and from Grandmother to the portrait of Isabella Wyncourt.

It stood in my part of the divided hall, but it did not belong to me. Grandmother had willed it to Oliver. That legacy had been something else that had shocked me. For the portrait, painted by Bernadino, should have been left to Magda. Grandmother had promised it to her many years ago, and I had been a witness.

On my eighth birthday Magda, five years older than I, was one of the people at my tea party. She had stayed on after everyone else had gone.

I had been admiring a little bracelet of pearls and garnets that my grandmother had given me. Magda had said, "I love jewelry, too."

Grandmother had laughed. "One day you will possess something far more valuable than any jewels I could leave you." She had led her to the portrait that hung on the wall in the wide paneled hall.

It was of the first Isabella Wyncourt, who had been at the court of George II. In the full glory of white satin and emeralds, her hair a pile of autumn flame, her eyes the color of dark honey, she seemed to watch our little group with amusement.

My grandmother had laid her arm across Magda's shoulders. "That was painted by Marc Bernadino in the year your ancestor founded the Wyncourt Glass Works."

Magda had said, without taking her eyes off the portrait,

48

"I know. You told me when I was five years old, and I remembered."

"I shall leave it to you in my will. You don't appreciate it now, but you will one day. It is worth a very great deal of money. In an auction, perhaps as much as thirty thousand pounds."

"It is *me*," Magda had cried. "It will be *really* me when I'm older. I have eyes that color, and hair ... I've got a necklace of green beads like those."

"Beads?" my grandmother had snorted in disgust. "Those are emeralds. And you most certainly do not possess anything so valuable."

"Where is the necklace now?"

My grandmother had said, "Gone. Gone like so much we had to sell because the company was in financial difficulties. We managed to save it, and then there were the taxes—"

"What are taxes?" Magda had asked.

"The payment you have to make for the right to exist."

"Who do you pay it to?"

"Oh—men."

"Men?" Magda had tossed her head like a young racehorse. "I shan't pay them anything."

Old Isabella had looked at her. "You know," she had chuckled, "I don't believe you will."

Magda had grown up, as she had known she would, to be as beautiful as the painted Isabella. Whenever she came to Roseheath, she would look at the portrait, and I could sense her thoughts, beating out a rhythm. "Mine ... Mine ... Mine ..."

But when the time came, the Isabella was not hers. My grandmother had willed it to Oliver.

He had said more than once, "I hate the damned thing. It's too forceful, too blatant. And did she have to wear

49

emeralds round her neck and a ruby the size of a sparrow's egg on her finger? It's vulgar."

So, I had thought, as he hated it, he would give it to Magda. He would say, "Here you are. It's yours by right." And she would hang it in triumph in her huge, vivid drawing room.

But Oliver had not made a move to do anything with the portrait. It still hung in the hall in my part of the house.

It was good that Justin would be down. The house was too large; too full of lofty empty rooms; too silent. I supposed he would talk again about wanting to marry me, and I wished the idea excited me. But I wanted no hold on him, and yet I needed his cheerful company. His voice was loud, and had a ring to it like some free and not very musical bird. His big bulk made the rooms seem smaller, more cosy. He came and went like a friendly bear. I thought with pleasure of the moment tomorrow when his awful little car would jerk and rattle up the drive.

The weekly newspaper had been delivered some time during the day.

Mrs. Jo brought it to me. "There's quite a bit about your granny in it," she said.

I opened the newspaper, flipping through the pages with a mixture of sadness and interest. Wyncourt Glass Works gave employment for two hundred people in Amesdale, and the death of the head of the family would be news.

It was on an inside page. What first caught my amazed attention was the photograph. It was not of my grandmother, nor of Oliver. It was a reproduction of Marc Bernadino's portrait of Isabella. The paragraph accompanying it reported the death of the oldest Wyncourt at the age of eighty-six, gave a brief résumé of her life, and commented how, in her youth, she had been a dynamic personality in the city. It mentioned the artist and then the value of the painting.

But who had told them? Who had brought the newspaper's representative into Roseheath to photograph the portrait? Danielle? Oliver? Certainly not Mrs. Jo, although I went and asked her.

She said, when I showed her the page, "Nobody came while *I* was here. I'd have told them that they'd have to get your permission first. I thought you must have let them in sometime to photograph it."

"The portrait isn't mine, Mrs. Jo. It belongs to Mr. Wyncourt. He must have given permission."

"Why doesn't he take it, then?"

There was no time to explain that everything in his house had its place and Oliver had no intention of rearranging his treasures in order to hang a picture he disliked.

She said, "Well, I'm moving in here tomorrow, and then we'll see about people walking into your house without your knowing anything about it."

It would be a relief to me to have her sleeping in the house. It was too empty, too full of memories, too echoing. It was a house that needed people.

CHAPTER

6

I FELL asleep quickly that night and awoke with a start, knowing that something had disturbed me. The luminous hands of the clock pointed to a quarter to one. I lay listening, but there was only silence and I concluded that Ming had been on the prowl and had knocked something over. My eyes heavy with interrupted sleep, I turned on my side and as I lay quiet, this time I actually heard a sound. It was a soft scraping as if something were being pulled across the floor below my room.

I got out of bed and slid into my dressing gown. Ming was perhaps chasing a field mouse that had strayed into the house. Cats were supposed to be able to walk through a collection of rare china without breaking anything. But not Ming. Graceful and elegant though he was, one paw too often managed to send some object flying. Sometimes I wondered whether he was a devil-cat—it seemed that that destruction was deliberate, if he was in a mood.

I crept to the head of the stairs and called him. Nothing stirred. From the landing I flicked on the hall lights. They glowed over an innocent, empty hall with the west-wing door tightly closed.

Nothing had stirred in my part of Roseheath. Perhaps behind the thin partition which divided us, Oliver or Danielle had not yet gone to bed. Or one of them had gone and had risen, restless and sleepless, disturbed perhaps by the persistent hooting of an owl.

Although I had reassured myself, I continued on my way downstairs, still prepared to find Ming skittering across the rugs in some wild game of his own making. I would take him up to my room.

I called him and waited, looking about me.

The hall had tall glass doors leading onto the stone terrace that ran along the back of the house. A draft of air blew on me as I looked for Ming. But I always closed and locked every entrance to the house before I went to bed.

The long brocade curtains billowed slightly. Of course, it was just possible that I had only thought I had shut the windows and the wind had blown them open. *But there was no wind.*

I went cautiously toward the windows, pulled aside a curtain, and reached for the catch.

Something above me creaked. My hand shot away from the window and my head jerked up. It all happened in a few swift seconds—the movement of my hand, my upward glance, my step back. But I was not quick enough.

The heavy double-lined curtains crashed down on me. I put up my hands to my head, ducking sideways to avoid the impact with the solid mahogany pole that would have knocked me out.

I struggled with the crimson folds, but it was like being in a nightmare where you never come to the end of what is tormenting you. My hands tore and pulled at the thick, unyielding fabric; my breathing became more difficult as I fought first with one great layer of brocade only to find another enfolding me. The smell of dust was in my nose, the taste of it in my mouth. I think I screamed, but the sound must have been muffled.

I was fighting a losing battle with the huge curtains and realized at last that my only hope was to try to crawl under it. I dropped to the floor and as I pushed my way forward, I had one panic thought. Who was waiting for me? Who had entered the house, forcing one of the locks on the window? Whose body had caused the curtains to billow out? But whoever was there, I couldn't stay shrouded forever. At last I crawled free of the huddle of curtain and stood up, shaking and shivering, my robe half torn from me in my struggle, the sash lost somewhere under the curtain, and myself in a flimsy nightgown exposed to the sharp air. I stepped over the mound of fallen curtain and closed the windows. Immediately I felt safe. If someone had broken in, he had escaped by now. No one lurked in the shadows to attack me. Why should they? What on earth had I got that anyone would want to steal?

A few pieces of costume jewelry, a gold watch. Oh, and of course, the ruby ring.

I looked automatically toward the portrait. In it, Isabella wore a great ruby on the third finger of her left hand; far larger, more splendid, than mine. I had half turned away when something made me look again.

The painting was no longer hanging straight in its heavy carved frame. It had tipped sideways, crazily, as if someone had knocked it in dusting ... *or tried to lift it from its place on the wall.*

Of course, the portrait. The local newspaper had made much of it and its value. Someone had been here, and the fallen curtain was no accident. I looked up and saw that one of the brackets had been torn from the paneling.

Oliver would know what to do; but Oliver would not be amused by being awakened at one o'clock in the morning. Then just for once he would have to be unamused. I turned and ran across the hall.

The door between the two wings of the house was ajar. I saw a floating movement of pale green on the other side. "Danielle ..."

She hesitated, her hand going out to the door. I pushed it wide, and we faced one another. She looked composed and very pale, her prematurely white hair like an aureole of little feathers. "What is it? What's wrong?"

"Someone broke into the house. I heard them. And the french windows were open. When I went to look, the pole gave way and the curtain fell on me. I . . . I don't know how he got in . . . I haven't looked to see if the lock on the windows was forced."

"Then we'll go together and see, shall we?" Her voice was calm; her hand on my arm steady. "And if there has been a break-in, we must call Mr. Wyncourt."

I said, "Did something disturb you, too?"

"You mean because I'm wandering around at this hour? No. I couldn't sleep, so I came downstairs for a hot drink."

We crossed the hall, and Danielle looked up at the place where the bracket had been.

"But it's obvious what happened. These curtains are very heavy, and the bracket just gave way with age. You sleep in the room above here, so that's what must have wakened you."

"The bracket didn't give way until I pulled aside the curtain."

"Then it was ready to fall. And as for the french windows, you can't have secured them. Some odd gust of wind blew them open. You once said you sleep lightly, so they could have banged and that disturbed you."

"But there is no wind."

"A sudden gust . . ."

"You make it sound very feasible."

"I think it's obvious." She was searching among the folds of the curtain for the broken bracket. When she found it, she held it out to me. "This must have been loose for some time. It has been up there for a great many years; in fact, it should have been checked long ago in case of such an accident as this. If it had fallen on you, it could have killed you." She put the bracket down on the floor and went to the windows, opened them, and looked at the locks.

"Perfectly clean," she said. "No scratch marks. Nothing. It's quite clear what happened."

I turned and pointed to the portrait. "And I suppose the nonexistent wind blew that out of place." I hadn't meant the note of cold derision that had crept into my voice.

"Or the curtain touched it as it fell."

I wanted to say, *You have an explanation for everything, haven't you?* But I couldn't, because if our positions had been reversed, I would have used the same arguments.

"Look, Suzanne, let's leave it all until morning, shall we? And I'll tell Mr. Wyncourt."

Always "Suzanne," but always "Mr. Wyncourt" . . . I said, "I'll tell him, too. I want that portrait out of here. To have advertised thirty-thousand pounds' worth of painting in a half-house lived in by one woman is making me nervous."

"I know exactly what you mean. Of course it should be in the west wing." She gave me a long look. "You're cold, Suzanne. And it's a warm night."

"Fright," I said. "I know I locked those windows."

"Sleep on it," she told me softly. "In the morning you'll probably remember."

Remember what? The very moment when I had turned the key and pushed the bolts? Remember how I had glanced at the portrait as I turned away because it was so flagrantly demanding of attention that it drew my eyes, although I had lived with it all my life . . . and saw that it hung straight?

"I know what we'll do first, just to reassure you," Danielle said. "We'll go round the house." She took my hand.

Together, flicking on the lights as we went, we searched every room. In the kitchen Ming sat upright, head stiff, affronted at being disturbed, eyes like rubies until the electric light changed them to sapphire. There was, of course, now no stranger in the house. Whoever had been there had escaped by the garden. He had been clever. He must have known where I slept; perhaps he had been watching the house for days, so that he had taken the precaution of checking any possible chase after him. First, by standing on the side table, he had managed to loosen the carved bracket sufficiently for it to give way if anyone pulled the curtains aside. And obviously, if I were disturbed, I would go to the french windows immediately below my bedroom, because the noise had come from there. Nicely planned, to envelop anyone who might give chase in thirty yards of heavy curtain. And since the Isabella was still there, he would try again.

I said as I went to the wing door, "Whether he likes it or not, Oliver is going to have that painting in his own wing."

She said, "Of course. Of course. Now, go to bed, Suzanne. You know the house is all locked up." As if it hadn't been before . . . as if I were a slave to imaginative fears; *as if I did not possess the stability to own Roseheath.*

Danielle had her hand on the handle of the door. She said, "I'm not going to close this tonight. So you'll feel more secure knowing that there are two of us within call."

"Thank you."

I went into the kitchen and picked up Ming and carried him to my bedroom. I said to him as I put him at the foot of my bed, "One live cat is better than a long deadly nightmare. I only have to reach out and feel you and everything will be all right." And that, I thought, was the stupidest remark, since Ming was neither a jungle tiger nor a bodyguard with a gun.

I lay awake for a long time telling myself that the police would have to be notified. The intruder had, of course, been a stranger. Perhaps he was one of a gang of thieves who stole for rich collectors. For the more I thought about it, the more certain I was that the portrait had been the objective.

I was surprised when I woke the next morning to find that my sleep had been untroubled.

57

Mrs. Jo was standing by my bed with a cup of tea, and Ming was glaring at me from the tallboy.

"You had a scare last night."

"Who told you?"

"Mrs. Goddard. She came in when she heard me arrive. She wanted to know how you were. I said you seemed to be sleeping late, so I thought I'd better bring you up a cup of tea and make sure you were all right."

I sat up, stretched, and took the tea. "I suppose Mrs. Goddard told you that I imagined what happened."

"Oh, no. She said that one of the brackets in the hall gave way and woke you."

The tea was very hot and strong enough to be refreshing. I drank gratefully. "It sounds such an easy explanation, but it's not correct. Something woke me. I heard movement downstairs. The bracket didn't give way until I pulled the curtain aside. Then it buried me."

She went to the window. Outside, the sky was like pale blue gauze with the tops of the trees painted on it. Everything looked so ordinary, so safe, making last night, as Danielle believed, a figment of my own imagination.

I said, "Mrs. Jo, I *know* someone broke in. The portrait—"

"That big one in the hall?"

"Yes, I believe someone came to steal it."

"My goodness gracious!" She stared at me, wide-eyed, her first reaction one of disbelief, then gradually working out the possibility in her mind. She folded her arms across her stomach. "Mrs. Goddard didn't say nothing about that. But a young girl living alone in a house with a valuable painting, that's enough for some of them thieves to see it as easy. Well, I'm moving in today, bags and all, and it's goodbye to that tumbledown cottage I've lived in for forty years. And there won't be no more scares in the night, not with me around. Come to that," she demanded, "who told the newspaper men about that painting?"

"It must have been Mrs. Goddard."

"On Mr. Oliver's instruction." She gave a snort of indignation. "What was he thinking of? Or did he hope that someone would steal the thing so that he could collect the insurance? Oh, don't look like that. I'm not here to pretend things aren't what they are. That Mr. Oliver hates the painting; he always did. But by the terms of your granny's will he can't sell it."

"How do you know?"

"Things get around."

The village grapevine of course. Even the walls had ears at Magnon Down...

"Oh, my dear saints!" Mrs. Jo gave a shriek. Ming had leaped and landed on her shoulders. "This dratted cat..." But she put up her hand to steady him. Secretly she adored him. Ming yawned in her face.

Mrs. Jo's idea that Oliver had arranged to have the portrait stolen was, of course, quite outrageously funny. To Oliver, the law was sacred. But I had sometimes felt that this respectability was a façade, and that he obeyed every law of the land, not because of principle, but out of fear of the consequences. There was a power in all the Wyncourts that could have had its origin centuries earlier in some merchant-adventurer ancestors who were hell-bent for riches. I could well believe, when I thought of their strong, aquiline features, that they could have plunder in their blood. But in the generations since then, they had acquired an overt social sense.

Mrs. Jo had never liked Oliver. She was no respecter of persons, and nothing would stop her voicing her opinion of him, of Magda, of all of us. But the picture of Oliver standing on the table to remove the Isabella was so funny that the thought lightened my mood.

Before it was time to leave for the Works, I saw that Mrs. Jo had propped the pole up against the wall and folded the two curtains, with the broken bracket on top of them.

In the light of day, with the thrush singing in the ash

tree and Mrs. Jo in the kitchen humming "The Road to the Isles," Danielle's explanation of what had happened last night seemed almost acceptable.

Oliver sounded his horn and I ran into the kitchen saying, "Will you get a room ready for Justin, please? I think the attic next to yours would be best. It's large, and he likes the view of the caves from there."

"That's more than I do," she gave a little snort. "Haunted, that's what they are. Full of the ghosts of those silly young men who died crawling around down there. But there's no telling with these artist fellows. They're usually temperamental, aren't they? Perhaps looking at them caves gives them in-spy-ration."

Oliver sounded his horn again. I ran through the house, down the steps, and got into the car.

He said, as I closed the door, "Danielle tells me you had a scare last night."

"That's right, I did."

"From what she says, it was perfectly clear what happened."

"Not to me."

"Then give me your version. Perhaps she has got the story wrong."

"I'm sure she hasn't. I'd tell you exactly the same story, but with a different conclusion."

He said a trifle impatiently, "Someone entered the house without breaking a lock? Danielle tells me that she went round the house with you and there was no sign that anyone had entered any other way than with a key—and we who live in the house are the only ones with those. So," he wound up, "you can see how wild your conclusions are, can't you? Danielle and I talked it over during breakfast. She thinks you are letting the house get you down. It's a responsibility, you know, Suzanne."

"I like responsibility."

"I know you love the place, but—" He left the sentence open, waiting for me to urge him on. I didn't, and so he continued, "It's far too much for you to handle. I've thought of a way around the difficulty."

"I don't find Roseheath a difficulty. I shall use the shares Father left me in Wyncourt's for the upkeep."

"I'll buy the house from you at a fair price. If I did that, then you could live here for as long as you liked—you could have, say, the top floor for yourself. And you would be entirely free of responsibility."

"I'm sorry. I can't do that. Roseheath means something deep to me."

"You should never make snap decisions. Think it over."

"I won't change my mind." I thought, unhappily, *I can't*. However unfair Grandmother's will was, she must have had some reason beyond mere malice and dislike of her blood grandson. All that was certain was that if anything happened to me, if I should die, Oliver would inherit the house. *If I should die* . . . I pushed the unlikely thought away.

"Of course," I said, "I shall have to call the police."

"Let me examine the place first. I'll know if anyone forced an entry."

"We found nothing, and neither will you."

"There you are, then," he said in triumph. "The police wouldn't thank you for wasting their time."

"Please take the portrait. It's yours. Hang it in some shadowy place where you don't have to look at it."

"I intend to. But I must find the corner first. Everything I possess has its special position, you know that. And for the moment I have quite enough to cope with without rearranging my house."

I said crossly, "Then for the time being, hang it in the bathroom, but *please* get it out of my hall."

CHAPTER

7

WHEN I arrived home that night, Justin was happily settled in the living room with a drink at his elbow.

He rose, folded me in his arms, and gave me a smacking kiss. "I like you with that headband around your hair."

"There's so much of it," I said. "I have to keep it out of the way while I'm working. Of course, I could have it all cut off."

He seized it and pulled it gently. "You do, and I'll divorce you even before you marry me. It's a gorgeous mane."

"You make me feel like a horse," I said and laughed with relief that was here with me.

He explained with a reluctance I knew to be sincere that he could not stay for the weekend after all. There was a big intercities—Bristol, Bath, and Amesdale—Students' Exhibition in a few weeks' time, and some of his pupils were coming during the weekend to work on the sculptures they were entering.

He said, "You understand, don't you?"

"Of course." I joined him at the window.

He slid an arm around my shoulders. "I often think how wonderful it would be to work here all the time. I hate the noise and gasoline smells of the mews."

"You'd be fine in summer," I said. "But you'd freeze in winter. The hut isn't built for a home, and the roof leaks, as you well know."

He said sadly, "Freezes and leaks accepted, I couldn't, could I?"

"There's no reason why, except your own discomfort."

His voice lightened. "You mean that?"

"Yes. Why not? If you really wanted to work here."

"Suzanne, I've told you before, you're wonderful. You see—" He was rushing with his arguments before I could change my mind. "I'd make the hut habitable. If you would let me—"

"Oh, I'll let you, but you'd probably spend part of the winter being nursed for pneumonia."

"I'm a healthy animal." When he grinned, his black beard slid sideways.

After dinner we went down to the hut together. It was a warm night, and the stars were so thick and clear that they were like silver flashes from some distant fireworks display.

Danielle was on the terrace, and I saw Oliver's shadow in the room behind her.

Justin had the key to the hut and unlocked the door. It always stuck a little.

During the summer weekends he had already managed to turn the place into a workshop. His tools lay untidily on racks; anatomical sketches were scattered over a trestle table. On a block stood a small wooden sculpture of a girl that, to my surprise, was finished. I knew he wanted to enter it in an exhibition in London in the autumn. The floor was littered with chips of wood, scrapings, and gray dust.

He left me and entered the second room. "I really could make this place livable. Dump a bed and a chair and a table in here, and get some sort of a stove. I'd be fine."

"You'd be more comfortable living up at the house," I said, "and then you could use both rooms, one as a studio, the other as a storeroom. If you had the roof tarred or whatever it is they do to make roofs waterproof, and the windows enlarged, it would be a really fine studio."

"I *could*?" He came back, standing in the doorway, legs

apart, a young giant of a man. "You mean I could do what I liked with the place?"

"Yes."

I did not know how he covered the space between us, but I was in his arms. "I love you. Suzanne Wyncourt, I adore you."

As I fought for breath, I understood how bears kill their prey.

"Please give me back my ribs."

He laughed and let me go. "So you really intend to stay here? I mean, a house of this size . . . and you—well, you're so small and young."

"Yes, I'm staying here, and that's final," I said. "Come on, let's go back to the house."

There was no light on in Mrs. Jo's room. I knew she had gone to her cottage to fetch some plants from her small garden. There was a hornbeam hedge at Roseheath that enclosed a lupin garden. The plants had gone to seed and should long ago have been dug up. I had given this little garden to Mrs. Jo, and her nephew was helping her dig her plants up from her cottage and bringing them around in his van.

Justin and I walked quietly side by side, and I thought how lovely the setting for Roseheath was at moonrise with the trees like uncurled ostrich feathers against the sky.

I had left the front door ajar when I went out.

Voices met me. Danielle's, raised and strong:

"But you can't do this, Oliver . . . No, *you* listen to *me*. If you don't . . ." She stopped speaking, and I knew that she had heard the sound of footsteps.

They were standing in front of the Isabella portrait.

Oliver saw her head turn, and he, too, looked over his shoulder and saw me.

My smile was cold. "Do you want something?"

"I was just looking at the portrait." He paused. "And, incidentally, at that bracket. It's quite obvious that the wood was rotten, that's what caused the accident. Grandmother preferred to buy model clothes rather than have the necessary repairs done to the house. You'd better get it seen to quickly. You don't want to live with gaping windows for anyone to peer in."

"I'm not worried. No one will look in. There'd be no reason. Tom closes the gates at dusk, and no one would be tempted to climb over them. Neither you nor I go in for orgies." I began to laugh, but the sound went hollow. At some time when I wasn't here, someone had done just what I was protesting could not happen; someone had peered in and seen where the Isabella hung...

I was fighting a surge of resentment against Danielle and Oliver. They were in my wing without invitation. Oliver's wing was locked against me, but I had no means of safeguarding myself against their intrusion, in spite of the fact that Roseheath was mine. They could unlock the door on their side any time they liked. My retaliation would be to have a lock on my side, too. But my annoyance died a quick death. My sense of justice reaffirmed Oliver's right to feel that this house was virtually open to him.

Danielle moved away from the painting. She gave me a smile half over her shoulder and said, "Come, Mr. Wyncourt, we are intruding. I'm sorry, Suzanne." Apologizing for Oliver as well as herself with a new quiet authority.

I said, "Please take that portrait, Oliver. I've had enough of it. I don't want any more 'accidents.'"

"What happened here last night was nothing to do with that." He nodded toward the Isabella.

"On the contrary—" I checked my protest. I was wasting my breath. They were walking away from me toward the west wing.

"Good night, Suzanne," Oliver said.

I heard the key turn in the lock.

I started when Justin asked, "What's this talk about an accident here?"

65

I had forgotten that he was in the hall.

"Oh, I haven't told you, have I?"

He put his hands on my shoulders and walked me in front of him into the living room, sat me down, and said, "No, you haven't. But you can tell me now."

He sat quietly while I talked, his big hands dangling over his knees. Ming sat unmoving between us like royalty, tail splayed over the Bokhara rug.

When I had finished my story, Justin said, "If you think someone broke in, then why in the name of goodness didn't you go to the police right away? Leaving it for a whole day was idiotic."

"I know."

He said fiercely, "Don't you see, you little ass, that they could now argue that you'd worked the thing up during the past twenty-four hours from a slight aberration on your part to a grand threat to your life and property?"

I got up and walked the length of the room. "It seems to have occurred to everyone that I'm possibly creating drama out of nothing. All right, forget it. It's too late, anyway, to go to the police now."

"I didn't say I thought you were making up some drama. I believe you. I'm just trying to point out to you that you should have rung up the police immediately."

"I know. I know. And if I act now, as you so rightly say, they'd think I had cooked up the story to relieve the dullness of an uneventful life."

"Of course, you could have been going to close the window and something took your attention ..."

I turned on him fiercely. I had a silly, unreasonable feeling that he was letting me down.

"So your accusation that it's ridiculous of me not to go to the police was just to appease your own principles. You really want to believe what Oliver believes—that I made the whole thing up." I had no more breath left. I took a deep one and stormed on. "You men hate the thought of the law, don't you? I suppose it's a throw-back to robber ancestors."

Justin threw his head back and roared with laughter. I watched fascinated as the beard went sideways. I was sure that if he shaved it off, I would see that his laugh was actually a one-sided thing—impish and gentle and quite out of keeping with the threatening power of the black fuzz.

I bent down and picked up Ming from the rug. "You heard Danielle call Oliver by his Christian name. Yet it's always 'Mr. Wyncourt' when anyone is around."

"Fair enough. You should know what village gossip is like."

He had a point there. I let a struggling Ming go and heard his light thud as he leaped toward his favorite place on top of the lowboy.

"It wasn't just the use of Oliver's Christian name. When we came in, she was angry with him. What she said sounded like a threat."

"Oh, come off it!"

"She said, 'You listen to me . . . If you don't' . . . And then she saw us and stopped. But she was obviously warning him."

"That if he didn't listen, she'd put arsenic in his coffee?"

"Justin, be serious."

"Then stop wasting time conjecturing about their relationship and get on to a more fascinating topic. Us."

We discussed people we had known at the art school; we argued about students' rights and the idiosyncrasies of the Principal of the College who always rode a bicycle and kept a skull in his room. "Probably to prove," said Justin, "that art is long, life is short."

He left me at ten o'clock to return to Amesdale to cope with his pupils' entries for the exhibition. He promised to return in a few days with the first load of his possessions.

I went down to the car with him and watched it disappear. The great emptiness of Roseheath was now only a temporary thing. My spirits soared like a crazy barometer.

CHAPTER

8

I NEEDED more immediate action.

Ming sat on the stairs.

I said, "Let's go and turn out the drawers in the attic to make room for Justin's things."

He raced ahead of me, ears pricked, sensing some sort of game I would play with him.

The attic was a large, low room, with an oak floor and windows at either end.

I had a fine time clearing odds and ends from the drawers, things collected over the years. I came across a faded satin sachet filled with Grandmother's handkerchiefs, two with wide edges of real Brussels lace and her initials in the center of each one. I.W. I found old postcard albums, Edwardian photographs, and a fascinating heap of phonograph records ... "Alexander's Ragtime Band" ... "In a Monastery Garden." I carried the things cleared from the drawers to a landing cupboard. Then, when I had relined the drawers, I went to one of the windows. The view in daytime was glorious, reaching far out over the grounds of the house, over the meadow rise to the spires of Amesdale.

From the window at the opposite end of the room black Mandrake rose out of the moors like an army camped for the night before an attack, menacing in towering immobility.

The telephone bell rang. When I heard Sarne's voice, I said airily, "Oh, hullo."

"I've been trying to get through to Oliver, but there's no answer. Do you know if he's already left?"

"Left for where?"

"He was going to Paris to clinch a deal with Marignon Frères."

I said, "Oh, I didn't know."

"It was a last-minute arrangement. We were sending Leo Cripps, but as it was such a big deal, Oliver decided to go himself."

"As there's no reply," I said, "Danielle has probably taken him to the airport. Or the telephone might be out of order. Shall I go and see?"

"Thank you, Suzanne."

I laid down the receiver and ran to the communicating door. It was locked as usual. I went to the french doors and opened them and crossed the terrace. The west wing was in darkness, but to my surprise the window leading to the drawing room was on the latch. I pushed it open and went in and called. No one answered me. It wasn't like either Oliver or Danielle to be careless about locks, and just before I went out, I paused and listened again.

It was then that I heard the sound. Somewhere back in the house a floorboard creaked and something rasped softly. Without thinking, I took a few steps across the room toward the light switch. Suddenly, remembering the other night, I stopped quite still.

The night closed round me. I called, "Is anyone there?" and before my voice had died away, I realized that if Danielle had been in the house, she would already have switched on the light and answered me. If someone were there illegally, he wouldn't come out of his hiding place in order to give me a brotherly kiss.

A sudden draft of cool air swept into my face from the hall. I crept to the door and peered round. The front door was open, and someone was running lightly down the steps and into the garden. I could not see the face, but I knew that flowing white housecoat. It was Danielle. And she didn't want me to see her.

I was disturbed as I went back to the telephone. Why had she sat there in total darkness and not answered me? Why had she been afraid I might search the house for her?

I picked up the telephone receiver thinking that Sarne, not noted for patience, had probably hung up. He hadn't. But he was calling impatiently. "Are you there? Suzanne . . .?"

I said, "There's no one in the house." And that, at that moment, was no lie. I said, "If it's urgent, you could, of course, put a call through to the airport and catch Oliver there."

"It doesn't matter. Are you all right?"

"Of course. Why . . . ask?"

"Because you sound a bit breathless."

"I was hurrying to look for Oliver—or Danielle." Then I added, "It's a bit eerie in this house on my own."

"Then you'd better come over here. I'm just going out, but Magda is here. I'll come and fetch you."

"Please don't. I can walk. But I'd like to come."

"Then wait till I pick you up. You should know by now that I like any excuse to walk. I get too little exercise."

"But you said you were going out."

"Into Amesdale and taking the car. But I have plenty of time. Wait at Roseheath for me." The line went dead.

I had no idea what time Mrs. Jo would be back, nor did I know whether Danielle had hidden, watching me return to my own part of the house. The great emptiness of the high-ceilinged rooms hung around me and I felt that, if I could only tune in to their wavelength, I would hear their voices —the voices of the walls of Roseheath murmuring their secrets.

When Sarne came for me, I was at the door. I had left

the lights on in the hall, but the east wing was still in darkness.

I closed the door and ran down to meet him. Tall tree branches nearly met over our heads as we walked down the avenue. We swung along like two athletes in the brisk night air, breaking our silence with inconsequential remarks about the weather, the unusual prevalence of owls in the woods, the need for better lighting along the minor road that ran between our two houses.

Sarne's car was parked outside Amber Court. The front door was open, releasing a blaze of light.

"Go right in," Sarne said.

As he spoke, Jason bounded up to me. He was outsize, even for a setter, and he was one of those dogs that are more dangerous to their friends than their enemies. He lunged at me with flying front paws, feathery tail waving like a windmill. His weight caused me to stagger back. Sarne was behind me and caught me. His arms went around me as he said, "You idiot dog, go and greet someone your own size."

"He probably thinks he's a Pekingese."

I turned, laughing up at Sarne while Jason, who never seemed to believe anyone could possibly reject his heavy advances, backed a little way and stood with lolling tongue, watching me.

I moved out of Sarne's arms. But not quickly enough.

"Ah, Suzanne . . ." The voice came clearly from the steps of the house. "I was wondering why Jason was barking."

I swung around. Magda was at the door watching us. I said, going toward her, "Jason nearly knocked me over. If it hadn't been for Sarne, you'd have found me flat on my face in your drive."

I heard the door of Sarne's car open and close, heard the engine start up. I climbed the three steps to the front door and Magda stood aside for me to enter. She said, "I'm sorry to disappoint you, but Sarne has a date for tonight." Then, before I could protest that I hadn't come to see Sarne, that I just needed company, she said softly, "*Et tu*, Suzanne?"

I had crossed the hall and thrown my coat on a chair before I got the inference. The ancient classic comment on betrayal. *And you ... Suzanne ...?* Of course, Magda dismissed the excuse of the dog bounding at me. She must have come to the door when Jason had bounded back, watching me in Sarne's arms. To Magda, we would have seemed like lovers, clasped together in the darkness. But if so, would she have minded? I could almost guess her thoughts. "So it's true what they say. The little dark horse is in love with Sarne. Well, she'll learn that he's just amusing himself ..." I'd heard her say that about married friends, and I was certain that she would be as objective toward her own husband.

Hugh greeted me, and then Maurice Trent, whom I always now connected with Sarne's first visit to England. His wife, Estelle, was with him. She was a big, comfortable woman with long, mouse-colored hair that never stayed tidy, and a wide mouth. She said as she kissed me, "I heard you've had a scare. Something to do with a curtain bracket giving way. It's a very old house, Suzanne, and a lot of things there will need renovation." She was reassuring me in her kind way, trying to warn me not to let imagination take hold of me now that I was relatively speaking alone at Roseheath. Because she had heard the old stories of my supposed hysterical tendencies.

I always had a sense of restlessness when I was at Amber Court. It was perhaps partly due to the hot, exciting coloring of the room and partly to Magda's own personality. Even when she was sitting still and quiet in a chair, there was a kind of electric current hovering round her.

I was standing by the window, a coffee cup in my hand, only half listening to the flow of conversation, when Hugh joined me. There was always the delicate scent of some expensive lotion around him.

He said, "I hear you have a *lot* of valuable furniture at Roseheath. I wondered if you were thinking of selling any of it."

"No."

"You should, you know. Antiques fetch a big price abroad these days."

"I happen to like what I have too much to get rid of it."

"But you can't like *everything*." He had a way of italicizing certain words. "You're young and modern, and if you sold what you didn't particularly care for, you could buy things that you really liked."

I drank my coffee, aware of his face thrust at me; my own turned away towards the dark, quiet garden.

Encouraged by my silence, Hugh said, "Now if I were to come round and make an inventory of everything—"

I drew back from that too-close face. "I don't think you understand. I have no wish to get rid of anything. If you want the truth, I don't feel it is mine to dispose of. I'm not a Wyncourt, you know, so I feel that the house and its contents have been left in trust to me for my lifetime. After that, it goes back to the family."

He said in surprise, "Was that a stipulation of the will? I didn't know."

"It is also my stipulation," I said coldly.

As I moved away I heard him say with amusement, "You have such high principles, Suzanne."

After an hour, I sought an excuse to leave. My car was at the garage in the village being overhauled, and I had been told I could fetch it that evening. The main gates of Amber Court opened out on the village street, and it was only a short journey down the drive to reach it. I looked at my watch and decided that it would be best to ring the garage first to see if it was still open.

73

When I asked Magda if I could use her telephone she said, "Of course. You know where it is."

It was in an alcove at the end of the hall. There was just room for a small table, a rack holding telephone directories, and a chair.

I sat down and dialed the garage number. There was no reply. I dialed a second time and waited, listening to the distant buzz of conversation in the room down the passage. The forlorn ringing continued. I decided ruefully that, as usual, Ernie Plover, who owned the garage, had shut up shop on the stroke of nine.

I replaced the receiver, switched off the light in the alcove, and went back toward the main hall.

Someone moved in the deeper shadows at the far end. Whoever it was seemed to have been about to come toward the main hall, then, seeing me, had darted back. There was a tall white chair in a corner. It moved slightly, and I heard the scrape of its legs on the floor as whoever darted from me fell against it. There was a whisk of some dark color— a girl's skirt catching on the chair.

Whoever was there did not want to see me. It could be Mai Chang wanting to use the telephone and, shy of doing so with someone else around, she might have tried to hide. Very well, then, I would pretend I had seen nobody. I turned from the telephone table. As I did so, I heard a sound between a hiccup and a sob. I looked back. I saw a small triangular face peering out at me and recognized Magda's young maid who helped Mai Chang.

I said in a friendly way, "Hullo, Pauline."

She was sixteen and not very bright. She had a pretty little flower face full of what I sometimes thought could be a deceptive innocence. She came every day from the village.

"Please . . . don't say you've . . . seen me." She jerked the sentence out, fumbling in her sleeve for a handkerchief. While she sniffed and wiped her eyes, I remembered how

74

the news had reached me through the village grapevine that when Magda had found a piece of her costume jewelry in Pauline's handbag, she didn't dismiss her, nor did she report it to the police. She had called her into her bedroom and talked to her. What had been said, nobody knew. Pauline never told and neither did Magda. But, tearful at first, then returning gradually to her ebullient self, Pauline had remained at Amber Court.

I was surprised that Magda had behaved as she had. It made me feel that I had misjudged her in thinking her ruthless. She must have realized that a piece of costume jewelry was, to Pauline, like something as precious as diamonds.

She was saying, still sniffing, "I'm sorry, Miss Wyncourt. I ... I'm all right now." Her wide blue eyes gave a frightened look past me.

"You're not all right. Pauline, tell me, what's wrong?"

"Nothing. Nothing at all."

"Oh, come. You don't stand cowering and crying in a dark corner for no reason."

"It isn't anything. Really it isn't." She was trying to edge around me as she spoke.

I stood in her way. "Why aren't you home? You usually leave at six, don't you?"

She nodded.

"I'm sure Mrs. Eskinholm doesn't know you're still here? Or did she ask you to stay on for some extra work?"

Her head moved from side to side in a slow denial.

I said, "Then run along."

"I can't."

"Why not?"

She was crying again.

"Pauline, why not?" I was beginning to regret having stopped to speak to her.

She said sulkily, "If you must know, I'm scared."

"You mean of going home in the dark?"

75

She didn't answer me.

"But you're a country girl, you're used to the lanes round here. You've walked them enough times."

"It's—different—now."

"Why? Oh, no, don't tell me you're frightened of nothing. You've too much common sense—" I doubted if she had, but I was trying the approach.

She gave a husky laugh. "Common sense? Me? Oh, yes, I got it all right. That's why I'm scared."

"Someone has frightened you between here and your cottage. That's it, isn't it?"

She stared at me in the half-darkness. From the living room that seemed so far away I heard voices mingling, falling away, brief silences.

I said again, "Someone in the dark drive? Some man—"

"Yes. Yes, that's it." But she spoke too fast, seized on the idea too eagerly, almost with relief, as if she had been alarmed that I might hit upon the real truth.

I chose to pretend not to know that she was lying. I said, "If some man has made a nuisance of himself, then you must tell the police."

"Oh, no. I couldn't. You see, I don't know his name." The whites of her eyes glinted sideways at me in the shadows, covert, watchful. She was lying again.

I said sharply, "You live in a small village where you know everyone. That means that you don't choose to tell me his name. But you must. Don't you realize, if there's someone—" I broke off.

Through the small window above the Spanish chair, the moon swam from a cloud, silver-bright, overblown . . .

"Let me go!"

I hadn't realized that I had seized Pauline's arm. The muscles under the short cotton sleeve writhed between my fingers. I said, "I'm sorry. Only, this is important. You know something that you have no right to keep to yourself—"

76

She said with sulky obstinacy, "You can't make me tell."

"No, I can't. But I can repeat our conversation to Mrs. Eskinholm..."

"No! *No!*" Her voice rose in a small harsh scream.

"Look, for goodness sake get a grip on yourself. Mrs. Eskinholm isn't going to sack you because you are scared to go home in the dark. She'll probably arrange for you always to leave in daylight or have someone walk with you. It'll be quite all right."

"Gaw! You just don't understand, do you?"

I said impatiently, "How can I do anything but make a guess when you give me half-hints and evasions?"

"Then leave me alone."

"Fine. I will. But you can't spend the night huddled in that corner. Listen. Just get your coat and wait—"

"While you go and tell Mrs. Eskinholm that I'm scared?"

"No, not if you don't want me to. But just to find someone to walk home with you—oh, without telling her." But who was there who wouldn't tell Magda? Only myself... "All right," I said, "I'll take you, and I'll bring Jason with me. Have you got a coat? Then go and get it and wait at the door."

"The *back* door," she whispered.

I went down the passage and into the wide, white painted hall. Magda wasn't the one to talk to about the girl's nameless terrors. She was fearless herself, and she would have no patience with cowards. Besides, the girl was obviously afraid for her job. Had Pauline been reported for her theft she would have been punished and placed on probation. But she had not, and quite obviously she was frightened of anything that might induce Magda to report her to the police. She knew nothing about the treatment of first offenders, and the prison at Amesdale probably loomed like a giant bat on her terrified horizon.

I reached the living room and sought out Magda.

I said, "I've just tried to call the garage, but there's no reply. Can I take Jason out—just for a brief walk? I need some air. I've been shut up with my drawing board all day."

"Of course. Take him. He usually goes with Sarne."

As if he had some sixth sense, the slim red dog was by my side, intelligent eyes urgent with questioning.

"Come on," I said. "We're going to look at the trees by moonlight." With Jason bounding ahead, I went round to the back of the house and hissed, "Pauline?"

She was waiting for me, hugging a dark sweater round her shoulders, her hair and her small face the only lightness about her.

She said, "You're thinking me daft, aren't you? Being afraid, I mean."

"Of course I don't. We are all of us afraid at some time in our lives."

"You—?" Her tone was disbelieving.

"Yes," I said. I supposed the biggest fear of all was of something threatening and unknown.

CHAPTER

9

PAULINE lived with her mother in a cottage at the edge of the village. We walked in comparative silence up Amber Court's drive, and I knew that both of us were listening for some sound, some disturbance of leaf or crunch of gravel. I was beginning to wonder what safeguard Jason would be on my return walk. He was a dog who loved everyone.

As we passed the lodge at the gate, I said by way of making some sort of conversation that would break the stillness, "That's a charming house for someone. Now, if you had a husband who was a gardener, wouldn't you love to live there?" I slowed down at the cottage. "Look at those windows opening out onto the little private garden."

She shied away from me like a restive horse, and I had to sprint to catch her up. We shot through the gates and into the main road, legs flying, Jason leaping ahead of us, loving it. I was panting, "Don't be so silly . . . there's nothing to be scared of . . ."

She didn't answer me. She was breathing so harshly out of sheer nerves that I doubt if she heard me. I plunged after her and seized her arm. "You can't on go like this. Either tell me—"

She was in the lighted road and safe. She stopped. A string of cars passed us, and by their headlights I saw the bright relief on her face. "Ta," she said. "Ta very much.

You're awfully kind, Miss." And then she was gone, running up the small neat path between the privet hedges. As I turned away, I heard the cottage door slam.

I called Jason and fixed the lead on him. During our walk to the village I had been too aware of Pauline's fears to notice the night. Now, with Jason as my chestnut guard, I had time to look around me.

The rising moon turned the tops of the trees to dark silver. In the undergrowth an occasional small animal stirred and scuttled from me. The gates of Amber Court were only a hundred yards or so from the village street, and as the breeze tossed the leaves of the trees, the lights of the house were like yellow eyes winking at me.

Jason was pulling at the lead, his head turned in the direction of the lodge. I said, talking to the dog, and wanting to hear my own voice, "There's no one there, so it's no use looking. Ben grew too old to look after the garden, and so he retired. Jason, come *on*, don't be an ass ..." Try to pull a big dog that doesn't want to be moved, and you know something of the feelings of an ant attempting to dislodge a stone. I said, "All right, Ben spoiled you giving you bits of biscuit and chocolate when Magda wasn't looking, but that's over."

I was laughing, glancing at the cottage in its rich setting of cherry and laburnum when something moved in a downstairs room. Something—or someone? A tramp, perhaps, or a couple of adolescents from the village with no other place to go.

I had no intention of investigating. I would suggest that Sarne checked the doors and windows and explain that I saw someone moving there.

I pulled at Jason's lead. This time he obeyed me, and we walked briskly up the drive.

I could have been mistaken. The movement I had seen

at the window could have been the reflection of a tree branch blown by the wind. Or my own shadow. But I had not been in the line of the moon. Suddenly I remembered how Pauline had run past the cottage. Was it the hiding place of someone dangerous to women walking alone? The moon was round and silver as a witch ball. The thought came that this could be someone's moon madness.

I began to run and, ashamed of my sudden attack of cowardice, pretended to Jason that I was playing a game with him.

At Amber Court, I found that Maurice and Estelle had left. They lived quite near, and a walk across the lawn and through the woods would take them home.

I let Jason go, and he raced around the house to the patio. I followed. The windows were folded back, and Hugh sat alone in the drawing room. He looked sulky and was flicking through the advertisements in one of the glossy magazines Magda subscribed to.

Jason bounded up to his chair, and Hugh pulled him close, fondling him. He said, "The Trents like to go to bed early." He added bitchily, "Estelle really does need her beauty sleep."

"Where is Magda?"

He shrugged. "In her room, I suppose."

I went to find her. It was unusual for the house to be so quiet. Amber Court was made for people.

I went up the sweep of shallow stairs that rose and opened out onto a wide gallery where two yellow chairs made a splash of color behind the wrought-iron balustrade. The lights glowed on emptiness. I had always thought that whoever had planned this house long before Magda and Sarne had bought it and intended it for a large family.

The door of Magda's bedroom was open. I caught a glimpse of ivory walls and grass-green silks at the window. Magda was sitting at her dressing table doing something to her hair. She never looked quite at ease when she was alone.

She had heard my footsteps and swiveled around. "Hullo."

"I've brought Jason back. Or rather, he brought me. He's like a lion."

"You didn't keep him on a lead? Oh, Suzanne, he hates that."

"He was free part of the time. But—"

"But what?" she asked without interest, her restless hands playing with a gilt lipstick.

I said, "I went as far as the village." I had no intention of mentioning Pauline. "And when I passed the lodge, I thought I saw someone inside. It could be a tramp. I was glad Jason was on the lead. I needed a protector near me, just in case—" My laugh was intended to infer a joke against my own cowardice, but it failed. "I think you ought to tell Sarne."

Magda's eyes had narrowed into golden-lashed lines. "Oh, there's no need. He knows all about the lodge."

"You mean he has given someone permission to use it?"

She lifted her shoulders. "If you like to put it that way." She got up, went to the window, and said with her back to me, "That 'someone' you saw in there was Sarne himself. He uses it."

"Uses—the—lodge? But he's got this house. He can't want more rooms."

"On the contrary, he needs somewhere away from us all. A secret place, if you like."

I fought a losing battle with myself not to ask questions. Intuition warned me to say "Good night" and go. But another part of me, too curious, too human, could not resist probing (with no right of explanation) the forbidden treasure-house of a man's privacy.

"A secret place?" When she didn't answer, I repeated the words.

She dropped the curtain she had been holding and began stroking the silken fold. "You may as well know, Suzanne. The lodge is Sarne's love pavilion."

I couldn't speak. I stood there staring at Magda and shuddering inside myself at the memory of myself wondering, as I had repassed the lodge on my way back to Amber Court, if I had enough courage to go up and look through the window to see who was there. It had been so dark inside that room. Adrienne and Sarne had disappeared together . . . Adrienne and Sarne . . .

I felt Magda's cool, amused eyes on me.

I moved toward the door on shaking legs and said the most banal thing that came into my mind. "I . . . must . . . go . . ."

She laughed. "You're embarrassed, aren't you? Oh, Suzanne, you little idiot. You're in love with Sarne, and don't deny it—you're not a very good actress, you know. But you aren't the only one. And do you think you—or they—really matter to him? They don't, you know. They are his distractions after long hours of work. *Work*, Suzanne, ambition. That is where Sarne's heart is."

"I don't want . . . to . . . to talk about it."

"It's as well for you to look facts in the face, my dear. It'll save you heartbreak in the end." She took a step toward me, and her face hardened. "I am Sarne's wife, and together we hold a great number of shares in Wyncourt's. There are only two other persons alive who hold any appreciable number, you and Oliver. It will be interesting to see how Sarne manages to get hold of them. And he'll try. I can promise you that. But, so far as you are concerned, my dear, it won't be through my husband's second marriage to you, so don't go flying up on any wild hope to some romantic heaven."

A kind of despair exploded inside me. Since she had no fear of losing Sarne, I wondered why she hated me so much that she had to thrust her daggers of malice at me.

I cried, "How can you live with him and say the things you do about him? How can you bear to live with someone you ... despise?"

She said boredly, "You really must grow up. You see life too seriously. It's a game, really, and you play to win. I do. I remain with Sarne because I know his little affairs are just diversions, and because I like an ambitious man and I do not in the least mind his ruthlessness."

I said slowly, "You are so sure of yourself and of Sarne. I wonder—"

"Wonder at nothing, my dear. I know my fate. Nothing threatens my marriage, neither Adrienne, *nor anyone else.*"

I felt cold and very tired. I wanted to leave. I said, turning to the door again, "I don't want to talk about it any more."

"There's nothing more to say," she answered. "Except this. You may as well know, Suzanne, that if there is ever a struggle between another woman and me to possess Sarne, I have the final and most powerful weapon." She waited for me to ask what it was. I stayed silent, still edging to the door, knowing that she wanted to talk, to prove her power to me, "the little Suzanne" who was maturing so late that she had not yet fallen seriously in love. Magda was trying to show me the harsher side of living. She went on, "Sarne has strong physical desires. I know exactly how to rouse them. Even if he came to me and told me he intended to leave me, I would only need to go to him. Just go to him and touch him. The fire would be lighted ..."

I thought, Oh yes, you could make yourself irresistible. But it would be a moment of weakness in him and he would despise himself afterwards and it would make no difference.

As if she read my mind, she said, "I am not impetuous. I know exactly what I would do, and he would be powerless because he is a man of strong passions. Afterwards I would ask him to wait, to think over any break between us just for a little while." Her smile was like the result of a secret she was sharing with herself. "I have a 'love voice.' Once, I remember, as we lay in the dark, Sarne said, 'Just say something, anything... The words don't matter, but I can drown in your voice.' It was one of the odd, poetic things that startle you about Sarne. So," she put up her hands and ran her fingers through her flame of hair. "A woman's hair, too, can drown a man. It's a primitive sensuality; it excites."

Something in my expression must have alerted her to the distaste I felt. If I didn't stop her, she would go on, preening herself like a lovely bird before me, her solitary listener. I said again, "Don't talk like that. I don't want to hear any more."

"But you're going to, my dear—now, rather than later. It's best for you to be forewarned before you think of doing something silly. Because, you see, in spite of all those beautiful shares you have in the business, Sarne won't leave me for you."

I said, choking over the words, "Me? Good heavens, it isn't me... Adrienne..."

"Oh, he's momentarily infatuated with her. Perhaps. But you are the one with the important possession—those pretty Wyncourt shares. They might—just *might*—make you irresistible. Do you know what I'd do if ever you gave Sarne encouragement to leave me? Oh, I wouldn't get hysterical, or whine. But I'd possess him again, just for a short time. It probably wouldn't last. Sarne would be weak for a while, for long enough for us to have one of those desperate, helpless reconciliations. That would be it, Suzanne. You see, I would play my ace card. I would tell him that I was pregnant. That, dear, would be the price of that temporary reconciliation. It has been Sarne's dream to have children. He would never leave me after that."

I watched her shake her hair again and felt sick. Blackmail through a child...

I had been so long rooted to the spot while she talked that I was not quite certain how I managed to move, to turn and fly from the room. I sped down the long gallery and pulled myself up short at the stairs. I stood hesitating, grasping the banister, trying to pull myself together. The curlicues of wrought iron were cool to my hand; I breathed deeply and momentarily closed my eyes. Behind me I heard the door of Magda's room close.

She had, of course, misunderstood that moment in the garden when Sarne had rescued me from Jason's over-enthusiastic greeting. He could have been my brother, then. But she could not know, surely, about that other morning, that dawn meeting. Or had someone seen us and told her? It was quite possible. Country people rose early. So had she believed that ours had been some prearranged meeting?

I heard a sound from the hall below and began to move down the stairs. Hugh was in the drawing room. I avoided him and went out into the bright garden.

Sarne and Adrienne . . . Sarne and I . . . Sarne and other women. And Magda, like a lovely spider in her orange and gold web, watching and laughing at us all.

CHAPTER

10

AS I walked up the steps of Roseheath I was vaguely aware of a distant cry. An owl somewhere in the trees.

The crash came as I opened the door, and I knew then that the cry I had heard had been human.

It was the silence that followed which electrified me. I raced down to the hall and heard sounds from the other side of the locked door.

I hammered on it, and it opened. Danielle stood staring at me. Her face, which seldom had much color, was chalk-white. Her eyes were enormous.

"There's been an accident. Go and ring for Dr. Simmons. Quickly . . . Quickly . . ."

I had a swift impression of Oliver lying spread-eagled at the foot of the stairs as I flew to the telephone. I nearly fell over Ming, whose inveterate curiosity could not allow me to move without knowing where I was going.

I dialed Doctor Simmon's number and told him that Oliver had had an accident and that I didn't know how badly he was hurt. He told me he would be over in three minutes.

Danielle had covered Oliver with a blanket and put cushions behind his head. His coat and shirt were open, and she was on her knees by his side.

"There's scarcely any heart-beat," she whispered.

I pushed her aside and lay over him, putting my mouth on

his. I had no idea how to give the kiss of life, or even whether it was the right treatment, but I acted on instinct. I gave him my breath, only lifting my head so that he might be able to breathe out. Danielle stood at my side, and her mist-blue housecoat brushed my arms. She watched me without speaking.

There was no time to ask what had happened, or even at what time he had returned from Paris. He was unconscious, and nothing I could do stirred his heart to more than the faintest flicker.

When the doorbell rang, Danielle opened it and Doctor Ralph Simmons went straight to Oliver, knelt by his side, and gave an examination.

Without a word, he went to the telephone and called for an ambulance. Then he came back and looked at Danielle.

"Where are his tablets, Mrs. Goddard?"

"He usually carries them around with him. His pocket—"

"They aren't there. Go and find them."

Danielle turned and went swiftly into the drawing room. I heard drawers being opened and slammed shut. Then she went past us up the stairs, her housecoat swishing softly.

I said faintly, "Tablets?"

"You surely knew he had a heart condition? Or no, perhaps not. He said he wanted it kept from everyone except Mrs. Goddard."

"But—why?"

"He had a big job to hold down."

"But surely he could have told me, trusted me . . ."

Ralph Simmons didn't answer me. He turned toward Danielle as she came down the stairs with a little box in her hand.

"They were in his dressing table drawer. He has just returned from Paris. He may have put them there absentmindedly when he unpacked."

Ralph Simmons said, "What happened? He fell, I know that. But where was he?"

Danielle said, "I . . . I heard him on the stairs. I think he must have felt dizzy and fallen."

"There are no broken bones."

"So," she said. "He must have clung to the banisters. Or perhaps he wasn't very far up."

I said, "There's the ambulance. How quick it's been." I ran to the door.

It was all very efficient. Oliver, still unconscious, was carried out. Since my car was at the garage, Danielle drove to Amber Court to tell Magda. As his nearest relative, it was she who would have to go to the hospital for the formalities.

When the ambulance had taken Oliver, I remained in the hall, sitting in the carved Italian chair with the arms like eagle's claws. Shock sealed us together, the chair and I. I stared at the opposite wall with the three landscapes, at the huge open fireplace which had never had that lovely living movement of logs and flames.

If Oliver had felt ill, why hadn't he asked Danielle to fetch his tablets? What was the meaning of the cry before the crash of his fall? If a heart attack was coming on, how had he found the breath for that cry? But perhaps fear that he was about to fall had given him one last burst of explosive power, enough to cry out so that I, approaching the house, had heard.

I got up and, leaving the lights on, went through the door into my own wing.

I wished Mrs. Jo were back, or Justin. I wanted someone to relieve the waiting.

As soon as I heard Danielle's key in the lock I ran to meet her.

We looked at one another without a word, and I followed her into Oliver's drawing room where every piece of Chippendale and Sheraton had its place to within an inch and the glow of a lamp Danielle had turned on pointed directly to the woven peacocks of an Ispahan rug.

Danielle tossed her coat on a chair and sat down, leaning

her head back. She kicked off her shoes and curled her toes. I recognized the way she did it, because it was a habit of mine. When I was tense, my toes seemed to stiffen and I could not relax until I did exactly what she was doing now. She had beautiful feet, and I watched the rhythmic contracting and relaxing of her muscles.

I asked, "Why didn't you tell me that Oliver had a heart condition?"

"He didn't want anyone else to know. *I* had to, in case he hadn't his tablets near him when he felt an attack coming on."

"But you weren't always near him."

"On those occasions I saw to it that he had them in his pocket."

"But not this time."

She said, "No," very quietly.

I moved around so that I faced her. "What happened?"

"I don't know. I was in the drawing room, and I heard him fall."

"And the cry?"

She jerked her head up. "What cry?"

"It came before the crash. I was outside the house at the time."

"The television was on."

"But the cry didn't come from that."

"No. But it must have been the reason why I didn't hear it. I suppose Oliver felt dizzy as he went up the stairs."

"He must have gone for the purpose of getting his tablets. But why not send you?"

She stood for a moment, biting her lip. Then she said icily, "Why ask me all these questions?"

"Going to fetch the box of tablets himself doesn't quite seem the kind of thing a man would do if he felt ill and knew that exertion was the last thing he should have."

Quite suddenly I saw something like anger cross her usually calm face. "But it happened, and that's all there is to it."

The bitter silence surrounding us was broken only by the wind rustling in the hydrangeas on the terrace. I turned to go. I felt that I could not face any more tension and tragedy that night.

I was nearly at the door when Danielle said, "Doctor Simmons says that if Oliver takes care, he can live for years. *If he took care.*" The amended last sentence hung on the air, the past tense ominous.

I said, "But he's not going to die. No limbs were broken."

She said shortly, "He suffered shock."

"When Oliver regains consciousness, we'll know exactly what happened."

"Yes. Yes, of course." She turned her back on me. "Isn't that your telephone ringing?"

It was. I pushed open the door saying: "If you don't want to stay here alone tonight, you know you'd be welcome in the south wing. I've got spare bedrooms—"

"Thank you, no. I'm quite all right. That telephone ..."

I sped to answer it.

Magda was saying impatiently, "For heaven's sake, someone answer! Is there? ... Hullo ... Oh, Suzanne, when there was no reply I thought I must have the wrong number."

"You saw Oliver?"

"No one was allowed to see him. He was unconscious. I gave the hospital the particulars they wanted. Then I had a word with the doctor."

"What did he say?"

"That he may not recover."

The words came so baldly over the telephone that it took me a moment to digest them. "They can't mean that ... that he might die. Magda, there were no bones broken, no internal injuries ..."

"With Oliver's heart condition, the shock of the actual fall could kill him. And he *did* fall. There are a number of bruises that he couldn't have suffered by just flopping down in the hall. And one wrist is badly wrenched—"

"Where he hung on to the banisters?"

"I suppose so. You'd better ask Danielle."

"Danielle knows nothing. She's in a state of shock herself."

"Then she'll have to get out of it and answer some questions."

"What—sort—of—questions?"

"As to why Oliver fell. As to whether he really *did* become giddy because a heart attack was coming on. Or because he was deliberately jerked off balance and that was what brought on the heart attack. Haven't you asked yourself whether it could have been that way around?"

"No, I haven't. And I won't! I won't think anything so horrible as . . . as a deliberate attack on him . . ."

"Snap out of it, Suzanne. You're dealing with human beings, not angels."

"Oliver had an accident," I heard myself shouting down the telephone. "He was taken ill, and he fell. And I won't listen to any evil hints from you. Just stop, do you hear?"

"You're getting hysterical again."

"Think what you like. I—"

"Oliver told Sarne that you were quite hysterical the other night. Something about a curtain pole."

"I don't believe he said I was anything of the kind."

"You have a history of hysterics, haven't you?"

A terrified child of seven in the Mandrake Caves . . . a voice mocking at me four years ago in the same caves. Fear, yes, terror even . . . but never, never hysterics.

Magda was saying, "Sarne said he thought it bad for you to be living in that great house. And now that Oliver may not live . . ."

There comes a time in every argument when one has talked it all out and only exhaustion remains. I replaced the telephone receiver very quietly.

A floorboard creaked behind me. I swung around. Danielle

stood in the doorway. She still had the look of a sleep-walker on her face.

I held out my hand. "Come and sit down. What would you like? A brandy? Tea?"

She shook her head. "I just came to tell you that I have to pack a case of Oliver's things."

"I'll do it. I know exactly what he'll want. Leave it to me."

"No, I can't. I must—"

I said again, "Leave it to me."

I ran into the west wing and up the stairs, flicking on the lights as I went. In Oliver's bedroom there were a few pieces of beautifully polished furniture and a wide bed with a coverlet in sapphire silk. The room was as spartan in tidiness as a monk's cell. I found a small case and collected his toilet things from the bathroom, his pyjamas, and a dark red dressing gown. I picked up his reading spectacles and a book that lay on the bedside table. Before I packed it, I glanced at the title. *The Living Truth.* I looked inside and was not surprised to find that it was a religious book. Oliver never went to church, but he had a strong secret interest in religion. He talked about it to nobody, as if, like a schoolboy, he were slightly embarrassed by it.

I wondered, as I packed slippers and book at the bottom of the case, how he saw religion. Being with him, talking to him, aware of his absorption in the family business, all of us who knew him would have been startled to hear him even mention the word "God." Perhaps his interest was purely intellectual. I did not know. In fact, I had never begun to understand Oliver.

When I came downstairs with the suitcase, Danielle tried to take it from me. "I'll go, this is my job."

I said lightly, "Don't let's have a fight. Just relax, have a drink if you want one, and leave everything to me." I felt suddenly the stronger of the two.

CHAPTER

11

I TOOK Oliver's car.

The road into Amesdale was almost deserted. It surprised me until I realized that I had quite forgotten to look at the clock, and because I hated the feel of anything on my wrist, my watch remained in my dressing table drawer.

After ten minutes of driving, my headlights lit up the suburbs of the city. I drove halfway through them and turned right for the new hospital building.

I could have left the case with the porter at the lodge, but I wanted to know if there was any change in Oliver's condition, so I asked to see the Sister-in-charge. She was kind and slightly formal. He was still unconscious, but he was holding his own. She had instructions to telephone Mrs. Eskinholm if there was any change in his condition.

On my way home I had to pass Amber Court. Some instinct impelled me to turn in at the drive gates. I had no idea why. What Magda had said on the telephone had repelled me. Perhaps, subconsciously, I needed to believe that I had misunderstood her and hoped that a meeting would reassure me.

The house was always somewhat like a stage set. The lamp over the door lit up the glass-and-wrought-iron door. The windows were usually uncurtained at night, lights blazing, the swimming pool floodlit whether anyone was using it or not. This was Magda's way. Her needs, like Grandmother's, were always for the grand scale. She was as much a Wyncourt as the jeweled Isabella of the portrait in my hall.

Magda and Hugh were together in the living room. Hugh, caught off guard in an inelegant attitude, legs stuck out, toes turned up, leaped to his feet.

I said, "I've just come from the hospital."

Immediately I felt the quickened tension in the room. Magda said, "I suppose they told you nothing?"

"There's nothing to tell yet. I just left Oliver's night things. He was still unconscious."

Magda motioned me to a chair. "Maurice will be here any minute—I rang him and told him about Oliver. I suppose Estelle will come with him—she can't bear not to know everything that's happening. Stay, Suzanne."

"I must get back. Danielle is alone."

"Do you think that will worry her?" Magda flashed at me. "Because I can tell you that it won't. Wait for Maurice. You must tell him what has happened."

As in a play, he arrived on cue. Magda had just leaned forward after speaking to take a cigarette when the doorbell rang. She went into the hall, calling to Mai Chang. "I'll open it. Bring in the coffee, will you?"

Maurice and his wife entered, and the room was immediately full of the sound of voices. I was certain that Magda would find some propitious moment this evening to interrogate him obliquely about the affairs at Wyncourt's. I knew what was in her mind and there was a question in mine, too. But it wasn't the same one, although both concerned Sarne.

What I was asking—without being able to answer myself —was "Where is Sarne?" What Magda wanted to know was, "If Oliver dies, will Sarne succeed him?"

Magda poured out coffee saying to Maurice, "Oliver

95

should have told you about his heart condition. After all, a company like Wyncourt's must be prepared for a crisis."

"Like this one? Yes, you're right. But his secret is out now. When he's well enough, we'll have to be realistic and discuss his possible successor. Where is Sarne?"

Her eyes smiled at them. "Oh, he had to dine with a client in Amesdale. He doesn't yet know about the accident."

"You probably know where he is. Couldn't you ring through to the restaurant?"

Estelle said in her heavy voice, "He usually takes people to the Martinelle, doesn't he? Maurice and I have seen him there."

Magda reached out her hand for Estelle's empty coffee cup. "But he may not be at the Martinelle this time. No. I'll wait. He can't do anything, even if I can find him."

If I can find him ... As she spoke the last words she glanced at me. I knew exactly how she intended me to interpret that clear golden glance. *You and I know where he is. In Adrienne Wand's penthouse on top of Amesdale Hill.*

I bent to pick up my handbag and said, "I think I'd better go now. I want to get home."

Magda didn't stop me, but as she said goodbye to me, I sensed both a tension and an excitement about her.

When I let myself in at Roseheath, I went straight to the communicating door and crossed to Oliver's drawing room. Danielle sat in the darkness, huddled in a chair so that, if the moonlight had not beamed upon her, she would have been invisible.

I saw her raise her head and look my way. But the rest of her body remained perfectly still. Her voice came hollowly out of the luminous corner of the room. "They say he can't live till morning."

I was dumb, staring at her.

Oliver Wyncourt, aged only thirty-seven, was slipping

quietly out of our lives. And there was nothing, *nothing* I could say that would not sound banal.

She said in explanation, "I got my car out because I couldn't stay here. I intended to drive around the lanes, and on over the moors, but I found myself at the hospital. I don't really know how I got there."

"Magda must be told."

"They were going to telephone her immediately."

The call must have come as I left Amber Court. I closed my eyes, and the night sounds beat upon my ears, accentuating our aloneness. Our night companions, the persistent owls, were hooting; floorboards creaked as if ghosts walked over them. The night express to London tore along the mile-distant tracks with that curious nostalgic melancholy of trains in the night.

Danielle, usually so calm and competent, was like a lost child sitting in a stranger's house waiting to be rescued. She had slid her legs up under her and, crouched like that, the chair enveloped her, making her look small.

I went over to her, bent, and kissed her cheek. She didn't respond. But as I turned away, she said my name softly.

I waited, wondering if she wanted me to stay. But I felt that she didn't. Although I would have welcomed it, we had no contact.

When the telephone began to ring, it was so quiet in the house that I jumped as if a gun had gone off.

"They've called from the hospital," Sarne said without preliminaries. "There is a change in Oliver's condition. We are going at once. Will you come?"

"Of course."

"We'll call for you in three minutes."

I realized when he had rung off that I had not asked what kind of change had taken place; whether Oliver was, as Danielle had indicated, worse or whether he had rallied and his resilience had carried him over the crisis. I went

97

to tell Danielle. She had not seemed to move from the position in which I had left her.

"That was Sarne," I said. "We're going to the hospital. Will you come, too?"

She unwound herself and sat up very straight. The hollows under her cheekbones were so dark that she could have painted them in.

"No," she said, "I'm not coming with you. And Suzanne, if Oliver is conscious, please don't listen to anything—" She stopped and turned away from my eyes.

I waited, watching her take a cigarette and light it.

"What might he say?"

She flicked on the table lamp. "Never mind. He won't regain consciousness. He can't. I ... know ... he can't ..."

"But if he does," I insisted, "what are you afraid he might say? What mustn't I listen to? *Danielle, what happened tonight ... ?*"

She said, "Nothing that has any bearing on the future."

It was an ambiguous answer.

I cried, "If I could only understand!"

She lifted her head. "I can hear the car. You'd better go." She turned away from me with a finality that forbade any more speech between us.

I left her, picked up my handbag, and went to the front door.

Magda sat, as she always did, in the back of the Humber. She disliked front seats in cars. Sarne had the door of the front passenger seat open for me.

Just before I got in, I looked toward the lighted windows of Oliver's drawing room. Danielle stood well back, watching us. I raised my hand to her, but she gave no indication that she saw me.

As the car purred down the drive, I turned to Magda. She was wrapped in a dark coat, her extraordinary hair undimmed in the darkness, like something burning with a phosphorescence.

I asked, "What did the hospital say when they rang you?"

"That there was a stir of consciousness and we should come just in case Oliver could recognize us before—"

"Before?"

Magda said, "He won't live. You'd better face that."

Danielle had said it, too, yet I sat in stunned silence watching the dip of our headlights as another car approached us along the main road.

I had a picture in my mind of Oliver not so many hours ago, as I had seen him at Wyncourt's in the engraving department, bending over one of the abrasive wheels to watch the deep cutting of a jug. The man working at the wheel had joined us only a week earlier from a factory in the North of England and Oliver made a point of personally inspecting the work of new engravers. It was not a popular move on his part, and once the whole department threatened to strike because they called it interference. It had been Sarne who averted trouble, and Oliver continued to leave his splendid isolation on the top floor and inspect a newcomer's work, ignoring his nervousness at what the men called among themselves "the boss's bossiness." I recalled how alert he had been, how interested in the man's delicate skill. When he turned to me, I had explained that the man was working to a design of mine, and Oliver said, "I congratulate you both," and walked away.

Only a matter of hours ago and now, because of one false step on a staircase, he could die.

I heard myself say, "No one is so loved by the gods that he can promise himself another day." The quotation had sprung involuntarily from somewhere at the back of my mind, read long ago, and recalled in this moment of terrible awareness.

Magda said impatiently, "What on earth are you talking about?"

"It just came out. It's a quotation from one of those Greek philosophers—Seneca, I think. But it's true, isn't it? This morning, when we got up, none of us would have dreamed that by the evening Oliver might die."

"None of us? I wonder."

Sarne said sharply, "Magda, be quiet."

"Suzanne is sufficiently of the family to know its thoughts and suspicions—"

Sarne interrupted her. "She isn't 'sufficiently' of the family, she *is* family. But you'll please keep these particular thoughts to yourself."

I asked, "What thoughts?"

Our voices collided. I waited. No one answered me. I said, "I suppose you mean that you think Oliver should have told us about his heart condition. I don't see why. It was *his* affair, after all."

"Danielle Goddard knew."

"Of course. She had to. If he felt a heart attack coming on, he would need her."

"He needed her this time, but she wasn't there. Or was she?"

"*Magda!*" The car swerved.

She said with a small, unamused laugh, "Free speech, darling. You can't stop me asking myself, and others, if it really *was* an accident."

I said, "It couldn't be anything else. Oliver felt ill, went for his tablets, and became dizzy on the stairs. He fell and was concussed. His heart couldn't stand the strain and the shock." I was using layman's language, but it was simple and accurate.

"Oh, yes, that's what happened. But whether it was strictly an accident is quite another matter."

Sarne said, "Don't make mysteries, Magda."

100

"And don't try me too much," her light voice came back at him. "Or I'll give you an answer to that."

He said shortly, "I've no doubt you would," and swung the car into the hospital grounds.

So much must have been said between them before they came out. They both had tempers, Magda's a matter of words that could cut and wound while spoken in a light, almost offhand voice. Sarne's was more violent, a fury quickly unleashed when he was goaded.

He parked the car in the hospital drive, and I sat tightly in my seat, not wanting to get out. Let Magda and Sarne go and see Oliver. If he were conscious, he would almost certainly know the danger his life was in, and all his resentment against me for possessing Roseheath might well up in bitterness. If he was about to die, his last thought must not be of bitterness toward me. I crouched in the darkness of the car, sick with a foolish and oversensitive self-condemnation.

Sarne's arm pulled me out of the car. Cowardlike I said, "You two go in. I'm staying here."

"If he is conscious, he may ask to see you."

"Oh, no," I said. "No, he won't."

Sarne said, "Don't be silly," and linked his arm through mine.

Like that, as if we were close in compassion—or in love —we followed Magda's tall dark-coated figure into Amesdale General Hospital.

CHAPTER

12

WHEN we entered the hospital, the porter first telephoned up to the Floor Sister and then waved us to the elevator. I entered after Magda and stood well back.

"... it's quite all right, Suzanne. The elevator can stand on its own. You don't have to prop it up."

My arms had gone out like two buttresses, my palms pressing against the elevator walls. I said, "It's me I'm propping up."

Sarne said, "We won't be staying many minutes, Suzanne. Bear up." How gentle he could be, when he chose; and how I wished he would be harsh or indifferent, for kindness was like taking an unconscious but unfair advantage of my reeling emotions.

Oliver's impending death; Sarne's powerful effect on me ... sleep; sleep was what I wanted, here and now ...

Sarne guided me down the cool hospital corridor. Then suddenly Magda reached out and took my hand. Her fingers were so inflexible, so taut, that I realized that underneath the beautiful, rigid exterior, she was shaking like someone caught in a wild panic or an unbearable excitement.

We walked abreast to the door of the Ward Sister's office.

She met us there, a thin, brown-haired woman in a navy blue uniform.

Oliver had died without regaining consciousness.

Sarne dropped Magda at Amber Court and then drove me home. They had both tried to persuade me not to return to Roseheath but to stay the night with them.

I was grateful, but I refused. "I'll be all right. And, anyway, I can't leave Danielle alone."

I think Magda murmured, "How protective of you!" as she got out of the car. But the wind caught her voice and as Mai Chang opened the door, she entered the house and did not look back.

Sarne and I did not speak as he drove out of the lodge gates and down the road, turning a sharp right angle toward Roseheath.

There was a light in the west-wing drawing room. My hands fumbled for my key. Sarne took it from me and opened the door.

I crossed the hall, dropped my coat on a chair, and said, "Go in, Sarne, and tell Danielle. You will be gentle with her, won't you?"

He walked away from me.

I went into the living room and crossed to the mirror above the fireplace.

I put my hands to my face, smoothing the tired lines, flicking back my hair, which felt almost too heavy for my head. I hadn't really loved Oliver, so why this emptiness? I didn't have to spell out the reason to myself. Isabella Wyncourt was dead. And now Oliver. We had never been close, but we had lived in the same house all our lives. And now I was alone. I could not count Magda, for she was not really in my orbit. Of other relatives we had scarcely any knowledge. The rest of the Wyncourts were spread across the world, living in Canada and Brazil and Australia; a bachelor uncle somewhere in the far north of Scotland interested only in wild geese, an aunt in the south of France who was not on speaking terms with us . . .

"Your hair looks fine."

I dropped my hands from my head and turned.

Across the space of the room Sarne and I looked at one another. Then suddenly, somehow—although I had no idea whether he made a movement or I, or both of us, I was clinging to him and sobbing.

I heard him say, "It's easier to cry sitting down," and felt myself being led across the room. I fumbled in the handbag on the table and dug out a handkerchief and buried my face in it. Sarne took me by the shoulders and pushed me down on the settee. Then he sat by my side and let me cry. My outburst was short and sharp, and when I stopped I knew that I must look terrible, my face swollen and blotched, my eyes probably screwed up to slits. As Sarne put a hand under my chin and lifted my face, I jerked away.

"Don't. I look hideous."

"Just a bit puffy. But that's natural. People only weep picturesquely in novels. I'm sure Helen of Troy looked terrible after she had wept for Paris."

I said, "I haven't cried like that for years."

"Do you want a medal for it?"

I said, "It's horrible for a man to be alive and then so suddenly dead."

"Suzanne, listen." He put his hand behind my head, cradling it. I think he wanted me to look at him, but I was too embarrassed by my drowned face. He said, "If Oliver had to die, it was a good way to go. He can have known nothing from the moment he hit the floor of the hall."

"When you told Danielle—what did she say?"

"She was prepared for it. She knew." He drew away from me, and I had to clench my hands to stop myself holding on to him. I sensed his sudden restlessness, his desire to leave.

I said, "Of course, you must go. It's late, isn't it?"

"It's only eleven o'clock."

I got up. "Thank you for being kind."

He said curtly, walking away from me, "Let it pass."

My overwrought state interpreted his words and manner as sudden boredom with me. Words fell over themselves, gushing from my mouth. "Yes, Sarne, let it pass. You calmed me as if I were a child crying in the night. My emotion is just a sort of superficial shock, isn't it? I'm not really touched by Oliver's death, am I? I'm still too young, aren't I, to feel very much? That's the prerogative of maturity. I'm not mature. I'm just—"

He seized me and shook me hard. "Stop that. Do you hear?"

"Oh, go, please go . . ."

"What in hell's name have I done?"

I said wearily, " 'Let it pass,' you said. As if crying on your shoulder was no more than a lonely puppy would do—"

He put his hand over my mouth. Our bodies were close; our eyes blazed at one another.

"God in heaven, Suzanne, what do you want? *What,* girl, what?"

"Nothing." I pulled his hand away. He was too close to me. The irises of his eyes were clear silver; his lips were long, firm. I leaned away from him, unable to bear the nearness. I said, "I must go to Danielle."

He bent his head; his fingers slid between the strands of my hair, pulling my face back. I felt that my tear-suffused skin was bathed in lamplight. There was an exhilarating violence in the hard pressure of his mouth. I held back, giving nothing of myself, and the fight to hold on to my unresponsiveness exhausted me.

He let me go with a suddenness that nearly unbalanced me. "Now," he said, "don't accuse me of boredom."

I said furiously, "Damn you, Sarne, what do you think—"

He interrupted me again. "What I am, what I think is my own affair. But be sure of one thing. My actions so far as you are concerned have nothing to do with the relief of boredom. As for you, you've let off steam and got shock out of your system. Now go to bed. There's nothing you can do to stop events. When death takes a hand, it is final."

I stood with my back to him and let him go, burning with shame and despair. He had stressed his freedom to be and to live in his own way. *What I am is my own affair.* I looked in the mirror over the mantel and smoothed my hair. Oh, he wasn't bored with me, because I was a woman and he liked women. To give a woman what he thought she asked of him was a pleasant pastime. *"What do you want? What, girl, what?"* And as he had asked, some malevolent demon had made me lower my eyes to his mouth. And Sarne had obliged.

CHAPTER

13

DANIELLE and I walked in the herb garden.

It was six days since Oliver had died, and we didn't find it easy to talk together. Ming followed us, sometimes walking sedately by our sides, sometimes leaping ahead in an ecstasy of lithe, springing life.

Danielle kept bending down to touch a herb. I think it was because she needed something to do to break our obvious quiet with each other. I watched her fingers touch the strong green leaves of basil; the feathery fronts of chervil; thyme and marjoram. She was wearing a gray dress with a string of pearls around her throat. She looked conventional and very withdrawn.

Once, when she paused to clear a weed from the mint bed, I turned to look at the house as I waited for her. From this view, over the hornbeam hedge, Roseheath seemed to lie in the spell of sunlight. The wide fanlight over its front door was spread like the blanched tail of a peacock; the windows gleamed in the bright, moorland air. The avenue of white poplars, the lawns, the stone terrace with the two time-worn urns were mine, and now, in his will, Oliver had left me enough shares in Wyncourt Glass Works for the complete upkeep of the house.

Death duties would take a large slice of his estate, and Danielle Goddard was to inherit the residue. She was also to have the portrait of Isabella, with the proviso that she must on no account sell it. "It is for her and her heirs." A will similar to my grandmother's. Whoever owned the Isabella must never let it go, the inference being that Magda should never own it.

Like an afterthought, she was remembered. Oliver had left her his rare pieces of Sheraton furniture and the Tabriz and Ispahan rugs. The fact that it was known to all of us that she had no love for either antiquity or priceless rugs made the legacy a mockery. Like my grandmother before him, he had made a last ironic gesture. I was sure that Hugh would seize Magda's inherited treasures and she would fly to Italy to be dressed by Valentino; or buy the bracelet of rare pink topaz she had seen in Bond Street.

I wondered whether Oliver had had a presentiment that he might suffer an early death. Otherwise, how could he know that a housekeeper as young and attractive as Danielle would stay with him long enough to inherit a valuable painting? Or, had they planned to marry? If so, Danielle was not telling.

As if she sensed my absorption in her, she turned her head and gave me a long, grave look. We had come to the end of the path, and we walked slowly back, the sun in our eyes, the scents of herbs like part of an old, nostalgic dream.

I kept my eyes on the house as if it held the key to the Wyncourts' strange quirks of character. First Grandmother and then Oliver must have sat alone gloating over the dispersal of their possessions. *To Magda, nothing that she wants.* It was, I supposed, almost a love-hate relationship between them all; an acknowledgment that the Wyncourts shared strong characteristics which they knew to be in themselves and hated in each other. A cold dominance, a selective covetousness. Only my father had escaped. He had loved Roseheath without any sense of proprietorship and had instilled that love into me. Neither he nor my mother had had any desire to play malicious jokes.

As if I had spoken my thoughts aloud, Danielle asked suddenly, "Why did he do it? Why did I have to inherit that portrait?"

We paused together at the terrace steps. I said, "You knew Oliver well enough to answer that yourself."

She didn't contradict me.

"Perhaps the will could be broken."

I had no idea whether it was suggested as a wish that it could be, or a fear that someone might try. I chose to believe the former. "I doubt if you can do that," I said. "Oliver was of perfectly sound mind."

It was Sunday morning, and the church bells rang with a distant sadness across the fields. A light wind lifted the long grass on the moors so that it swayed like a green sea before the approach to the Mandrake Caves.

I said, "Have coffee with me. I'll bring it out onto the terrace."

In the kitchen, Mrs. Jo and Ming were having a conversation.

"You talk too much." She rattled cups. "I never knew a cat like you. Why don't you go and lie quietly in the sun like other sensible animals?"

He answered with a yawn and rolled on the floor in ecstasy, a paw curled around one ear, watching us.

Mrs. Jo saw me in the doorway and said, "I know what you've come for." She gave me a cue, sniffing meaningfully.

I said obediently, "The coffee smells good," and perched on the table edge and watched her, finding comfort with this down-to-earth woman.

She looked into the sugar bowl. "But you don't take sugar, do you?"

"Mrs. Goddard does."

She shot me a look and put the sugar back on the tray.

"You know, I've been thinking. That was a good Christian will of Mr. Oliver's."

"Good? But—"

"Of course it was, and don't you go having any conscience over it. You love this house, and now you've been left those shares, you can afford to keep it going. So you just live here and enjoy it."

I said, "I'll keep my fingers crossed that Wyncourt shares hold their high level."

"Oh, Mr. Eskinholm will see to that. Everyone in the town says that he's the cleverest one they've ever had there—and he so young, too. What *I* want to know is why Mrs. Goddard should get so much." She waited, giving me a sideways look.

"So much? A few thousand pounds, after the death duties are paid, and a painting."

"They say it's worth a fortune."

I said vaguely, "Oliver had his reasons," and picked up a biscuit from the plate and bit into it. I knew that Mrs. Jo would go on talking about it until she hit on a point where I would have to give her some concrete answer. She was a good woman, but relentless in her determination to know all that went on.

She had her head cocked now, waiting for me to say something. I munched the biscuit and said nothing.

She said thoughtfully, "Of course, your granny was old. But Mr. Oliver going like that. It don't make sense."

"His heart...and that fall..." I finished the biscuit.

"People live for years with bad hearts. They do say in the village—"

"*What* do they say?"

"Well—they talk..." She left the sentence in the air, heavy with meaning.

I didn't take my eyes off her.

"Well?" I asked, after too long a pause.

She said, half enjoying the enforcement of her piece of gossip, "They do say that Mrs. Goddard's job didn't stop at the bedroom door."

I slid down from the table and picked up the tray. "Then from now on, when you hear any such rumors, I trust you to squash them flat. What happened—or happens—in this house is our affair. Do you hear?" I went on as she kept silent. "You've been with us for years, and I hope you'll stay. But you've got to be loyal—"

"Loyal?" She slapped her hands down flat on the table. "God strike me dead if I'm ever disloyal to you."

"And to those," I insisted, "who live in my house."

She gave a heavy sigh. "It doesn't worry me what Mrs. Goddard was or wasn't. I'm just glad you've got security. They say in the village, 'That's a slap in the eye for Mrs. Eskinholm, that nice Miss Wyncourt inheriting like that.'"

"Mrs. Jo . . ."

"Oh, all right," she grinned at me. "I'm only telling you what they say. You ought to be glad. It's nice to be liked." She added slyly, "And one day when you get married—"

I said lightly, "Oh, perhaps I'll found a dynasty here." She gave me a puzzled look and I explained, "A family, I mean, who will have a family—oh, that will just go on and on."

"You and Mr. Justin?"

"The picture isn't even on the drawing board yet." Again, I knew she didn't understand what I meant but, carrying the coffee tray, I left her to puzzle it out and walked out to the terrace.

Ming padded ahead of me. Siamese cats are not partial to milk. Ming was the exception. His saucer was on the tray, and if a cat could get drunk on anything so innocuous, Ming of Trebizond would be an alcoholic.

CHAPTER

14

"IT'S outrageous!" Magda stormed round her living-room. There was a pile of fashion magazines on a low table. She picked one up and flung it across the room. It just missed a rare cameo-glass jar. "That woman inheriting Oliver's money."

I said, "Oh, damn the money. Oliver is dead, and Danielle is grieving."

She turned on me. "What an old-fashioned word to use."

"Grief isn't old-fashioned. It belongs to all ages. Danielle cared for Oliver."

"She cared for what she thought she could get out of him."

I had come to Amber Court because I felt bad about the will. But my sympathy for Magda died under her wave of rage. "Look," I said with weary patience, "if you're going to resent what Oliver did with his own possessions, then you must resent me, too. After all, I've inherited a lot of Wyncourt shares."

She leaned against the side of the settee, her golden eyes incalculable. "Yes, you have, haven't you? But I'm thinking of all that lovely cash—"

"A few thousand, after death duties."

"And the portrait . . ." She left the sentence unfinished and crossed to a mirrored panel on the wall. I watched her run her fingers lightly through her hair. I watched her thinking that mirrors, to Magda, were like candle flames to moths.

When she was a child, she must have loved the story of

the Sleeping Beauty ... *Mirror, mirror on the wall; Am I not the fairest of them all?* the jingle danced in my brain.

"Of course," she said, "there's a chance that I shall contest the will, anyway."

"If you took it to court, there'd probably be very little of anything left when the case was finished," I said. "And Danielle has a right to something. How do we know that Oliver wasn't planning to marry her? If he had lived a little while longer, perhaps none of us would have inherited anything."

"Or perhaps," her eyes narrowed, "he was planning to dismiss her, and she knew it. Perhaps she knew, too, the terms of the will and got in first."

"Got—in—first?" The repitition was to give myself time to adjust my mind to the horror of it. My voice burst on the room. "You said something like that in the car going to the hospital. Stop hinting at things that aren't true."

"How do you know they aren't true? What do you know about all those ... those subterranean thoughts that tear people apart even while they are smiling and sweet-tempered? Oh, for heaven's sake, get wise, Suzanne. I opened your eyes the other night, didn't I, about Sarne? Well, maybe one of these days you'll learn to open them for yourself."

It was not the first time her conviction that I was an idealistic innocent had annoyed me. She always made me feel I wanted to go out and live it up so much that my antics would shock Somerset from north to south and east to west.

"Why don't you stop thinking of me as dreamy-eyed?" I demanded angrily. "I'm out in the world, earning a living, mixing with people, understanding them—"

"Do you understand Sarne, for instance?"

I caught my breath.

Magda didn't wait for me to reply. "If you think you do, then you're under an illusion. Because you're in love with him, you refuse to see him as he is. You've created a dream image and fitted Sarne into it."

"I won't listen to any more."

She moved toward me. "You will, you know, because you can't help yourself. We always have to squeeze out the last ounce of information about someone we love. You won't face the fact, will you, that Sarne isn't interested in your pretty face? I've told you before, you *have* got something he wants—Wyncourt shares. I warn you, Sarne is devious. He'll find a way of getting them. Grandmother is dead; Oliver is dead. You are the only one now to stand between him and his monstrous dream. Wyncourt Glass Works. *Wyncourt's . . .*"

"It makes no difference what you say—and keep saying —I don't believe you."

She said softly, "Poor Suzanne. Like a kitten in a lion's den. And in the end, my little sweet, he'll crush you and break your tender bones." She paused. Then she said, "Was Oliver's death an accident? And if not—who . . . ?"

I turned on my heel without another word and began to walk away.

I hoped she wasn't watching me, for my knees shook and I wasn't able to steer a straight path.

The telephone bell rang. Pauline called from the living-room. "You're wanted, Mrs. Eskinholm."

Magda swung around. "How many times must I have to tell you not to shout across a room like that?"

I paused and looked around.

Pauline's light hair hung over her face like a sheep-dog's. She was a thin little thing, but even so, her pink dress was too tight; it was like a child's dress passed on to her. She was my size, and I made a note to choose a couple of my own summer dresses to give to her. She was saying sulkily to Magda, "I didn't know where you were, and the house is too big to go running all round it when the phone starts ringing."

"That's what you're here for. You're young and agile. Who wants me?"

"Mr. Gayer. He's hanging on the line."

I pictured him slung up on telephone wires, elegant to the last. In spite of my dark mood, the thought was irrepressibly funny.

Magda went into the house, and I heard her run up the stairs to take the call in the privacy of her own room.

I turned back, crossed the living room, and looked into the hall. Pauline was flicking a duster at the banister. I said, "I hope you haven't had any more scares."

She shook her head. "No, but if I do, I won't ever come and work here again."

"You still haven't told Mrs. Eskinholm?"

Pauline made a finger-stall of one end of the duster and was probing the curlicues of the wrought-iron work. "I've been in trouble with her once, and that's quite enough. She'd think I was making it up—"

"I'm sure she wouldn't. She would see that anyone frightening young girls in the village would be dealt with by the police."

"Don't you talk to me about the police. She'd tell them—" she closed her mouth in a thin, tight line.

She hadn't forgotten the episode of the piece of costume jewelry.

I wondered, as I looked at her, why she remained at Amber Court. She was pretty and personable, and she was a good worker. She could get a job in Amesdale, and the bus stop was almost outside her door. She would not then have to run up Sarne's lonely drive.

I said, "I've a spare flashlight somewhere at home. I'll let you have it."

She moved to a carved white table on which stood a blue jar of lilies and delphiniums. "Thanks, but it won't make me less scared."

"All right, it's your scare," I said, and walked away.

CHAPTER

15

WHEN I returned home that night, I found Justin on the lawn. He was staring across at the burning afterglow in the northwestern sky.

"Justin, you're back!" Then I laughed. "It's one of those idiotic comments on the obvious, isn't it?" I caught his arm and hugged it, more pleased than I would admit to myself that he was here with me.

"I've brought some of my stuff," he said. And then, with doubt in his eyes, "You haven't changed your mind, have you?"

"Of course I haven't."

"Then, what's the matter?"

I made him sit down, and I told him about Oliver.

"You should have called me and told me to stay away for a time. Why didn't you?"

I said, "Because you and Oliver scarcely knew one another and, besides, I wanted you here."

"There must have been quite a bit about Oliver in the local paper, but I don't take it, and if it was in one of the national dailies, I'm afraid I haven't had time to do anything but read the headlines. Oh, Suzanne, it's horrible—a man dying so young, and so suddenly." He let me talk about it, quietly listening, until Mrs. Jo called us to dinner.

Afterwards, Justin said, "Let's go for a walk."

I liked the idea. I wanted to shake myself out of this

shadow of sadness that had overcome me as I had talked about Oliver. Justin loved the moors, and the caves fascinated him. He had once said that no sculptor could ever create anything as fine as the Mandrake.

The outline of every bush, every hummock, every jagged tip of the cave, was sharp against the yellow twilight.

Justin was a compulsive talker, using his hands to stress a point, his big laugh ringing out across the silence.

He talked about his dream of making a fine studio out of the hut if he could raise enough money. "The Old Man is rather proud of me. He'd like to bask in reflected glory, if he lives long enough to see my success. I might be able to get a loan from him." "The Old Man" was his uncle, Forster Norton, who lived in a drafty mansion in Forfarshire.

So, as we made our way through the high thick grass, Justin talked. The star Venus was brilliant just where the aquamarine of the sky deepened to sapphire. A wind at our backs kept blowing my hair across my face. I was happy in a serene, unexcited way, accepting the present, closing my mind to the immediate past. I loved Justin's enthusiasm, and I was grateful for his companionship.

Justin stopped some yards from Mandrake. "I think it would help me if I were a caver."

I said, not taking him seriously, "What would it be? A new kind of publicity stunt? An underground cave for a studio?"

But he didn't laugh with me. "Can you imagine what it must be like to come suddenly upon an interior world of caverns as big as cathedrals and mauve and golden stalactites and red waterfalls? And I'm not painting a pantomime picture." He jabbed a finger downward. "Somewhere deep underneath where we are standing, there could be more inspiration to a sculptor than he could use in a lifetime."

I looked at the black mouth of the Mandrake and remembered that nine men had lost their lives over the last sixteen years trying to find what Justin dreamed of.

He said sadly, "I think my bulk might be the obstacle. I can see myself getting stuck in some eighteen-inch-high tunnel, and I don't fancy that sort of death."

I said, "If the caves interest you, there are dozens of photographs in the Amesdale Museum, taken by cavers who have actually swum the lake and penetrated Mandrake."

"Second-hand vision is no good. I need to see for myself, *feel* the rocks, trace the formation with my fingers. That's the only way to get the excitement right into your bones so that you have to re-create it." He sat down on a large flat stone, put out his hand, and drew me down by his side.

The wind was warm, and the afterglow had faded. We sat in the solitude of rolling moorland and I picked a piece of long grass and chewed it.

Justin pulled his pipe out of his pocket, looked at it, and put it back again. He picked up a stone and twisted it in his fingers. "You've no idea what it means to me to be able to live at Roseheath."

"It's nice for me, too."

He turned me around to face him. "Of course, we could make it more permanent—though God knows I've little enough to offer you. You can't make a bed out of blocks of stone, and you can't pay the bills with sculptor's tools. At the same time, I'll get where I want to go." He added with a schoolboy's enthusiasm, "It'll be Moore and Hepworth, here I come."

"I'm sure it will."

He kissed me and his beard teased my chin. But it was a gentle kiss, as light and sensitive as his hands were, touching my throat, my hair. But there was no response from me, and he knew it. He drew back. "You'd like me that way if you gave me a chance, Suzanne." He waited. "All right," he said cheerfully, "I can wait. Time is on my side. Now that I'm to live at Roseheath, you'll find out for yourself that I'm easy to live with, tidy about the house—except in my own room. But that'll be clean, not grubby, chaos. And I'm only temperamental in spots."

"You don't have to give me credentials, Justin," I said.

This time, when he took his pipe out, he lit it. A comforter, I thought, an alternative for me. "All right, so we're just good friends."

"Stop muttering clichés." I clasped my hands about my knees and stared into the darkness feeling suddenly deflated.

"At least, they state truths," he said. "Clichés, I mean. You may as well know that I intend to get married. I'm not the type to drift. I've had my wild adolescence. Now I need someone I can make love to in the comfort of my own home. I want permanency. Perhaps I'm just a nice, old-fashioned kid. Or an old-fashioned kid without being nice."

"You're nice," I said. "You're very nice . . ." (*Oh, Sarne . . .*) I closed my eyes. Justin was kinder, gentler than Sarne, who was my world inside myself. If he had asked me to the empty lodge at the gates of Amber Court I would have gone to him without a thought for anyone or anything else. Love is a hunger, even a greed. Mine was. I had battened it down like a frail ship in a storm, and it threshed about inside me all the more fiercely for being imprisoned.

"What do we do now, if we don't make love?" he asked on laughter.

"Go back home and turn on the television or talk. I'm getting cold." I stood up and put out my hand to his.

Still laughing, he tried to resist me. I said, panting, "It's like pulling at a mountain."

"But muscle and good healthy bone. Not fat."

He got up so suddenly that if he hadn't caught me around the waist I would have fallen. He held me and kissed me again.

"With a promise of more to come," he said.

We argued lightly over what he should pay for the hut and his keep. He wanted to give me more than I felt it was fair to ask. In the end we compromised. He was so desperately anxious to be a good tenant. He was also, I knew, thinking of me and the alarming expenses I would find hanging over my head as owner of Roseheath.

The hut was obsessing him. He could not give his mind to any other topic, and at last he gave in and asked: "Do you mind if I go back there for a while?"

"Of course not. Go. And if you don't come up with some brilliant work as a result of owning a new studio, then I'll send you back to Amesdale."

He strode away from me across the terrace. And as I watched him, Danielle called me.

"Suzanne? I think it's time you came and had a look over the west wing. You haven't really seen it since it became yours."

But I knew every corner of the house. I had played hide-and-seek in the alcoves and the great wardrobes with school friends and had terrified myself through games of "Murder" at Christmas time. I felt that Danielle's suggestion came from a personal loneliness, a desire to have someone there with her.

We went through the west wing together. As I stood in the drawing room I thought: Every piece, the grand piano, the Chippendale tables, the lyre-backed chairs, they all belong now to Magda, and she will sell the lot to Hugh with no more emotion than if it were a discarded coat. The dining room was oak-paneled and too dark. Upstairs, four of the bedrooms had dust sheets over the furniture. A fifth, which was Oliver's, was dominated by a French Empire bed and two carved-fronted wardrobes filled with his carefully pressed clothes. The whole place depressed me. It was beautiful and bland and without personality.

Opposite Oliver's room was a closed door. Danielle went toward it. "My room—"

"No," I said. "I don't want to see it. Nor the attics upstairs."

She said, "They're almost empty. Oliver never hoarded."

I said, "I've seen enough. Let's go into my place and have a cigarette, or something."

She came, but she wouldn't sit down. She wandered restlessly to the window and back. I had never seen her so pale, or perhaps it was that since Oliver had died, she had not bothered with make-up. With her white face, her snowy hair, and the gray dress that she kept wearing as if it were a mourning outfit, she was like a half-ghost.

I wanted to know her plans and said, "I'm sure it's too early for you to have decided what to do, but I want you to know that if you would like to stay here—*live* here, I mean—then, as I said before, I would love it. If you took a job in Amesdale you could travel in from here every day as I do. Oliver has left you the car."

She turned her head away from me, and when she spoke it was as if she were clenching her teeth so that her words came indistinctly. "I want to leave. I *must* get away."

"Of course. Though I'll be sorry."

She still didn't look at me.

"Roseheath has nothing for me but—" She hesitated. Then added, sharply and bitterly, "but haunting."

I reached down to the coffee table and picked up an enameled box, opening it. "Smoke?"

She took a cigarette eagerly and lit it. I said steadily, watching her, "There's nothing haunting about this house. No ghosts. No unquiet spirits—not even Oliver's. He enjoyed his life in his way and—"

A great shiver shook her whole body. "You don't understand, do you, Suzanne? Ghosts don't have to be dead. We can haunt ourselves."

"You mean conscience can. All right, but if we let ourselves be haunted by every silly, thoughtless thing we've ever done, we'd go crazy. Oliver had a good life. He died quickly and without a long period of pain. You don't have to be your own ghost. You have a right—"

"I wonder what you think constitutes 'a right,' as you call it? Never mind, don't answer."

She left me so swiftly that I had no time to say anything. I heard the door to the west wing close.

Had she loved Oliver? Or had they been two people, emotionally lonely, both with broken marriages behind them, thrown together by circumstances? Had they used one another secretly, not out of love but because of the deep inner need to assuage that loneliness?

I watched Ming sitting on the tallboy like a piece of cream sculpture, contemplating nothing. I called his name softly, and he flicked the tip of his tail, but he didn't come to me.

After a few minutes I pushed open the french windows and stood on the terrace. It was so quiet that I could hear the soft crunch of gravel on the drive. I stood listening. The footsteps were those of a man. Sarne? *Please, please, Fate, Circumstance, Heaven—whatever you call yourself—let it be Sarne* . . . Let me be assured that Magda spoke out of malice; that Sarne has no devious plan for taking from me my interest in Wyncourt's and even, perhaps, Roseheath.

"Suzanne?"

My heart did a heavy plunge downwards. Hugh Gayer came up the terrace steps, the lights of the house shining on his bland, complacent face.

"May I come in?"

"Of course."

As he stepped into the room, his eyes flashed about him. Like the expert he was, he made a swift mental assessment of the furniture. "You have some beautiful things here. That Queen Anne cabinet." He moved toward it, stroking the patina. Then, with a completely unexpected movement he swung around. "Do you like it?"

If he hoped to take me by surprise he was mistaken. I said, "Very much. And even if I didn't, I'm not going to be startled into promising to let you have it."

He said huffily, "My dear Suzanne, I wasn't thinking . . ."

I didn't like being called "My dear Suzanne" by him. It savored too much of patronage. Also, I knew perfectly well that Hugh *was* trying to do exactly what I had accused him of. I said, "I told you the other day that I look on everything here as being left in trust for others who come after me."

"And I told you that you have too many scruples."

"Or, you could put it that while I am alive, I enjoy living among beautiful things."

"But you can't possibly love everything in this huge house. There must be *some* things—"

"Nothing."

"And, after all, who is there now to benefit after you? I mean, who is left? Oliver is dead. There is only Magda, and she wouldn't give house room to the furniture here."

"She can do what she likes with Oliver's furniture in the west wing, just as I intend to do what I like with what I have. You're fighting a losing battle," I went on. "There's nothing for you here. And if I don't want to sell, why should I?"

He said softly, "Mink coats and emeralds."

I laughed outright. "I'm not a mink coat person, and I don't like emeralds."

"You're splitting hairs."

I thought, "Oh, do *go . . .*" and watched him walk toward a carved wall cupboard. It didn't seem to interest him very much, and he turned to the long refectory table with the lions' claw feet. "Shall I tell you a secret?"

"It depends if it's worth telling." I felt rude and irritable and impatient for him to go.

He had been bending to examine the table legs. He straightened up and turned and smiled at me. "Sarne wants Roseheath."

I said in amazement, "What for? He's got a perfectly good house of his own."

"Prestige. Photographs in the illustrated papers. 'Sarne Eskinholm, owner of the Wyncourt Glass Works, whose export sales have broken all records, seen here at the door of his beautiful Somerset mansion . . .' "

I said coldly, "I can't think that he discussed the matter with you, so I can only imagine that this is pure idle gossip with no foundation at all."

I saw his small mouth tighten; his eyes had an angry glitter. I suppose that, again, I sounded rude. I wanted to.

"Magda talks to me," he said, "and she knows her Sarne."

"I'm not interested."

"But you are, aren't you, Suzanne? And I'll lay a bet with you that you pretty well hate Adrienne Wand."

"On the contrary, I like her."

He shook his head slowly. "You can't. No woman in love with a man likes his current girl friend."

"Look." I backed away from him. "Let's get one thing clear. I'm not discussing Magda or Sarne or Adrienne with you. In fact, I'd rather you went. You're wasting my time."

He shrugged his shoulders. "Of course I'll go. I expected you to be angry with me. I'm sorry. You see, I was only trying to warn you."

"Of what?" My voice shook with anger and secret despair that my love for Sarne was as public as if I had shouted it from the housetops. "Well?" My voice rose. "What are you warning me against? Sarne's invasion of Roseheath? Has he massed a secret army to rout me out of my home? Or will he smoke me out? Or—"

"It isn't a joke, Suzanne."

"Did I sound as if I thought it was? Oh, do *go!*"

He crossed the room to the french doors. "Why don't you stop to ask yourself what I stand to gain by warning you that Sarne wants Roseheath?"

"The furniture, if I sold out and fled."

"Oh, yes, I'd like that. But there's plenty to be had in other houses. I haven't nearly scraped the bottom of the antique furniture barrel yet. So, I'm not talking for my own ends. I thought that, living more or less alone here, you ought to know."

"And you've told me. Thank you."

He went through the glass doors and then paused on the terrace. "Get out, Suzanne, before you're forced out. By fear, perhaps. Get out."

I didn't hear his footsteps fade away along the gravel path. I didn't hear Ming, prowling and calling for companionship. One thought went through me with a violence that shook me. Suppose Magda had been right? Suppose Oliver had died because someone wanted him dead . . . and now I was the only one who stood in the way of someone's ambition?

CHAPTER

16

I WAS still standing, shaken with the realization that my life—or death—could be important to someone when Justin entered. His voice boomed across the room. "Who was that standing in the window like a tailor's dummy?"

"Oh, *Justin—*"

"You sound as if I'd thrown you a lifeline."

"In a way, you have. I've been feeling furious enough to throw something hard at someone and hope I didn't miss."

"Your visitor?"

"Yes. Magda's friend, Hugh Gayer, the antique dealer. He wants to buy up my furniture and make me rich."

"Well, being rich never hurt anybody. And I suppose a lot of this stuff is very valuable. But you aren't going to sell, are you?"

"No," and then I went up to him and hugged him. "It's so good to have you here." It occurred to me suddenly that I should have remembered to tell Hugh that there was going to be a man about the house from now on. I should have said, "With Justin Norton around, nobody's going to scare me out of Roseheath."

The house seemed oppressive. I felt I wanted air and space. I said, "Let's go down to the studio. Or, at least, let's get out of here. Don't you sometimes feel that after someone has been in the house, you want to throw open all the windows and doors and blow the place clean of their personality?"

Yet the evil had not been in Hugh himself, but in the evil he had warned me of . . .

We walked across the lawn, through the copse of whispering trees toward the lighted hut.

Justin perched on the lower rung of a pair of old steps and stared at a little figure carved in elm wood.

He said, without turning around, "I know what I wanted to do. And I haven't done it. Damn it, it's pallid, soft, God-almighty sweet. Look at it," he thrust his hand towards the carving. "All nice curves and insipid features like something that's sold in fancy goods shops along the Brighton Parade."

He got out his pipe and without lighting it said, "I've wasted weeks on this. And look what I've produced." He leaped toward the figure, seized it, and threw it to the ground.

"Justin, don't be an idiot. It's good—"

"Go on, add 'of its kind.' And you'd be right. Here," he picked it up, unbroken, from the littered floor. "Take it. Put it in the attic or the tool shed. But keep it somewhere so that one day I can look at it and wonder how these damned great hands of mine could model such a *pretty* thing." He made the word "pretty" sound hateful.

"I'll have it in my room."

"Your bedroom," he thrust his head at me like a belligerent ogre, "because every time you stand in front of your mirror without your clothes on, you'll see that that girl is supposed to be you. Small, neat, perfectly proportioned. Don't you know that I had you in mind when I carved it? But I didn't want to show what you looked like photographically. I wanted your strength to come through, your fierce independence. And what have I done? Shown a little nude looking like a nymph in some forest pool in Arden."

I held the small statuette at arm's length. "It flatters me, but *I* like it." I added with a laugh, "I would, wouldn't I, because I don't understand modern sculpture. I know it's supposed to arouse sensations. It does, but mine are not particularly complimentary to the artist. I'm a philistine."

He seemed to realize that he held an unlit pipe between his fingers and struck a match. Furious bursts of smoke billowed over the hut.

"I'm not good with wood, that's the trouble. I need something hard that will resist me so that I have to battle with it. I suppose it's like wanting to conquer an element. I need stone."

He went to the trestle table and flipped over a pile of sketches. All the power and the spirit in Justin were directed toward his work. It was his real world, his absolute reason for living. In the other world of existence among people and the hazards and complications of living, he needed peace, protection, calm. A woman would need to be a complement to his work.

Sarne, too ... Sarne, whose world was Wyncourt Glass. Or how did I know? How could I possibly know the depth and ferment of his love for Adrienne? Suddenly I longed to be older, to have left all my futile emotions behind me in some far-off, mature peace. But perhaps peace was being offered me. Fate was saying, "Here is a way out. Justin will demand so much of you that everything else will be pushed out of your mind."

My chance was now. I could go to Justin and put my arms round him and reassure him that his failure was just that wood was not his medium. I could kiss him into forgetfulness. It was in my power. I even moved toward the bench to put down the little elm wood model of myself and go to him with my arms free.

There is always a moment when something becomes too late.

Justin said, "I've ordered some stone. It was to have been

delivered to the Amesdale studio. Now, it'll be all right if I ask them to send it here instead, won't it?"

My arms fell, relaxed, to my side; I felt a great sense of relief that the impulse had been stillborn. "Of course. The hut is yours. You can do what you like with it, enlarge it, put in a studio window, refurnish. So long as you don't paint the outside scarlet." I laughed and went to the door hugging my gift of myself in elm wood.

Mrs. Jo was on her way upstairs. She paused as I entered, and I held out the statuette for her to see. The likeness to me was only in Justin's eye, so she saw it just as a little nude.

"Oh, my," she said. "Now that's pretty, not like them modern things you can't make head nor tail of."

I didn't tell her that "the modern things" were just what Justin intended to do.

She said, "I've just answered the phone. Mr. Eskinholm was on the line, and he left a message. If you should need him, you've only to say."

"What does he think I need him for?" I flashed at her.

She looked slightly shocked. "Well, I think *he* thinks you'll want some sort of advice about the house and things. After all, my bonny, it's a big responsibility for a young girl to find herself mistress of a place like this, and you haven't got Mr. Oliver to help you now."

I said vaguely, "I'll see Sarne at the office in the morning."

As I crossed the hall, my eye registered the huge brown blank of paneling near the french windows. I stood quite still and stared at it.

The portrait of Isabella was gone.

Of course Danielle had taken it. I said, "So Mrs. Goddard has taken the portrait."

Mrs. Jo's eyes followed mine to the empty space. She put up her hand to her mouth and let out a yell. "Oh, my dear holy saints! Oh, Miss Suzanne..."

"Mrs. Goddard didn't come in, then? Or at least, you didn't see her?"

She shook her head, her eyes popping.

I went to the door of the west wing, opened it, and called Danielle.

There was no answer and, except for the five lights of the chandelier in the hall, the place was in darkness.

I called to Mrs. Jo, "Fetch Justin. He's down at the hut. I'll ring the police."

She said, "Hadn't you better just see if Mrs. Goddard hasn't perhaps taken it before you call in the law? After all—"

(After all, it belonged to Danielle.)

I said that I supposed she was right. But I went into Oliver's drawing room and flicked on the lights. There was no Isabella, nor did it seem to be anywhere else in the house. I even looked in the attics.

When I returned, Justin was in the living room with Mrs. Jo. His hair sprang all ways, strong and dark and wiry; his green shirt was covered with dust, as if he had been doing yoga exercises on the floor of the hut.

He said, "Mrs. Jo has told me. Well, did you find the painting in the west wing?"

I shook my head.

He said, "I gather that Danielle is out. She must have taken it with her. Perhaps to show some expert friend of hers. Paintings don't walk. Do you know where she's gone?"

"No."

"Then, do you know the names of any of her friends?"

"Only a few she made through Oliver."

"Ring them, then. You can't go summoning the police unless you're certain the thing's been stolen."

"In the meantime, if someone *has* taken it, I'm giving him time to get clear away."

"He's done that already. He won't be waiting around for the fun of seeing your reaction."

Danielle was not with anyone I contacted. I came away from the telephone after four fruitless calls. "This seems to link up with the night when I came downstairs and the curtain fell on me."

"You told me that there was quite a bit of publicity about the Bernadino in the local paper when your grandmother died. Thieves can read."

"Justin, what do I do?"

"What can you do, except wait until Danielle returns? It's her painting. As I say, she could have taken it in to have it valued by some friend. You'd look silly if the police swarmed around here for nothing, wouldn't you?"

Mrs. Jo said, "You're going to sit down and have a nice cup of tea."

Justin said, "A whisky is more in my line." He looked at me.

I said faintly, "Tea, please." Not because I wanted it, but more because it was something to do. Then I asked Mrs. Jo, "Didn't you hear anyone in the hall?"

"I was upstairs in my room watching television. I suppose I wouldn't have heard anyone right down here. Oh dear, if Mrs. Goddard hasn't taken it, then—"

"We'll wait," I said, and went into the hall and looked at the place where the Isabella had hung. I half put out my hand to the wood, then withdrew it. If the police were sent for, they would not want my fingerprints over the spot. The hook was intact; nothing seemed out of place.

I was drinking tea when Justin, who was looking through phonograph records, said, "There's a car."

"Danielle!"

I sprang up, slopping tea into the saucer, and raced into the south wing.

She entered briskly and looked surprised. "Oh—Suzanne—"

131

"The Isabella . . ."

"What about it?"

"Did you take it?"

"Take it? No, of course not. I would have spoken to you first."

"Well, it's gone. You'd better come and see for yourself."

She threw her white stole on a chair and followed me into the south-wing hall. She flashed a look at Justin and then turned to the wall. For a moment she just stood there, and I could not tell from her face what her emotions were. Then she said quietly, "We must call the police."

CHAPTER

17

NICK ELDER, who had been our village constable for almost all my life, came at once. His motorcycle roared down the drive advertising his approach like a bull about to destroy the china shop.

I knew, by his questions, that he was quite certain the newspaper publicity had whetted the appetite of some thief in the pay of an unscrupulous art collector. But he called Amesdale police headquarters, and within a quarter of an hour experts were there, powdering for fingerprints, photographing, questioning.

Mrs. Jo stated indignantly that she had heard nothing. What did they think she was, a coward who hid away while thieves walked off with a valuable painting? If she had been around . . .

Detective Inspector Reid interrupted her firmly, assuring her that he quite understood that in a house of this size someone could easily move around downstairs while the occupants upstairs would hear nothing.

And Mrs. Goddard? He turned to her. She explained that she had been visiting friends in Amesdale. He could check with them. A wave of her hand indicated the telephone.

The inquisition continued while men worked, finding, as I had suspected, nothing. I remembered that I had read that thieves wore gloves and socks over shoes. I searched in my grandmother's great bureau, which I had not yet had the heart to clear out, for some photographs that had been taken many years ago of the Isabella portrait before it had been loaned for an exhibition of Bernadino's work in Paris. The Inspector took them politely from me. "And you must notify the insurance company. If I remember rightly," he added, "the painting was worth roughly thirty thousand pounds."

"Yes."

"And you are the sole possessor?"

"Oh, no. When my cousin died last week, he left the portrait to—"

"To me," said Danielle.

I had already telephoned to Amber Court to tell Magda. She had been out, and Hugh had taken the message. I remembered now, as the telephone bell rang and stopped the Inspector in the act of his next question, that Hugh had said, "Oh, my lord, this'll put the cat among the pigeons. Magda reckoned on getting that painting somehow or other . . ."

I crossed the room and lifted the receiver and heard Magda's voice. "Is this some silly kind of joke you and Hugh have cooked up, because if it is—"

"It's no joke. The Isabella has been stolen, and we have no clues."

"Let me speak to the Inspector."

"Why? Do you know something?"

Magda's voice was clear and carrying. The Inspector must have heard his name. The receiver was taken gently out of my hands, and he introduced himself to Magda. "What is it you want to say to me, Mrs. Eskinholm?"

I shot a glance at Danielle. She was sitting on the arm of a chair, her hands in her lap. It seemed to me as if she felt herself an onlooker, completely unaffected by what was happening. Her expression was neither unhappy nor particularly distressed.

The Inspector was saying, "Thank you, Mrs. Eskinholm." He replaced the receiver and turned to Danielle. "Mrs. Goddard—"

She looked up at him politely, like a mature child drawn into some adolescent game, a little bored but determined not to show it.

"I am told that there was a clause in the will that prevented the sale of the painting."

"That is true."

I held my breath.

He nodded gently and understandingly. *J'accuse* . . . But he didn't. He knew perfectly well that whatever he might suspect, she would not be forced to answer his questions now.

In the pause, I saw a faint smile touch her face. "Of course, I could have done all this myself, couldn't I? Pretended the painting was stolen, secreted it away, and collected the insurance. It's such an old trick, Inspector."

She was far more in control of herself than I was for her. I had a feeling that, in the circumstances, she was being too calm and that the Inspector was trying to make up his mind whether this was natural to her.

"There's one thing you ought to know," I said to him.

He turned his attention at once to me and I told him about the night when I had thought I had heard a sound in the hall and had gone down to see. I explained how the curtain had fallen over me.

He asked, as I knew he would, why I hadn't reported it. I said, "Because everyone else was so certain that it was an accident. The brackets were old and probably rotten."

He went to the window and looked up at them.

I said, "It's no use, Inspector. I've had new ones put up. It was, at the time, only an unfounded suspicion on my part."

He looked at us all in turn, but his face was so bland that I had no idea what he was thinking.

When the police had gone, Danielle refused to stay and talk. She said, "I'm very tired. And there's nothing we can do now, anyway. Good night, Suzanne...Justin."

I sent Mrs. Jo to bed and told her that everything was all right and she must stop reproaching herself for not having heard the intruder.

I had no idea how long we sat slumped in our chairs before a car tore up the drive.

Justin said, "More visitors? The police have found the painting under the rosebushes."

But when he opened the door, I heard Magda's voice. She swept in, her eyes brilliant with anger. "Really, Suzanne, you seem to have no regard for your possessions or anyone else's. You go out and leave the house open to anyone who passes and thinks there's something for the taking."

"I did nothing of the sort. I closed the front door, and the terrace windows were locked. And," I added furiously, "Mrs. Jo was here."

"Probably with a television set blaring."

The emotional exhaustion of too many things happening at once made me ask, "What did you expect me to do? Build an electric wall around the property? Or keep a kennel of bloodhounds? Or both?"

"Don't be silly."

Out of the corner of my eye I saw Justin's beard slide sideways, and I knew he was grinning lopsidedly at me.

Magda sat down with a slow elegant movement that was natural to her. "Of course, I can't expect you to feel as the rest of us would about property. Such a sense of responsibility is an inheritance—"

"All right," she was goading me and this I couldn't ignore, "so I have inherited something you think I have no right to. Very well, that's the mistake made by those who left me Roseheath, not by me."

136

She took a cigarette from a slim case in her handbag, and Justin lit it for her.

I said after the small pause, "I have asked you before. This time, please tell me the truth. Do *you* want Roseheath?"

Her eyes opened wide, and she waved a hand around the room. "Can you picture me among all this? Whenever I walk into the house, I feel I have stepped back in time. I don't belong to the past. But I do have respect for what is inherited, and I'm afraid you haven't even that."

"What," asked Justin, "should Suzanne be doing? Sitting all day long at the gates of Roseheath with a gun by her side? Oh, for God's sake, leave her be. She's had enough to contend with."

Most men found Magda either irresistible or a little terrifying. Justin did neither, and I think this intrigued her. For a moment I feared some cutting comment flung with perfect aim in order to hurt him. Then she shrugged her shoulders. "You have a Sir Galahad, Suzanne. Guard him carefully, he's a rare specimen."

I avoided the trend of the conversation. "Suppose we stop scratching at one another. The one to be upset about the theft is Danielle."

Magda leaned her head back. "Of course, she could have done the obvious thing. She couldn't sell the portrait, so she could have arranged to have it stolen."

I said coldly, "She suggested that herself to the Inspector."

"That doesn't exonerate her!" She drew a mocking, envious breath; then her low rich voice rang out. "Thirty thousand pounds of insurance money. What a scoop!"

"You're wrong," I said angrily. "You couldn't be *more* wrong."

She said exasperatedly, "And what a household! Justin defending you and you defending Danielle. Do you two belong to some new crustader's society—'In Defense of my Brother—my Sister.' Oh, really!"

I said, "I hate injustice. It's as simple as that."

"Then direct your moral indignation into the right channel," she snapped back. "That portrait is mine. Grandmother promised it to me. Then, when she was senile, she forgot."

My nails dug into my palms; I counted ten carefully. Then I said, "Grandmother had every faculty, including her marvelous memory, right up to the end of her life, and you know it."

Magda rose. "It really isn't important what we say here. What matters is that sooner or later the police will find the Isabella, and when they do I'll see to it that it comes to me."

Justin said coolly, "On the premise that to will to possess is to succeed. I wish you luck."

She walked to the door, turned, and looked directly at me. "The argument is a little one-sided. Sarne should have been with me to even it up."

I was still angry. "He's probably dining out with some French buyers who were at the Works today. You could have waited till he came home and brought your ally."

"Oh, Sarne will be late. But you couldn't exactly call his dinner guest a client." She left me, with a name hanging on the air. Adrienne ...

Justin heaved himself out of his chair and followed her into the hall. I stood at the mantelshelf, rubbing my finger along the carved molding, and heard the door close and then the car drive away.

"That cousin of yours seems to have quite a flair for an exit line." He returned to the big chair that took his weight without a hint of creaking springs. "Do you know what she said to me as she walked through the front door?"

"A final crack at my lack of responsibility."

"No."

"Go on then, tell me."

"She said, 'Did Oliver really die by accident?' "

Quite suddenly I felt drained of vitality. It didn't matter

what Magda said. "If the police never find the portrait, she'll blame me for the rest of our lives because there's nobody else to blame. She has lived for so long with the belief that the Isabella was to be hers. If only Oliver had left it to me."

"And you'd have given it to her and broken the terms of the will."

"Oh, I'd have been much more careful. I'd have had some clever artist copy it, kept that for myself, and given her the original."

Justin got up and put his arms round me. "You have the makings of a little criminal, my pretty," he said and laughed and kissed me.

CHAPTER

18

THE heat wave broke upon us the following day, and because I was one of those people who reacted badly to battering heat this added to my jumpiness.

During the daytime, I was too busy at the Works to be more than irritated by the way my hand stuck to the drawing paper. But when I was back at Roseheath and darkness fell, I had the recurring sensation that someone watched the house.

The Isabella was gone. There was nothing more in my south wing that could interest an unscrupulous collector. Of course, there were Oliver's valuable rugs and the furniture, which Magda had not even bothered to come and look at. But I doubted whether a thief would bring along a truck and blatantly load it.

So, nobody had any more reason to watch the house. I was merely caught up in the merry-go-round of my own imagination.

Yet every night, while Mrs. Jo was in her room watching television and Justin was at the hut, I would turn on all the downstairs lights and lock myself in like some voluntary prisoner. When Justin first returned after a long evening spent working at the hut, he laughed and asked if I were playing at being a princess in an ivory tower. I had answered quite seriously. "I'm just a coward in a big house, watching my own shadow."

"You're no coward," Justin had said. "And anyway, you've only got to shout for me if someone scares you."

"I'd need to trumpet like an elephant for the sound to reach you."

"I'll teach you the long Maori 'Coo-eeee,'" he said.

He did teach me, but I still locked myself in, and whenever I was out late, I would blow the horn loudly as I pulled the car up by the door.

Not once during those few days did Danielle and I meet and spend any time together. She kept herself as remote as ever. I sought my friends. They were young, and none of them had very much money. My inheritance thrilled them, and they kept asking me when I was going to start having parties at Roseheath. I kept saying, "Not yet. Not yet."

I began to have nightmares again. I would wake with a start and for the first few moments relive the nights when my grandmother had padded to my room to arouse me with some monstrous delusion about the house being on fire or someone downstairs lying in wait to attack us. Then I would shake myself fully awake and remember that it could never happen again.

Toward the end of the week, however, I dreamed again that my bedroom door opened. This time, though, it wasn't my grandmother who entered, but a figure moving silently as if it walked on air. As so often in dreams, there was neither face nor real form. "It" stood at the end of my bed, like all classic ghosts, and from it emanated a stream of cold air. I tried to cry out, and it must have been this effort that woke me up.

I lay quite still for a moment. The sickle moon made a faint pattern on the ceiling; the curtains billowed gently, and cool air blew in on me from an open window.

I reached out and switched on the bedside light.

There were two large windows in my room, one facing south, the other west. The frame of the latter was worn, and the window was difficult to open. I didn't bother with it because when the rains came from the southwest, they beat against this window and I had so often had to do mopping-up operations to the window sill and the carpet that I kept it closed.

I lay now, fully awake, and saw that it was wide open.

But I hadn't opened it.

I put on my dressing gown and crossed, barefoot, to the west window. Grandmother had told me that the windows in some of the bedrooms were not the original ones, for her mother had had casements fitted after a guest had hurt her hand one day when a sashcord broke on one of the original ones.

The bar of the north window hung loose. Even if, absorbed in thinking of something else, I had absently opened it, it would have been an automatic action on my part to have secured it on its notch.

I leaned out, looking down on the beds of delphiniums immediately below me. They swayed gently in the wind which, after the heat of the day, was a wonderful relief. Except for the slender stalks of the flowers, nothing stirred. But as I stood there, outlined in the lamplight, my eyes became adjusted to the darkness. I could easily have imagined that a shadow moved by a tree or crouched below the hornbeam hedge. But of course it didn't. No one was out there. I closed the window firmly and crossed to the door and checked it. It was closed.

I sat on the bed and tried to remember, movement by movement, what I had done when I came to my room. I had undressed, washed. I went downstairs for the book I was reading, came up, and closed my door. I opened the south window, but I didn't go near the other one—not even to draw the curtains. *So, not I, but someone else had opened the west window.*

Two o'clock in the morning is a bad time for fears, and

I needed someone to laugh me out of them. I thought, "Perhaps whatever woke me woke Mrs. Jo or Justin." With a wild hope that it had, I went out into the passage. It was quite dark, and the only outlines I could see as far as the turn of the staircase were those of the carved Italian *cassone* and a small table outside what had been Grandmother's room which we put there so that we could rest trays on it when we brought her meals in bed. Apart from those two familiar outlines, the place was deserted. I reached out and switched on the light, and the passage lost the air of eeriness. I went to the far end, where a curved staircase led to the attic rooms.

Halfway up, I tripped over my housecoat. As I untangled it, I looked behind me. I could just see part of the main staircase. It was dark and empty. I ran up the remaining stairs. The strange noises coming from Mrs. Jo's room told me that she was lying on her back in a state she would call "dead to the world."

Under Justin's door was a thin strip of light. The floorboards creaked as I stepped on them. I knocked softly.

"Justin?"

After a short pause, he came, wearing a purple dressing gown.

"Hey, Suzanne . . ." He scratched the back of his head, looking at me with sleepy surprise.

"I saw your light, otherwise I wouldn't have disturbed you. Something odd has happened." I told him about the window.

He yawned loudly. "The bar probably slipped when Mrs. Jo dusted the room."

"It couldn't. It's very stiff."

"Then you opened it and forgot."

"No."

"Windows don't open themselves."

"That's just what I'm trying to tell you."

143

He said with a laugh, "Then you walked in your sleep."

My flesh crawled. I put out a hand to the door frame to steady myself. "I didn't. Justin, I couldn't have." *Could I?*

"You'd better let me come and see what I really think about it. I'm using guesswork at the moment."

His practical tone steadied me.

"Come on," I said, and we crept down the stairs to the gentle accompaniment of Mrs. Jo's snores.

Justin stopped and looked around my bedroom. "Pretty," he said. "I like it. It's feminine."

"The window . . ."

He crossed the room and tested the bar on its notch. "It's firm enough when it's closed."

"So it couldn't have slipped off," I said. "So—?"

"Mrs. Jo opened it sometime when she was cleaning and forgot to shut it properly. Go back to bed, Suzanne."

I stood stubbornly resisting his hand on my arm.

"Go," he said and put up his hands and dragged my housecoat off my shoulders.

I leaped onto the bed, sat up, and dragged the bedclothes over my knees. Justin pushed me flat onto the pillows and bent and tucked them in. "Comfortable? That's good. Now turn the light out and go to sleep."

"You're wasting your time doing all that," I said as he still fussed with the bedclothes. "Because I'm going to get out after you've gone and lock my door."

He said, "You stay where you are. You're perfectly safe. No one came in here and opened your window. Why on earth should they? It's not a trick even a moron would play at two o'clock in the morning." He patted my check.

I lay quite still and heard the door close. What did Justin really think? That I had walked in my sleep? That alarmed me almost more than the thought of an intruder. There had been a girl at Magda's boarding school who had done just that and had walked into a pond in the school grounds. Fortunately it was not deep, so she had not drowned, but she had slipped and fallen in the water and so disproved the theory that if you left sleep-walkers alone no harm came to them. The explanation had been that she suffered a disturbed home life with quarreling parents. Sleep-walking was psychological, they said glibly. Well, then perhaps I was becoming psychologically disturbed. But I didn't believe it.

I lay and tried to sleep, but my mind was too active. The most unlikely possibilities slipped through my mind. Ming, in one of his wild games sometime today, leaping on to the windowsill. But Ming's delicate feet could never dislodge a well-secured bar. The window cleaner? But he hadn't been near us for a month.

Very well, then suppose someone had hidden in the house until we were all asleep and then entered my room. Why? What did I possess that could possibly be of value to anyone? A string of cultured pearls; some costume jewelry ... And the ruby.

Some years ago my grandmother, clearing out an old Victorian shell box, had come upon it among a heap of birthday cards, valentines, and little dance programs with their tiny pink and blue pencils attached. I remember having been surprised that she had kept such things. I had never known the Wyncourts to have any sentimental feelings. But the box proved that she must have had them at one time, for there were the relics of her gay Edwardian past. The television set had been on at the time, and with Ming on my lap, I was watching a program that didn't interest me very much—Grandmother had long ago been bored by it.

Suddenly, she had said, "Here, Suzanne. Take this. I don't want the thing," and a ring with a gleaming red stone had flown through the air to flip past Ming's sleek ear. With an affronted yowl he had leaped off my lap. I had said, "Is it a ruby?"

"Of course. My men didn't give me glass."

"It was an engagement ring?"

"He wanted it to be. He gave it to me just before he went to India. I never heard of him again. I believe he married a General's daughter. His will had the substance of thistledown, and she probably led him by the nose to the altar. I don't like rubies." Then, as I handed it back to her, she said, "Take it, child. It's valuable. And sell it if ever you need money."

I had had it valued for insurance soon after that. The ruby was a fine one set in an oval of clear blue diamonds. The valuation was eight hundred pounds. Worth stealing? Worth breaking and entering for? But who, except for the family, knew I had it? For I never wore it. Of course, there was always the common belief that if you lived in a large house you owned jewels and precious objects.

I pushed back the bedclothes wondering if I would ever settle down that night. But I had to make certain that the ring was there. I went across the room to the tallboy. In the second drawer was a blue leather box that contained my few pieces of jewelry. Set in its velvet-lined groove, the ruby glowed. I closed the case. In some odd way I was almost sorry it was there. It denounced my desperate theory that a thief had entered my room. I was back to the beginning of the puzzle. There is something terrifying about the inexplicable. I was one of those people who had to have an answer. And the only one left was what Justin had suggested. I had walked in my sleep.

Downstairs, the hall clock struck three. My father had always called it, laughingly, a "doom-laden" clock, because its tone was heavy and sinister. I made a promise to myself that if ever I could prove that I had sleep-walked I would, from that time on, have myself tied to the bed each night.

Before I went back to bed, I got the key from the outside of my door and locked it from the inside. But I did not feel safe.

146

CHAPTER

19

THE local newspaper gave the theft of the Isabella full coverage.

"A painting valued at thirty thousand pounds was stolen from the home of Miss Suzanne Wyncourt of Roseheath, Magnon Down. A reward of £3,000 is offered by the loss adjusters, Collet and Mason. Miss Wyncourt, who is a designer at her family's glass works, told our reporter..."

Justin and I sat at breakfast and read all about it. He said, happily munching toast piled with honey. "Three thousand pounds isn't going to lure the thief to find the painting, 'accidentally like.'"

"But sometimes someone overhears a conversation or sees something suspicious—"

"Unscrupulous connoisseurs don't employ amateur thieves. But who's suffering? Only the insurance company. Danielle will benefit by thirty thousand pounds; the receiver will gloat over the painting; and you won't have the anxiety of knowing you've got something worth stealing."

But somebody thought I had; somebody who had crept into my bedroom and opened a window to scare me into believing I had sleep-walked. Because even in the clear light of day, that was what I was convinced had happened.

I had told Mrs. Jo about the open window, and she had declared that she had never touched it. "There's always too much air in your bedroom, and even if you had both windows closed, the drafts would be enough to blow a man sideways. It's always the same in these old places, no matter how you block up the cracks. I think this house breathes through its walls."

That was one thing that last night had done for me. It had reminded me of a thing of value that I did not want. Grandmother had told me to sell the ring if I needed money, and I had Mrs. Jo's and Tom's wages to pay.

After breakfast I put the ring case in my handbag. I thought a little giddily that I would like to put a notice in the local newspaper. "Miss Suzanne Wyncourt has now disposed of her one and only valuable possession. She no longer owns anything of consequence but a house, some furniture, and a Siamese cat." Such a notice would certainly brighten up the "Personal" column of the Amesdale *Gazette*.

The house that morning seemed full of light and sound. Mrs. Jo was in the kitchen listening to the news on the radio, and upstairs, Justin was collecting his medley of suitcases to take back to Amesdale to refill with the rest of his belongings. His unmusical voice rose above the radio, delighting me, lifting my depression. He sang a tuneless song to his own bellowed words.

> "I have immortal longings, tra la; tra la;
> And they're going to come true, tra la, tra la;
>   I'll work long and late
>   For I'm going to be great.
> I'll be Justinian Immortalis, tra la, tra la."

He left the house ahead of me, and his red car rattled down the drive, giving long, sharp hooting signals as I followed.

If Grandmother had been alive, she would have flown at him for the extrovert din he was making. I tried to signal to him by flashlight my light, to stop rousing the neighborhood.

But he must have thought I was giving him encouragement.

"Noise is a killer," my grandmother always said. "It is like a dagger cutting through every nerve. Only morons and fools like noise."

But Justin was neither a moron nor a fool. Happiness impelled his fingers as he drove in triumph out of the gates and toward the city.

He had told me he would be away two or three days packing up the rest of his possessions and bringing them to the hut. He had already arranged for the local builders to come and give him an estimate for the rebuilding that would turn the hut into a respectable studio.

"Charm," he said, "that's what'll pay for the conversion. I'll 'magic' the Old Man into letting me have a few hundred. I'll tell him that my memoirs will be dedicated to him in gratitude."

I kept Justin in sight all the way to Amesdale. When I reached the town center he turned off by the Cathedral and I drove in the opposite direction to the Wyncourt Works.

I knew, of course, before any of them, that at the Extraordinary Board Meeting the day before, Sarne had been elected as their chairman in Oliver's place. But the news had only just been broken to the staff. The doorkeeper, who was a retired army sergeant, boomed at me. "Morning, Miss Wyncourt. You heard the news about Mr. Eskinholm?"

"Yes."

"Sad way for it to happen, but that's life. And you tell Mr. Eskinholm that we're all pleased for him."

"I will."

"It's he that's lifted this place out of the doldrums. I remember well, before he joined the company, how we wondered just how long we'd be able to carry on. And look at us now—winners of the Grand Prix for glass manufacture, orders all over the world, and now talk of a new factory."

It was true, of course, Sarne was the man who had brought

life to the sluggish industry; Sarne, dynamic and tireless, who had fought through old conservatism, through staid, dyed-in-the-wool ideas and revolutionized Wyncourt's.

The manager of the accounts department stopped and spoke to me as I waited for the elevator. "Everyone is delighted at the news that Mr. Eskinholm is our new chairman."

"I'm glad, too."

"We were afraid that some outsider—"

"Oh, never an outsider . . ."

The elevator doors opened and I got in. As the car moved upwards, I remembered how someone had said when Sarne had only been with the firm a few months:

"He'll never be content until he controls Wyncourt's. There's a lot of dead wood in this factory, and I've a feeling that he'll rip it out. He's ambitious, and he's probably ruthless. There'll be some redundancy before Mr. Eskinholm has the Works as he wants it."

But there had been no redundancy. Instead, the "dead wood" had proved to be still living; those who half slumbered in their easy jobs sat up and saw the red light of danger if they dared to sleep again. Work, that's what Sarne wanted, a hundred-percent efficiency; a whole-hearted attempt to make Wyncourt's the kingpin of the industry. He taught them to take a pride in achievement, in the beauty of the form and cut of the gleaming crystal, and not just carry on through the day with an eye to their pay envelopes. A new name joined the famous Bristol Blue and Stourbridge. It was Wyncourt's Peridot crystal—a glorious gleaming grass-green—which had become an instant success when it came on the market.

I was quite certain that the staff reminded each other of what had been said when Sarne joined us. "Mr. Eskinholm won't be content until he rules Wyncourt's." Well, Oliver was dead, and Sarne now ruled. Sarne, who had everything

—his beautiful house and his beautiful wife. His mistress and the job he had come to England to get ...

I was aware that the elevator had stopped, the gates were open, and already starting to close again. I squeezed myself out and went along to my office.

The design panel I was working on was an intricate one based on old Persian illustrated manuscripts. It could be a challenge to the engraver, but I felt there was too much detail. When I had finished it and it was approved, I had to design for a set of glasses, champagne, wine, liqueur, the lot, for a Coptic millionaire from the Middle East. I was to be given an opportunity to try my hand at this, but it had been pointed out to me that my design might not be passed. If I failed, the senior designer, who was also an engraver, would take over.

Halfway through the morning the panel design was finished. I relaxed and took the ruby ring from my handbag.

I held the stone up to the light. It had a marvelous depth, crimson within crimson, like the mirrors you see in palaces, reflecting other mirrors so that galleries go on endlessly into space.

"Marguerite dipping into her jeweled casket."

I looked up and saw that Sarne had come quietly into my room. My heart turned a somersault. I stood, very controlled, even managing a laugh. "Your imagination has stretched. One small ring case does not make a casket."

"It's a very beautiful stone." He took it from me and held it, as I had done, to the light.

"Grandmother never cared for it. She threw it into my lap one evening as if it were no more than a box of matches. I'm going to sell it."

"Why?"

"I don't *want* the ring; I don't even *like* it. Why shouldn't I ... ?"

"My dear girl, you have a right to do what you like. But where were you going to offer it?"

I told him. "Masons, in the Square. They're the best—"

"Let me do it for you. I'll show it to Adrienne. She'll know where best to sell it."

"Oh, no. I'm sure you both have too much to occupy your time together without—"

"What the devil do you mean by that?"

It hadn't been so much what I said as my taut, defensive manner that had made him flash his question at me. I could have bitten out my tongue. I knew that my face and neck grew crimson, and it was probably the first time in my life that I had blushed. It was not an involuntary shyness that suffused me but sheer anger at my own stupidity. The words were out and there was nothing I could do to drag them back. But, like an idiot, I tried and made it worse. "I didn't mean . . . if you think . . . I'm sorry if you . . ." I stammered and hesitated as if my tongue had gone berserk.

Sarne said shortly, "Start again."

"I didn't mean to imply that—"

"I suggest you tell me what you did mean."

I stood up. It gave less longitude between us so that I could meet his eyes, if not on a level, at any rate without the curious supplication one feels in bending the head back in order to look up. "I meant that you . . . you are both very busy people and—"

"And all *that* is what you did not mean."

"Sarne, don't try to cross-examine me."

He gave me a long, strange look, seemed about to say something, and then, tightening his lips, walked over to the little cabinet that held some special pieces of engraved glass. "In Uruguay, there is a whole forest of weird crystal trees created by lightning striking the sand dunes." He was deliberately changing the conversation so that our awkwardness should not hang on the air after he had left. I thought:

152

Like not letting the sun go down upon one's wrath; making a charming comment to sweeten the exit.

"I'd like to see that forest," I said. "Perhaps one day . . ." My voice tailed off. Whatever either of us said was anti-climax. Sarne had reacted to the asperity in my voice, and there was no cleansing process that could wash it out.

He wandered back to my drawing table. "Well, do I take the ring?"

"No, thank you."

"What is this—obstinacy or aversion? And if the latter, it's certainly new. I thought you liked Adrienne."

"Oh, I do. I do." Too quickly said, too emphasized. (I did . . . I did . . . until I learned the secret of the gardener's lodge at Amber Court; until I learned that Sarne's need for women held no love.)

He tossed the ring on to my desk. It rolled toward the edge, and I caught it. "All right, if you want to lose money on the sale, that's your affair."

And Adrienne was his affair, not mine. I had no right to feel angry or resentful or, in fact, stand in judgment upon them. It was the evil of the Mandrake Caves that parted us, and my grandmother's outrageous story that I was a hysteric, and Magda's confirmation of the fact.

His hand went out to close my door.

I called his name.

He turned, his eyes like blue ice, and waited.

I said, "I'm sorry. I'm in a bad mood this morning."

"No one is less susceptible to moods than you." He was not going to allow me even that excuse.

"How little you know me," I said.

"I'm beginning to think that's true." The door closed.

Suddenly I knew that I couldn't let him go in anger.

"Sarne . . ." I threw the pencil across the desk and ran to the door and flung it open.

He was in the corridor.

153

I called down to him. "The ring. Thank you, if you would ...let Adrienne see it."

He said with a touch of amusement, "You change your mind with the swiftness of light. You'd better be sure you mean it."

"Oh, I mean it." I hesitated. "And Sarne, I *am* in a mood —or you could say that I'm frightened." I was, but that was not the reason for my utter tactlessness. How easily and artfully I could defend myself to save my pride . . .

I darted back to my desk, fitted the ring into its velvet slot, and took the box to where Sarne waited in the corridor.

"Please," I said, "ask Adrienne if she will try to sell it for me. She knows the market. I don't."

"Very well. But what's this about last night?"

"Something scared me rather badly."

"Then for God's sake, why didn't you tell me right away?"

I took a deep breath. "I believe I walked in my sleep."

For a moment I thought he was going to laugh at me. "Oh, no, Suzanne, not you."

"I didn't believe it at first, then I did. Now—I don't know. I'm trying to tell myself that what happened was just— inexplicable. Odd things do happen—they do, don't they? Perhaps . . ."

"Suppose you stop trying to analyze it and give me the facts?"

"I . . . I woke up in the middle of the night. Something had disturbed me. When I turned on the light, a west window that looks toward the moors was wide open, and I always keep that one closed."

"Then Mrs. Jo opened it."

"Oh, no, I asked her. She hates open windows, anyway. Most of the villagers here do."

"All right. So the catch is weak. Roseheath is a very old house, and the window frame could have warped and loosened the latch in some way."

I said bitterly, "An easy explanation like the one I was given about the curtain pole."

"I'm a practical man. I usually lean toward the obvious. You really aren't letting yourself get agitated about an open window? There was a bit of a breeze last night, and very welcome it was, too, after the heat of the day."

Everyone was being too damned reasonable. "Oh, yes, there was a breeze, and it had fingers and it opened my window from the outside, just for the devil of it. And I—"

"Suzanne..."

I took a gasp of breath. "I'm sorry. Oh, heavens, I keep apologizing to you, don't I?"

He gave a sudden smile. "It's all right. I understand. You've been through some strains lately." He reached out and took my hand. "You mustn't let things get on top of you. There's no need. I'm here. I'll help you in any way I can. Do you understand?"

I nodded, not looking at him.

"And if you're worried or uncertain about anything, you'll come to me?"

"Oh, of course," I said flatly and without truth.

Sarne sensed it, and his quick temper rose. "For God's sake, what's got into you?"

I looked at him through a sudden shot of sunlight which broke through my open door and in which danced a million specks of dust. "Nothing's got into me. I just said 'of course.' You don't have to pick me up on that."

"At least pay me the compliment of being perceptive." The anger went out of him as swiftly as it had come, and his voice held a despair that was startling in so positive and proud a man. "Suzanne, what has happened between us?"

I said shakenly, "It's all my fault. Don't let me have to say 'I'm sorry' again. Just take it that I'm like a non-swimmer in a sea that seems to be getting rougher. Let me be, please."

"That's the last thing I intend to do. Face facts, Suzanne.

You've been landed with a responsibility that's too big for you, and it's getting you down."

Hugh's horrible insinuation the other night slid into my mind. *It's Sarne who wants Roseheath.*

I cried, my voice high with indignation and secret hurt, "I love my home, and no one is going to turn me out of it."

"You talk as if someone were trying to." He was watching me closely.

Outrageous though it may seem, somebody could be," I said. "I *know* someone came into my room while I was asleep and opened my window. I *know* somebody loosened the curtain bracket..."

"But to me both these things seem to have a very feasible explanation."

"And the theft of the Isabella?" I demanded.

"Oh, that was different. It was the craziest thing to advertise its value in the local paper. But to come back to Roseheath, if you're going to live there, then you'd better accept the fact that in old houses, odd things happen—wood creaks in the night, old brackets give way eventually, window frames warp..."

I said bitterly, "Everything always seems to have an easy explanation to those who haven't experienced the oddities. All right, Sarne, forget it."

"One thing," he said. "You're very young. You've got to have someone to whom you can go for advice, for help. You know I'm around."

"Thank you," I said quietly and thought that if I needed help I would go to someone like Maurice Trent, who had no personal interest in my house and my shares. And yet Sarne was here, offering me help—Sarne whom I loved and could not trust.

He said, "You're quite certain you want to sell the ring?"

"Quite."

I turned from him and went back into my office. I stood at the window staring out.

Take it; show it to Adrienne. "Little Suzanne wants to sell this. And now, let's forget business transactions." My tortured imagination saw them go to one another.

I put my face in my hands. What utter idiots we could be when emotion took control. Here was I, young and sound in mind—I hoped—unable to tear a hopeless obsession out of my blood. Obsession. That's what it was, and it was up to me to pull myself together and drag it out of me by the roots. I was behaving as though my own infatuation gave me the right to stand in judgment over Sarne. My grandmother and Magda had, for their own ends, taken the right from me.

And all the time I took myself to task, I knew that I had used the wrong word about myself. This was no infatuation.

In love, one feels either very young or very old. I felt the latter. It was as if all the time of my life, past and present and future, had been gathered together to weigh me down.

CHAPTER

20

JUSTIN was in London to visit an exhibition of Henry Moore's work. He told me before he left that some blocks of stone were to be delivered to Roseheath and he had given instructions for the men to put them in the hut.

When I came home two evenings later, Mrs. Jo told me that they had arrived. "The only thing Mr. Justin can do with *them* is to use them for tombstones."

It was a hot night, and she set my place for dinner at a small table pulled into the open terrace doorway. "You should have seen the to-do the men made of it, heaving and groaning and swearing, too. They said they wouldn't deliver no more like that unless they had a crane and pulleys."

"Mr. Justin has big ideas."

She said placidly, putting half an avocado in front of me, "One thing about him, he ain't temperamental, and if he were, he couldn't go throwing *them* about, could he?"

I said no, I supposed he couldn't. And anyway, if he had been temperamental, I wouldn't have let him come to live at Roseheath. "I'm not the patient type. I'd probably throw things back at him."

Later that night, I went down the garden to the hut. The path at the far end curved toward the copse, and I looked back at the house. The west wing was in darkness, so Danielle must be out with friends. I had hoped that, with

Oliver's death, some of her reserve would melt and we could reach a closer friendship. But Danielle came and went quietly, occasionally spending a brief evening with me or joining me as I walked through the gardens after the stifling heaviness of the city heat. But she never talked very much, never offered any information about her life. We had once more discussed her future, and I had suggested that she stayed at Roseheath until the will was proved.

"But that could take months, even a year. Oh, no, Suzy, I couldn't. Anyway, I must find myself another job."

She had, however, let herself be coaxed into repeating her promise to stay for a while, protesting that she must pay me rent. I told her that she was doing me a service by using the rooms and, if she liked, she could look after the herb garden as her contribution. That was something that did not interest Tom, and if he could dodge work there, he did.

But at the end of the first four weeks after Oliver's death, I knew no more about Danielle than when she had come to the house three years ago.

As I walked down to the hut, the risen moon made little patches like snow between the shadows of the silver birches. The door of the hut was closed. I opened it, switched on the light, and saw the blocks of stone.

Three of the smaller ones were piled on top of one another; the other two stood side by side. Justin had told me that it was Portland stone from some Dorset quarries. I touched the rough surface of one of the stones, testing the hardness with my nail. I had never seen Justin work in stone, and it would be fascinating to watch him, always supposing that he would let me.

As I stood back to look up at the three piled pieces, the floor seemed to rock under my feet. I felt my foot slide and as I tried to keep my balance, the floorboard gave a deafening creak along its entire length, split, and gave way. My sideways leap came from a kind of instinctive sense of self-preservation. I landed awkwardly on the floor as the top stone of the three rocked, settled, then rocked again as the part of the floorboard on which I had stood gave way completely. The top stone crashed almost on the spot where my sandals had made marks on the dusty floor.

I clambered to my feet, standing well away from the two remaining stones that were now tilted at an angle on the broken floorboard. Then the second began to rock like a living thing preparing for a leap. It was uncanny to see its movement as if it had a brain and was deliberating whether to remain or fall.

Gradually it stopped swaying, but I had backed from it to safety, leaning shakenly against the trestle table. The leather of my sandals was scraped, and one nylon was ruined. But I was whole.

I saw then that two other floorboards were sagging and ready to give way. If so, the rest of the stones would crash and might cause the whole hut to fall. I kept that danger well in mind as I went as near as I dared to examine the floorboards. I was certain that they were all the original ones. Perhaps the wood was worm-eaten; there was certainly no smell of dry rot. I bent and moved one of the sunken boards with my foot. It seemed in extraordinarily good condition for such an old hut, thick and strong. I thought, with a kind of relief in irrelevance, that they seasoned wood well in the old days. No green wood for them; no hasty work. Everything had been made to last by the stolid Victorians.

Perhaps, then, the nails were worn. But when I looked at them, they seemed strong enough.

But why was I making such an issue of it? The explanation was obvious. The weight of the stones must have weakened even these strong old boards.

I stood at a safe distance and realized how near I had been to a serious accident. Had my reflexes not been so swift, the stone would have pinned me down. So often later, when a crisis has passed, the terror of what might have happened attacks with almost the ferocity of the act itself. I thought, shuddering: *Just as with the curtain pole, the blow in a vulnerable place on my skull could have killed me.*

I stood, trying to steady my shaken nerves. All right, so I'm going through a cycle of being accident-prone. That was all it was. I would have to watch my step. I looked again at the three floorboards now tilted into the void below. The wood was so strong; the nails were not twisted by the strain of the breaking planks but upright—as if they had been prised away from the adjoining boards.

The result of strain on old wood? Of carelessness in placing three heavy blocks of stone on top of one another? Or a piece of deliberate planning? Had someone guessed that I would come to look at the stone or to see that the hut was in order for Justin's return? Someone who knew that Mrs. Jo would not come here again and Tom didn't work at Roseheath on a Thursday?

The thought was preposterous. I backed away from the wall against which the stones were piled as if I faced a man-eating tiger. The door of the hut was open, and the moonlight made little moving patches on the path outside. Moving . . . I stared fascinated, trying to make a shape out of the pool of darkness. Then I let out a long breath. A tree branch was swaying gently in the wind. No one lurked somewhere among the silver birches waiting for my destruction by a sculptor's blocks of stone. Accident, or design? Oh, come off it! Those stones weakened the old floorboards. *Hang on to that—and run for it . . .*

I turned and ran. The fact that I flicked off the electric light as I went was more out of luck that hand and switch met at the right moment than from any effort of mine. I left the door of the hut open and sprinted through the copse and over the lawn as if Lucifer and all his dark angels were behind me.

I had got out of the shelter of the copse before I realized that it had begun to rain. It had started quite gently pattering on my face like little cool pine needles. Then quite suddenly, as it often did in summer storms, it deluged.

Out of breath, my hair plastered about my head and neck, I nearly fell over Ming in the hall. I did a right wheel around him and caught sight of myself in the Regency mirror. I looked as if I wore a cap of some not very charming color —dull, wet brown. My nose shone, and raindrops clung to my lashes.

There were voices in the living room, and all I could tell was that one was a man's. Mrs. Jo came out into the hall. "Here she is. Oh, my goodness, and what's happened to you?"

"It's raining," I said unnecessarily and looked toward the living room. "Who?"

"Mr. Eskinholm."

There was nothing I could do about my appearance, and if I read in his expression that he was obviously thinking, "What a sight she looks," I wouldn't give a damn. I stalked into the room like an empress to meet her courtiers. Ming, tail erect, sapphire-eyed, was my page.

"Oh, Sarne—" My voice had a false brightness as I greeted him.

I heard Mrs. Jo in the doorway saying something about fetching me a towel for my hair. "And before you sit down to a cosy chat, you'd better get out of that dress."

I said, "It's a hot night. I'll steam dry."

Sarne took hold of me and marched me to the door. "Get out of it, or I'll drag it off you. You can dry your hair here while we talk."

I flew upstairs and changed, grabbed an orange towel, and ran back to join Sarne.

He said, watching me rub my hair, "I'm fascinated. I

want to see how that marvelous swing comes back in your hair. Go on, rub. Don't mind me."

This was Sarne being charming, and I suspected it. Magda, who knew him, and Oliver, who worked with him, could not both be wrong.

"And here's something for you," he said and held out the check.

It was made out for eight hundred and fifty pounds, and it was signed "Adrienne Wand."

Sarne said, "Adrienne herself bought your ring. She says it's a very fine ruby."

I thanked him and put the check on the mantelshelf and returned to drying my hair. "Pour yourself a drink."

"I think you should have one, too."

"You've no idea how true that is!" I looked at him between the folds of the towel wrapped round my head. "If I go on being accident-prone like this, I'll end up on the psychiatrist's couch."

"You?" he demanded in rich disbelief.

I said, rubbing vigorously, "I was nearly crushed by a ton of stone."

He gave me a swift look, which I could not quite interpret.

Aloud, he said very steadily, "You can tell me about it when you have sat down and relaxed and I have poured you out what you want."

I said casually, "I don't know. Be my doctor."

"Brandy, then. And I'll have a whisky if I may." He selected a glass and held it to the light. "I see you still have the Haggard glasses."

"Oh, we've guarded them well. Grandmother only allowed me to wash them." I glanced at the one he held up. It had been exquisitely cut by Sean Haggard, the greatest engraver Wyncourt's had ever known, back in the nineteenth century. The facets quivered and changed color like diamonds.

"Now," Sarne said when he handed me my drink, "what's this about a ton of stone?"

I flung the towel untidily to the floor and took the drink because I wanted to have something to hold while I talked. As I waited for Sarne to pour his own drink and to sit down, I found myself in sympathy with the old Chinese who played with pieces of jade while they talked.

Sarne leaned back and looked at me, prepared to listen.

I told him about the floorboards in the hut. I said, "If I hadn't jumped back when I did, I'd have been lying underneath one of them now. It's a good thing I'm quick on my reflexes."

"When you've finished your drink, we'll go down together and have a look. I'd have said it was pretty silly to dump blocks of stone on that old floor."

"It seemed solid enough."

He gave a short laugh. "That's a good old brandy, Suzy, from a better cellar than you'll ever have, if you have one at all. It's sacrilege to make such a face over drinking it."

I swallowed some more, but it only burned my throat and made my stomach feel as if it had been kicked.

"All right." Sarne put down his glass. "We'll finish our drinks later. I think I'd better come down with you first and inspect the damage at the hut."

He held out his hand and drew me to my feet. We walked in silence across the dark garden, and only the stars, scattered about the sky, watched us.

When we reached the hut, Sarne flicked on the light and took one look at the stone blocks. "Justin seems to have literal dreams of greatness!"

"He has."

He stepped carefully over the sunken boards. "If he possesses the promise the critics say he has, then we'll probably be able to commission something from him when we rebuild."

I said, startled, "You mean this rebuilding is now an actual fact, and not just a remote idea?"

He lit a cigarette, and I watched him thinking: Oliver had pride in the old place, outmoded though it is. But it has tradition and dignity...

Sarne was saying, "You can't be a hundred percent efficient with antiquated workshops. I've never paced them, but I should imagine the corridors in those buildings measure at least three miles. And it's a ridiculous usage of space."

I said my thoughts aloud. "You don't waste much time, do you?"

"Time is all we have." He was kneeling by the broken floorboards. The light turned his hair to gleaming corn; his broad hands examined the wood, felt the nails. "It must have been the wood that gave way, drawing the nails with it. They're so strong and not bent at all."

A million tiny icicles shuddered through me. "That's—what—what—" I gulped and tried again. "It didn't look to me as if the nails gave way, and the—the floorboards—aren't—rotten."

He got up and said, "There are such things as stresses and strains in wood."

"But you don't think that in this case—"

"My dear girl, it must have been. There's no other explanation."

"Isn't there?" I was running my hands over my damp hair. "*Isn't* there, Sarne?"

He looked at me in surprise. "What's in your mind?"

I said, "The fact that someone wants to scare me away from Roseheath and is trying to accomplish it by things that could so easily be near accidents. No shreds of evidence for the police; no reason for a closer investigation. And this is the latest—blocks of stone weakening floorboards, a window—" I stopped and shook with a new terror. "Perhaps someone is trying to prove me unbalanced. Perhaps they want me to believe that in some moment of schizophrenia I did these things ... because in my ... subconscious madness, I want someone else blamed ..."

Sarne gripped me so hard that I cried out, "You're hurting me," and tried to wrench his hands away.

"Good. Then perhaps that'll stop the nonsense."

"You can call it that because you're not involved. All right, so I have no proof that the things that have happened to me are deliberate."

"None at all," he said coolly.

"But I *know* it isn't nonsense. There's a thing called intuition ..."

"There's also something called imagination."

Imagination? Another name for delusion? ... madness ... ?

We faced one another. In the single hard light of the hut, our eyes flashed enmity. "I was an idiot to think that you would understand." I was suddenly afraid of him and his dominating matter-of-factness. "You understand nothing, do you, except ambition? ... Wyncourt Glass Works. 'Rebuild. Forge ahead ... Race to the top ...' 'I'm the King of Crystal.'" I flung back my head and gave a sharp bitter laugh, "I salute you!"

"Don't be so damned silly."

The bravado went out of me. I turned away, ashamed of the outburst that was as much due to my resentment of his power over my emotions as to his denial of my suspicions concerning my danger.

I said in a quaking voice, "Why *should* you understand? I'm probably just a neurotic."

He ground his cigarette out in Justin's huge metal ashtray.

I said, "Arguing that all these things were just accidents doesn't make me less afraid. My mother once said that I was intuitive. I hope I'm not—I hope to *heaven* I'm not— because my intuition goes on telling me that the things that happened were clever ways to scare me away from Rose-heath."

Sarne walked to the door and stood looking out. The storm clouds still hung over the face of the moon, and the only light came from the bulb hanging from the ceiling of the hut.

It seemed to me as if Sarne were bored by it all. I crossed the room and touched his arm. "It's all right, Sarne. Thank you for trying to reassure me. Let's go back to the house."

He turned slowly. "Have you made a will?"

I stared at him. "Of course I haven't."

"Then I suggest you do."

"In case I might die soon? In case—the next—'accident'—is—is the last?" I could scarcely get the words out. At twenty-one, dying seemed such a long way. Even the things that had happend to me had not brought it as near as what Sarne had just said. "Oh, no!"

He took my hands, and when I tried to withdraw them he held them more tightly. "Just listen, Suzanne."

"I don't want to." We had a tug-of-war, fingers dragging at one another.

Sarne said, "Let me finish. If you are honestly afraid that someone is deliberately trying to harm you—and I'm not saying that I believe it—a will is a way you can safeguard yourself."

"I don't see it."

"Suppose you stop interrupting and let me explain. Ring up Maurice Trent tomorrow and make an appointment. Tell him that you want to make your will. And . . . Suzanne, don't try to stop listening to me . . . Just use your head. Think before you see Trent, and make up your mind to leave Rose-heath to the most innocuous person you know—to some charity, if you wish. Then, when you've done it, make certain that everyone whom you know hears about it."

"So that," I said slowly, "whoever is trying to get me away

from here would know that any efforts would be useless."

"*If* anyone is—yes, that's the answer."

"But it could be someone whom I don't know. I'm not a Wyncourt, and there are relatives alive, all over the world. How could I make it known to all those scattered people?"

"If someone is really trying to harm you then he—or she —has to be somewhere near at hand."

Of course . . . "But who?" I thought suddenly of Oliver's wife. She was one; just one of how many Wyncourts the rest of whom I had never met?

I said, "You suggest this as if it's the only solution. There's an even more obvious one."

"Is there? What?" He watched me, eyes inscrutable.

"The police. We called them in over the portrait. I could go and see Inspector Reid and tell him of the things that have happened." But of course they were all too subtle to be proof that they were anything but accidents. "Oh, Sarne!" I cried in a sudden overwhelming sense of hopelessness. On an impulse I leaned forward and laid my face against him. "I'm superstitious about making a will."

"That's silly. It's the only practical way of keeping your house and your peace of mind."

But was it? A will could be contested. If I died, someone at the inquest would be certain to mention the things I had said had happened to me, and perhaps the magistrate would have no imagination and merely decide that I was a neurotic; that I had made a will 'while the balance of my mind was affected,' or some such phrase. Sarne had, though, given me a straw to clutch at.

"I'll give it a thought in the next few days," I said. "I'll leave Roseheath as a home for maladjusted children or something. And the Wyncourts all over the world will hate me."

"I doubt if that should worry you, since none of them visits the house."

But perhaps one of them had, watching me from some dark tree shadow . . .

I had moved around Sarne and was leaning against the door looking out into the blackness of the night. He was behind me. I felt his fingers touching my hair, and I bent my head back to hold his hand against my flesh. I felt his arm go around me, drawing me against him. Thought of Adrienne flashed into my mind and out again. I was here, and Sarne was with me in this ugly wooden room hung with a single electric light bulb. To me, in that moment, it was a golden place, the Forest of Arden, the Garden of the Hesperides . . .

I closed my eyes, and while my blood raced and my limbs melted I felt Sarne's rough cheek against mine. He said my name, very, very softly, and I thought, *Adrienne is miles away. Why not?* I wanted him enough, and if he, on some momentary impulse, wanted me, then why deny the leaping flame?

Sarne's hand stroked my throat . . . With my eyes still closed, I tried to remember who it was who had said, "Give me my moments, you can keep your years." My moments, all that I could expect of someone with a wife and a mistress. But a beggar is happy with a crust; he doesn't ask for what the giver eats at his own table, nor does he demand for himself a full banquet.

A beggar . . . I opened my eyes, and my mood swung like a pendulum from enchantment to anger. Damn him, damn all love that humbly begged a crust while someone else enjoyed the feast. I looked up straight into Sarne's eyes. I said, "What do you want? Another skeleton for your cupboard?"

His eyes blazed, and he went rigid. Then he turned and, without a word, walked out of the hut.

I stood without moving, listening to his striding footsteps crackling through the twigs and the leaves in the copse. It seemed an age before the sounds eventually died away into the silence.

And when I could no longer hear them I burst into tears.

The telephone bell was ringing when I returned to the house. I heard Mrs. Jo on the landing and called to her that I would answer it. I didn't want her to see me, because I knew she would ask why I had been crying and I could not have explained to her or, indeed, to anyone.

I lifted the receiver and heard Magda's voice. "Oh, Suzanne, is Sarne still with you?"

"No."

"Has he been gone long?"

I asked. "You knew he was here?"

I heard her laugh softly before she replied. "Of course. He made some excuse about calling on you to give you a check for something of yours he'd sold. A ring."

"That's right. He came. And now he has gone."

There was a moment's hesitation. Then she said, "Take care, Suzanne. You are the one who will get hurt." Then quickly, before I could speak, she continued, "Pauline has had hysterics, and I couldn't get any sense out of her. Now she has run screaming out of the house. Neurotics bore me, but servants are hard to get, and I want her back. Sarne can go and get her to snap out of her idiocy." She waited for me to say something.

I sat with the receiver to my ear, biting my lip.

"Suzanne, are you sure Sarne isn't with you?"

"Quite sure."

"Then run and see if you can find him."

I retorted, angry with her tone. "Why should I? You are much more likely to know where he has gone than I."

"On the contrary, you—" She stopped abruptly. "Well, never mind that now. If you want to be a silly girl, that's your business. But Pauline is mine. She's scared of something, or someone, and she says she daren't tell me about it. She probably saw some magnified shadow on a wall—her own, I wouldn't wonder—and thought it was something from a horror story. It's typical of villagers who live in these isolated places—they're crammed full of superstitions. I'd go after her myself only I have guests."

I wanted to demand of her what she meant by calling me a "silly girl" in that patronizing way of hers. But I guessed where that conversation would lead ... back to Sarne ... "Surely," I said, "Pauline gave you some idea as to whom she thought she saw?"

"My dear, hysterical people are incoherent. I've had experience ..."

"Go on." I said in a tight, hard voice, the bitter memory flooding back that she had once called me hysterical.

She must have thought twice about what she was going to say. Instead, she sighed. "Pauline was full of the dark threats and awful things that would happen to her if she told me what she knew. Be a nice girl and see if you can find Sarne. Even if he is not with you ... all right, I believe you. So, he isn't! But do go and see if he's somewhere in the grounds. Did you know that he adores Roseheath? He often walks there—I suspect playing at being the lord of the manor."

I said, to get rid of her, "If I see him, I'll tell him you're looking for him," and rang off.

I had no intention of trying to find Sarne. I went into the living room, frowning.

So Sarne liked to walk through the grounds of Roseheath, unknown to me. Could it have been he who had frightened Pauline? Somehow I would have to find out and if he sometimes stood in the shadow of a tree and watched my house, what were his thoughts? Did he sometimes actually dream that the house was his, as Magda had suggested? Was

Roseheath, with its age, its tradition, its old glory, more alluring to him that Amber Court?

Sarne and Roseheath...As unconnected as Roseheath and I. Two people loving it far more than those to whom it belonged as a right...

I saw my face in the mirror. *Oh, yes, you funny little thing, so small, so amusing, so scared that I might make love to you back there in the hut. So you turned on me like a little cat and scratched. "What do you want? Another skeleton in your cupboard?" You really amuse me, Suzanne Wyncourt. Do you know what I'm doing now? I'm walking over your territory, among your trees, chuckling over the fact that I so nearly caught you in a weak moment. What were you frightened of? My sweet Suzanne, I have my lover...*

I picked up Ming from the chair by the window and buried my face in his silver fur. He struggled and yowled. Well, fair enough. I had rejected Sarne, and now I was paid back in kind. My cat leaped from my arms and stalked off.

CHAPTER

21

JUSTIN returned to Roseheath while I was at the Works. I found that I was clock-watching, wanting to get home and greet him. I would feel more secure with a man in the house, and fear was a new emotion for me. In my lofty ignorance before it had hit me, I would have said, "I'm no coward." I was having my baptism of it now, and deep inside myself where it didn't show, my mind walked the lonely passages of shamed terror.

On the stroke of half-past five I did my face, grabbed my coat and bag and, too impatient for the elevator, ran down the stairs and out to the parking lot.

I saw Sarne in the distance, and I thought he made a sign as though beckoning me, but I didn't look again to make certain. In the car driving through the outskirts of Amesdale toward the moors and home, I sang completely off-key.

Justin was in the living room.

I said, "Welcome, boarder!" and peered closer. "You've lopped an inch off your beard."

He took both my hands, but he didn't look directly at me. Something had obviously gone wrong, and my mind reeled off the possibilities. He couldn't pay the final month's rent of the Amesdale studio; he had accidentally broken something he was working on—probably that mound of stone at the mews that he was calling "Jupiter Three."

I asked, "Is the removal now complete? Have you got everything? The hut is going to be a most marvelous place for a studio. I give you full permission—"

"Suzanne, wait." His eyes had an unhappy, wary look.

"All right. I'm waiting. What is it?"

"Something unexpected has happened."

I said lightly in order to hide a growing intuition of a disappointment to come, "Something is always happening. What's so special...?"

He walked away from me. Hands in his pockets, clinking money, he looked out over the lawn. A blackbird sang in the oak tree on which, as a child of seven, I had carved the name of the little boy I would love until death.

"You remember Gustav Svenling?" Justin said.

"The Swedish sculptor. Sarne's friend. Yes, of course. He came to Amber Court once, and they took him to see your work in Amesdale."

"I've heard from him."

"He's coming over again?"

I saw Justin square his shoulders like a boy expecting punishment. "No. He wants me to go over to Stockholm."

"But that's wonderful. I read an article once about the studio he has there. An enormous place—"

"It won't be just a visit."

"No?"

Justin said, "Suzanne, please understand."

"I will if you'll tell me what I'm to understand."

"It's so difficult. You see, I'm in a spot. In a way I hate the idea of going, in another way—"

"You may as well let me have it quite straight. You have been invited to Stockholm, and you won't be coming back?"

"Well, it's not quite like that. I mean—"

"Oh, come off it, Justin. It *is* that, or it isn't. But what's the idea behind it? That you're to work there with Svenling?"

174

"He has four sculptural assistants. They help him and learn all the time."

"You went to sculpture classes, and you qualified to teach." I knew it was wonderful for him and I should be glad about it. But I needed a few minutes to orientate myself, to face the loss of something that I had so looked forward to. I wanted to talk about it, to argue myself into acceptance of my loss. I wondered, too, if Justin wasn't leaping into a new future without looking first. I needed to hear more about Svenling and his world.

"Sweden," I said, "is a different nation; the language is strange. All right, I know thousands of people go and live in other countries and are perfectly happy. But you're like a bee, and you should live in a hive with a hoard of other bees. You like belonging and you hate loneliness."

"But I wouldn't be lonely. Svenling's four assistants live in bungalows on his estate; they're with him all the time; even in the evenings they sit round and talk. And artists come in and join them. It's a marvelous life. Oh, God, Suzanne . . ." His strong brown hand went out and brushed the air between us as if it were fogged. "Look, if you really want me here, I'll stay. I'll learn all I can in England, haunt galleries—"

His desperation brought me up with a jerk. I was seeing my own loneliness when he had gone. I was like a wife threatened with desertion.

"Of course you must go," I almost shouted in my effort to convince him. "It's a wonderful opportunity, and Svenling must think a great deal of your work. Now you can get us both a drink to celebrate."

He leaped forward, seized me, and kissed me. "You're wonderful. I was afraid you'd be terribly upset. After all, in a way I've let you down."

"Don't be an ass. Now, about this celebration drink—"

"I brought something in with me, just in case you wouldn't

mind. It's in the hall—I hid it under a newspaper so you wouldn't see. I thought if—"

"If I minded, you'd sneak upstairs with it and drink a toast all to yourself. What is it?"

"Champagne. A good one—"

"Go and get it," I said and ran past him to the kitchen to fetch the ice bucket and find out from Mrs. Jo when dinner would be ready.

She beamed at me. "I've made a special meal, seeing as Mr. Justin's come for good. You've got Scotch salmon with creamed shrimps first. And a soufflé—"

"It was a marvelous day for me when I asked you to come and live here," I said and gave her a wide smile. I hoped she would not be discerning enough to see the joylessness in me.

I dawdled back to the living room. There would now be just two women in a big house I would have to find a way to fill.

The champagne cork went off like a noonday gun. The dancing bubbles overspilled from the bottle. Justin had found two glasses and was filling them. He handed one to me.

"To you, to me, to us," I said, and lifted the engraved goblet.

He put down his glass, sat on the arm of the settee, and pulled me toward him. "Of course, if you'd marry me, it would all be different."

"Would it?"

"I'd find out if I could take rooms somewhere near the Svenling estate and go to work there every day."

"I suppose you aren't getting paid a great deal."

"It sounds fair enough, but then I don't think it's particularly cheap living in Sweden."

I said, "I've never believed in that silly cliché that two can live as cheaply as one."

176

"If I could manage it, would you come?"

"No."

His question had been a final gesture. I could feel his relief spreading like an aura around him, although he managed to look a little hurt. We sat gazing into our drinks, serious, thoughtful, friendly yet withdrawn. He still had one surprise for me. "I suppose I'll always be in Magda's debt for this."

"Magda?" I sat up.

"She wrote to Gustav Svenling and sent him an article about me that appeared some time ago in the Amesdale *Gazette*."

"She *did*?" I remembered the article, but I had no idea that Magda had even seen it.

Justin was saying something about how marvelous it was of her to take such trouble. I stayed silent, listening to his enthusiastic tribute. She had been busy doing this for Justin and telling me nothing. Why? Had she done it out of appreciation of Justin's great gift? But she had no understanding of art, and had never pretended to have. Then had she gone to this trouble for some angry personal reason? I knew Magda so well. Justin had never been attracted to her, and this was something she could neither understand nor forgive. So, had she decided to remove him from her orbit not as a punishment to him, for he was scarcely aware of her except as my cousin, but because he liked me?

While Justin talked—and *how* he talked—I watched him walk back and forth across the room, stepping over Ming's tail with an elephantine heave.

"... and I'll have to go and thank her properly before I leave ..."

I said "Yes." I was thinking that if Magda had lived in the fantasy of *Alice in Wonderland* she would have been more direct: "Off with his head!" Because tribute was Magda's right, not mine.

I started when some photographs were thrust under my nose. "I found them," Justin was saying, "in a magazine a long time ago and cut them out."

"Oh. They look like scenes from another planet."

He pulled my hair gently. "Don't be philistine. They were taken at Svenling's place just outside Stockholm.

Massive stone figures dominated a landscape; abstracts scattered over a rolling hill; a house with four white wings pointing upwards from walls of glass. And huts among the trees . . . Justin's strange new world.

I had always known that he needed to belong. There had been no difficulty in understanding this of him. He was an orphan; I had unknown parents. In that, we ran almost parallel. I thought: He's twenty-five and yet he's not ready for marriage; he's just a huge lovable adolescent with a great potential gift. He would be intensely happy in a community life. In Sweden, with Gustav Svenling he will live among people who share something far more important than the spoken word—the language of stone, of wood, of alabaster. They will work and plan and criticize, argue and talk half the night.

I got up and took my glass and went out onto the terrace. It was a cool, vivid night with a west wind blowing and the sky burning with orange and flame. Oncoming night from the east had blackened the trees, and I could see one speck of dusty gray through their thick trunks—the outline of the hut that would now never be used. A little dream that had expired quietly in the shadow of a great ambition.

Mrs. Jo put her head round the door, calling, "Dinner in ten minutes, and don't be late. You can't keep a soufflé hot."

I said, "You won't even start it until we've finished the salmon. Come in first and celebrate with us."

"Me?"

I re-entered the room and looked at Justin.

He said, "Sure enough. Come on. Champagne," and fetched another glass from the cupboard.

She said with awe, a hand across her mouth, "I've never drunk it in me life. I'll be sloshed."

"Not on one glass," Justin said. "You'll turn out the soufflé of your life."

"Well—" she took the glass, stiffening her nose against the bubbles. "Here's how, and I know you'll be very happy here."

"I'm afraid we're not drinking to that, Mrs. Jo," I said. "Justin is going to Sweden to study under a very great sculptor there."

"Going to Sweden?" I could have said the North Pole.

"The offer has come quite unexpectedly, and he can't possibly refuse. It's a most wonderful opportunity."

"You mean he's not going to live here?"

"No."

"And how long are you going for?" she demanded.

"Two or three years," Justin said. "Drink up."

Mrs. Jo looked as if her lips were suddenly stuck together. Then she lifted her glass and drained it in one go, turned around, and marched to the door. From there, she said, "Oh well, it takes all sorts to make a world," and tramped to the kitchen.

"She doesn't approve," Justin said.

Of course she didn't. She had seen something that she would call "a budding romance" between Justin and me. And now she was disappointed. She had probably told the village her "inside story" of what was bound to happen. "They'll be married before the year's out. You see if my words don't come true." And Justin's news had deflated her.

I said vaguely, "I'll just go out and see that everything is all right."

Justin laughed. "That she hasn't fallen flat on her face into the soufflé. You'd better. The way she downed that drink—"

179

Mrs. Jo was sprinkling parsley on the potatoes. She muttered without looking up, "Of all the things to do, letting you down at the last minute like that. I never—"

"Justin hasn't let me down at all. I'm glad for him."

She wasn't listening. "All that fuss carting them blocks of stone here."

"He'll do something about them. You won't have to worry."

"Well," she retorted, "at least we won't have any more of that peeping and prying."

"What *do* you mean?"

"Why, them people from the village snooping up here just to have a look at a bit of stone—or perhaps to gossip about you having Mr. Justin living here. They've got nasty minds, some of them have. But then there's little enough in their lives, I suppose." She spoke from her own lofty position as my helper and confidante; she worked at Roseheath, and so she was "somebody."

I said, "Why didn't you tell me this before?"

"I didn't want to bother you. But I saw—"

"Who were they?"

"I was too far away to see. And when he saw me he—or it could have been a 'she' in pants—ran."

"Then it was just one person?"

"That's all I saw, but you know what that village is like. One goes and tells the rest, and they come up here for a walk, like, and snoop."

I doubted if she had the right idea at all. It was far more likely that she had disturbed whoever it was who watched me. One person who wished me away from here. "When was this?"

"Last evening." She turned the potatoes into a bowl. "Some time before I saw you go down to the hut. I thought at first it was Mrs. Goddard, but she wouldn't have run away, would she?"

"Think, Mrs. Jo. This could be important. Wasn't there

anything familiar about this man—or woman? You know the people in the village, how they dress, how they walk. Wasn't there something that struck you as familiar?"

She stood frowning at me, trying to think. "No," she said at last. "Nothing. It was too far away, and dark among them trees. I think he—she—had fair hair, but I'm not really sure. I'm sorry, I'd have told you before if I'd thought it was important."

There were too many fair people around me. I said, "It's all right. It may have been, as you say, someone from the village who heard that Justin had come to live here and wanted to know what a sculptor's studio looked like." I argued with myself that it was a possible explanation. I wanted to believe it. I said with forced lightness, "I'm hungry. Let's forget it."

Justin talked incessantly over dinner. Now that I had accepted his news, he could relax. He said, "I can resell the stone—at a loss. But someone will buy it. Would you mind if it stays where it is until I find a home for it?"

"No, let it stay. We don't need the hut." I added ruefully, "The stones have gone through the floorboards already, and so it'll give me an excuse to pull the place down."

"Oh, my sainted aunt!" Justin combed his beard with his fingers. "You mean the stones have actually damaged the floor?"

"Don't let it worry you."

"But, Suzanne, I'd no idea they'd be too heavy. I know the hut is old, but it seemed to me so solid."

"So it did to me."

"You must let me pay for any damage."

"Don't be silly. When they've pulled the place down, I'll get Tom to stack the wood, and then in the winter I'll light huge fires in the hall and throw parties and roast chestnuts."

Justin pulled a face. "Why the heck am I going away?"

"I'll send you a chestnut," I said. I had no intention of

181

telling him that I was certain the broken floorboards were a deliberate act. He was not involved with me or with Roseheath any more.

"When are you leaving?"

"I'll have to go back to Amesdale tomorrow. I've got to get rid of the studio there—it's in the agent's hands, though I can't think what anyone will want it for."

So this was our last night with one another. The thought made me infinitely sad. I hadn't fully realized until this moment how much his huge company would have meant to me here.

He put his arms around me and rubbed his face against my hair.

"I'm so happy. I want to make love to you."

Firmly, but without speed, I moved out of his arms. "It's not mutual," I said. "Go to bed, or if you're not tired, you may as well start packing. Have you got a decent suitcase? Those you came here with were rather like bags you'd picked off a rubbish dump."

"Oh, I've got something respectable. But it's not respectability I'm interested in at the moment. Suzanne, it's my last night, and we could make something memorable of it."

I picked Ming up from the rug and held him as a fawn bulwark between us, laughing at Justin over the cat's humped body. "I'll see you in the morning. Pleasant dreams."

But mine weren't pleasant; they were the kind of dreams you could interpret as coming from a forlorn subconscious. I was running toward a group of people. I knew I loved them all, but the nearer I got, the farther away they seemed. I woke, slept, and dreamed again. This time I was crouched in the caves, and I called and called and nobody came. I thought, in my dream, "But of course, there's nobody *to* come. They've all gone ..."

CHAPTER

22

I WOKE depressed and cross. A shower and coffee revived me, and when Justin came down to breakfast I was laughing at a cartoon in the morning paper.

Before I left for the Works, Justin and I put our arms around each other and kissed.

I said, "One of these days I'll be seeing your work outside some big new building and I'll tell everyone 'We used to pick raspberries together.' Or I'll say: 'I've got an early Justin Norton, a girl carved in elm wood.' I might even tell them it's me."

"You make it sound as if I'll only ever be a memory, as if we won't meet again. We will, you know, I'll see to that."

So sincere, so honestly meant. I said, "You'd better have your beard trimmed again. It's still rather ragged."

"I feel ragged this morning. I thought of you all last night."

"You'd better start moving if you're going to catch the midday train to London. You've got a lot to pack up."

He grinned at me. "It's like a one-night stand! From Amesdale to here, and now to Stockholm."

"That's life." Whatever happened, he mustn't know how badly I was minding. He had his life to lead, and if I did not choose to be involved, then I must let him go. He was just one more familiar face I would never see again. Only, in Justin's case, he was going to a very bright future.

I went in search of Mrs. Jo. I wanted to bring her into Justin's happiness.

The clock in the hall was striking nine, and I knew I would be late at the Works, but I sauntered into the kitchen, sat on the edge of the table, and talked about Justin's marvelous opportunity. I could always influence Mrs. Jo if I tried hard enough, and presently she was saying, "Of course I'll help him pack. Men aren't any good at it. They make bundles of their things as if they're rags. You leave it to me."

I drove to Amesdale in a day heavy with threatening thunder. I had the roof of the car rolled down, but I could not get air. I felt as if a great wet curtain were hanging around me shutting out all the country's freshness.

Halfway through the afternoon Sarne came to my room. "I hear Svenling has offered to take Justin as an assistant. Is he accepting?"

"He has already left for London to make his plans. Justin knows of only one important moment of time, and that is 'Now.' He'll make his final arrangements from there."

"You're right. He doesn't waste much time, does he?"

I was silent, thinking: Did you, when you came to England?

Sarne walked restlessly to and fro across my room. "I've been shut up at a meeting since eleven o'clock this morning. I want to get out. Come and have some tea with me, and I don't mean in the canteen, nor do I mean on a tray in my office. We'll go down to the Evergreen."

We had done this on a few occasions, and I had enjoyed my twenty minutes' freedom with him. This time I tried to find an excuse. "There's going to be a storm. It's been trying to break all day."

"We'll go in the car and keep dry."

The Evergreen was an old barn with a vast thatched roof and beams a foot thick. The entrance lay under an arch of rowan trees and the lance-shaped leaves brushed the top of Sarne's head as we went toward an ancient, russet-brick building.

The place was crowded with a busload of tourists who had come to see over the Wyncourt Works. All through spring and summer, parties of people were taken by our two paid couriers—both of them retired Wyncourt workers —around the factory. Afterwards the visitors were let loose in the Reject Room where odd pieces of Wyncourt crystal were sold at low prices. The tour usually ended with a Somerset tea at the Evergreen. The tourists carried their parcels of Wyncourt crystal carefully, some unable to resist opening them, undoing string, peeling off paper for another look at some lovely discontinued piece, a goblet, a bowl, opaline or lustre or milk glass.

Sarne said, as we drank tea, "Do you mind very much about Justin leaving?"

"It was a lovely idea that he should live and work at Roseheath."

"I'm sorry."

I said in surprise, for Sarne was not a man for apologies, "It's not your fault."

"I introduced them in the first place when Svenling came last year to stay with me."

"I know. But Justin told me that Magda wrote to Svenling."

"That's right, she did."

"She sent him a newspaper clipping about Justin's work." I said.

He sat frowning into the room. "And told Svenling that Justin needed a chance to work with a master, that he was wasting his life in an unimportant place among people who couldn't appreciate what he was trying to do. If Svenling would give him a chance to work for him—" he broke off. Then added in a low fury, "Damn. Damn all interference . . ."

The tea was scalding hot, and it hurt my throat. It wasn't

185

in the least important that Justin either did not know, or hadn't chosen to tell me, the exact contents of Magda's letter. The odd thing was that it was she, totally uninterested in the arts, who had been the moving factor.

I said, "Oh, well, Justin has his chance, and that's the most important thing."

"It has disrupted all your plans."

We sat in a not very happy silence watching the tourists with their parcels fighting their way through huge Somerset teas of scones and cream and jam. The conversation roared around us. I poured out more tea, and our conversation was forced and desultory.

I said, only drinking half a cup, "I'd better go. I've got a lot of alteration to do to the panel design. Kris says it's too intricate."

Sarne looked at me in faint surprise as if he had almost forgotten I was there and had been deep in private thoughts that had no connection with Suzanne Wyncourt. "Oh, yes, yes of course. Come along."

He had been a very long way away from me.

When I got back to my office, I opened the window wide and leaned my elbows on the sill. The excuse that I had work to do was true, although it was not urgent.

At the Evergreen, I had sensed Sarne's mood. He had been restless and preoccupied, and if he had hoped that I would amuse him, I had failed utterly. That had been why I had cut the tea period short.

I began to think again about Magda, and my suspicions seemed even more founded. She might have been motivated by a wish for revenge because she looked on me as responsible for the loss of the Isabella. It was very possible that she had thought that she and Danielle between them could have worked out some scheme to break Oliver's will. Then, deciding against it, she had managed to avenge herself for the theft of what she had never ceased to look upon as her possession, by robbing me of Justin's company. Whether that was her motive, or whether it was simply that Justin preferred me to my lovely cousin, I was certain that the general idea was to hurt me.

As a child I had seen Magda tease a little girl into such blind misery that she had run away from school. A tougher child would have taken no notice, or paid Magda back in kind. That she would have understood and respected. But this particular little girl was oversensitive and timid.

I had actually fought Magda, small eight-year-old fists slamming into her, because this particular child was my friend.

Magda had said, "You don't understand, Suzanne. I don't want to harm her, but I hate cowards. That girl would cringe if somebody frowned at her."

I went on pummeling her, and she gave me a bored push and walked away.

I pulled away from the window and began making unconnected circles at the corner of my drawing paper.

But Magda hadn't completely scored off me this time. If I had loved Justin, I would have married him even if he was going to sit at the South Pole for three years contemplating the penguins.

The storm broke almost as soon as I realized that a heavy, burnt-umber glow had spread over the room. Lightning flashed over the twin towers of the Cathedral. One of the girls from the typing pool, running toward the storage block, gave a shriek and dived into a shed, clasping the letters she had typed.

I put my hand out of the window and felt the lash of hailstones, but there was no relieving coolness.

By the time I was ready to go home, the storm was over, but the clouds were piled in the northern sky, poised for the moment of return.

I found Mrs. Jo down at the hut. A thin trickle of rain

trailed across the floor; drips still fell from some split in the roof and landed in soft plops on the workbench. Mrs. Jo was collecting a pile of tools Justin had left. Her skirt clung to her, her hair was matted, and I knew that she must have remembered that the hut leaked badly and run out at the height of the storm to mop up and collect Justin's paraphernalia of chisels and calipers, rulers and mallets. He had probably left them all with a sense of wanting to make an entirely fresh start even with new tools.

"Mrs. Jo, for heaven's sake, go back and get dry."

"I'm all right. A drop of rain won't hurt me. I want to clear all this stuff up. Men are usually sentimental about their first set of tools, if that's what you call what sculptors use."

"First tools? I'm quite certain Justin started using something or other when he was a small boy. He probably carved the headmaster's head on the school wall."

"But I promised him I'd store all this up in the attic for him. You don't mind, do you?"

"Of course not, though I doubt if he'll ever come back to collect them. But I *do* mind you hanging around here in those wet clothes. Get back and change into some dry ones."

"Don't you worry about me—"

"Mrs. Jo—*go.*"

"But these things are soaked. This roof leaks like nobody's business."

"*Go.*"

She gave a long-suffering sigh. "My, you fuss!" she said and went.

When she brought in my dinner I saw that she was shivering and trying not to let me see. As she went to the door, I called her back. "You've got a chill. Will you go straight to bed?"

"Look," she said with exaggerated patience. "When I want

188

to be mollycoddled, I'll ask for it." She shut the door before I had time to think up a retort.

We had a succession of thunderstorms the next day, with torrential rain. In the evening they eased up, and I drove home through a watery landscape. I found Mrs. Jo, who hadn't heard me come in, sitting at the kitchen table with her head in her hands. She looked up when I entered and sprang to her feet. "Well, and here I am, day-dreaming—" She looked ghastly.

Persuasion would be useless. I knew that I had to use drastic measures. I lost my temper. "And what use do you think you'll be if you get pneumonia? Where's your common sense? Dragging yourself around the house, looking like death . . . Go on, go to bed. If you don't, then you can remove yourself and your belongings back to Magnon Down. You're an obstinate woman, and I won't—"

"All right, all right, don't go for me like that. I'll get to bed when I've done your dinner."

"I am perfectly capable of getting my own dinner," I said and took her by her square shoulders and pushed.

We had run out of aspirin—I couldn't remember when the last bottle had been bought—and I knew that if I went immediately the village shop would still be open.

I bought aspirin, some fresh peaches, and some weekly periodicals in order to try and keep Mrs. Jo in bed through the following day. I had not had a chance to watch the six o'clock news on television, but Jock Timms, who ran our single grocery store, told me that Shallwaite and Ladytree, two neighboring villages, had made news because of bad flooding.

He said, "Water inches deep in the streets, and there was a shot of the Mandrake Caves. The underground lake there is swollen. That'll stop the potholers this weekend."

I knew, since he was one of the cave rescue team, that

he was delighted that even experts would not dare to risk their lives in the flooded caves. All summer long, our cave rescue men waited, expecting some group of potholers to get into difficulties in the deeper caves.

When I reached home, I dosed Mrs. Jo with aspirin, made her a light supper, and put a peach on her tray.

She struggled up in bed, flushed and cross. "Bed and me aren't friendly," she said. "I hate—"

"Beds are kind to aching limbs," I said cheerfully.

"I don't know why you should be so good to me."

"Put it down to my egotism. I want you to be happy here." That made her laugh.

I wondered where Danielle was and whether the police had been to see her again with any news of the portrait. But it had been stolen from my part of the house, so if they had any lead at all, they would probably come directly to me.

As soon as I came home, I had flung open the terrace doors for air. But as night fell, blacking out the sullen saffron of the sky, I was nervous at my own isolation. With every scrap of my flesh crying out for air, I closed and locked the terrace doors and secured the windows. But I was still edgy. I told myself that thunder in the air had this effect on some people and now I was developing this odd allergy. But I walked like some prisoner back and forth through the lofty, silent rooms, and there was not even the comfort of knowing that Danielle was nearby, for I heard no sound from behind the west-wing door.

CHAPTER

23

IT was nearly nine o'clock when I realized that Ming had been missing for some time.

I went around the house calling, expecting him to spring out at me, yowling a protest that I hadn't noticed his disappearance earlier. But there was no Siamese greeting, nor the sound of his bell. Ming knew, with some cat sense, when it was going to rain, and if he wandered out, he would streak back before the first spots marked his impeccable coat.

I went onto the terrace and called him again.

A sound behind me made me start. I swung round and saw Danielle. "Oh, I thought you were out. There was no light—"

"I sometimes like the anonymity of darkness," she said.

She was wearing a long, loose blue kaftan, and she must have washed her hair, for it was like an aureole of white swansdown. She said, "I heard you calling Ming. I'll see if he's anywhere here, though I doubt it. He never strays beyond the wing door."

Because Oliver had hated cats and chased him out. If anyone threatened Ming's dignity, he never forgot or made a second approach.

I heard Danielle's light footsteps treading through the upstairs rooms, calling. Then she came down again, spreading her hands. "No Ming," she said. "But he'll be all right. He's got his cat door when he chooses to return."

"All the same—" I began.

"Give him five minutes more. Come and have a long, cool drink with me. I've got some news for you."

I didn't want the drink, but we stood in the terrace doorway in the thundery dark and she told me that a representative from the insurance company had called on her again.

She said, "He asked me the same questions he put to me the first time he called."

In the half light, with the glow of lamps from inside the house at her back, her profile had the contemplative look of a sphinx.

"There's a very large sum of money involved," I said.

"Of course. But this time there was something different in their attitude."

"You're imagining it."

"Oh, no, I'm as aware of what they think as I am of the villagers' opinion of me."

"But they like you."

She shook her head. "They're as suspicious of me as if I were a black mamba."

"You're so wrong—"

She gave a sudden laugh. "Whether I am or not, it doesn't worry me. I shan't have to spend my life here. Magnon Down has nothing for me. Now, let's try to think where Ming could be. It has stopped raining for the moment." She rose and went to the terrace edge and I knew that, for some reason I could not fathom, she was as restless and disturbed as I.

A cloud swam over the moon's face—a large, endless cloud, presaging another storm.

I put down my empty glass on a table just inside the door. "I'm going to look for Ming." I went down the terrace steps and kept to the garden paths because the grass was still sodden. I kept calling him and listening for the light jingle of his cat bell. I wandered along the paths between the wet, exhausted blooms of the gentle delphiniums, and zigzagged through the copse aware that if Ming chose to, he could be playing a game with me. But, with no sight or sound of him, I reached the hut. The door was closed, and I had no idea how even a lithe cat could possibly get in, but I searched the place.

The blocks of stone were as I had left them—one plunged through the broken floorboard, two others still perched like displaced boulders after an earthquake. I called Ming twice, then I went out and through the white gate onto the moors.

I doubted if he was there; in fact I began to doubt my own sanity in searching for an animal who was perfectly capable of returning home in his own good time. But when a series of odd, unexplained things happen, the mind becomes bogged down with wild imaginings. Ming could be some-where out there in that rolling darkness. How did I know that someone from the village hadn't defied the law and set a trap for a rabbit or a hare and Ming was not crouched with one fastidious paw crushed in it? He might be too injured even to cry out. I had not brought a flashlight, and I had no animal sense that would lead me to him in the dark.

I ran back to the house. The light was on in Oliver's draw-ing room and the curtains drawn.

I knew that a powerful flashlight was always kept in the chest in the hall. It lay on top of a folded tartan blanket. I took it out, tested it, and found the battery strong. On the moors again, the strong grass flicked like little wet whips around my ankles, and occasionally a hummock tripped me. It was absurd to find myself being unnerved, I who had loved the moors all my life. I told myself that something of Pauline's terror had brushed onto me. Somewhere, in this lonely place of moor and hamlet, someone menaced our peace of mind.

I walked on, tilting the primrose beam of the torch down-wards, occasionally calling Ming in an unnecessarily loud voice as if, with his marvelous extra sense, he didn't know I was around.

"Ming . . ."

Then, in the utter stillness as I stood listening, I heard the faint, dancing tinkle of a cat's bell.

I swung my flashlight in an arc. He must be crouched on the ground. A trap . . . My original fear rose up and half-choked me as I called him again. "Ming . . . ?" Then angrily, "Ming, you idiotic animal—"

The sound of the bell came again, just ahead of me. The moors were dotted with clumps of wind-bent thorn bushes. I went slowly forward, listening for his voice—no cat is more garrulous than a Siamese. But he was either playing dumb or was hurt. I walked slowly in and out of the bushes as if I were taking part in a medieval maypole dance. And all the time, the intermittent sound of the little bell was just ahead of me.

"Ming. Don't play games with me." My voice rang through the empty air of the moorlands. The stars were veiled, and the broom and thorn bushes did not move. If Ming had had the training of a St. Bernard dog on the high passes of the Alps, he could not have been more insistent that I follow him. The silences between the tinkling of the bell lay like a spell. Twice I stopped in my tracks, turned sharply, and raked the darkness behind me with my flashlight. No one was there. The broom and thorn ahead of me made a low avenue leading to the Mandrake Caves.

I was near enough now for my flashlight to illumine the piled rock formation at the jaws of the cave. The little silver bell agitated again, and this time it came from inside. I ran forward.

"Ming—you ass cat, come out. Don't run ahead of me like that."

The shadows of the cave folded in on me like black wings. I was inside, and the darkness was like a rancid

194

scent. My heart began to thud, and as I stumbled over a piece of uneven ground I cried out. My cry echoed like a banshee's wail. Then, as it died away, I heard a familiar and beloved sound. Ming yowled at me. I turned the flashlight swiftly in the direction of the sound, beaming it onto crevices and ledges, but I could not see him.

"Ming?"

For a moment or two, only the steady drip-drip of water somewhere deeper in the cave answered me. Then Ming cried again.

In the center of the cave was a vast hole eighteen feet wide. At the bottom of it was a lake. There had been some experienced potholers who had swum those turgid, malodorous waters to find a magnificence beyond. Caves, they had said, like Arabian Nights palaces; crevices of stones that glowed like rubies and stalagmites rising up like petrified plants in an underground garden...I walked to the edge of the lake and looked over. The sight was slightly sickening. The first part of the hole sloped gently enough, with footholds of rock. That gentleness has fooled so many. For suddenly the sides fell straight and steep, and ropes were the only means of reaching the water.

"Ming...?"

This time his voice came, loud and demanding. Ming had been mine ever since he was a kitten, and I had learned to understand his language—the varying intonations registering hunger, a need to be loved, a desire just to talk—and fear. Fear was in his voice now, as he raised it to answer me. I heard the little bell jangle somewhere below me. My blood went cold. Ming was caught on one of those fiendish ledges between me and the swollen waters of the underground lake.

I crouched down and looked over the edge.

"All right. I'm coming down. Ming...it's all right...But where *are* you?"

I swung my flashlight and saw the dozens of small ledges jutting out of the higher part of the abyss. It was just possible that I could reach Ming, but if a piece of the rock face should give way with my weight, or I should slip, there was nothing along the smooth lower drop to break my fall. A plunge into those waters would be the end of me, for once in them, no gymnastic prowess could find me a foothold on those steep, smooth lower edges.

I knelt shaking and uncertain of the way to go about saving Ming.

If I could only see where he was, I might just be able to reach him. He must have seen me, for his calls to me became fierce and prolonged. I lay on my stomach on the wet rock, and I thought with a new horror that the light from the flashlight seemed fainter. I prayed wildly to all the gods I'd ever heard of not to let its light fade out on me. I knew Ming would be able to see me, or sense me, more easily than I, human and minus his extra sense, could see him. But wherever he was, he was obviously unable to clamber up to me, or he was too frightened to do so.

I let the light move from rock to rock, slowly, peering into every shadow.

Suddenly I saw him. Two gleaming ruby eyes pierced a dark place I had missed. I swung my flashlight and saw the eyes change in the light to blue, the heart-shaped sable face looking up at me, mouth open, tiny needle-sharp teeth bared. The noise he made echoed horribly round the cave.

I edged around the chasm until I was immediately above him.

I said through chattering teeth, "You silly cat, what made you go hunting in the Mandrake? All right, I'll get you. At least I hope to heaven I will." I was talking as much to reassure myself as Ming. "Perhaps," I said testing a ledge just below me, "perhaps I ought to go for help. But if I do, will you stay where you are? Or will you try to climb up? If you do, you'll probably fall. Even you won't find footholds easily on slippery rock. Oh, Ming, you ass, you utter arrant ass, how—did—you—get—there?"

Could I leave him and go for help?

His eyes mesmerized me. With every bit of will he had, he was asking to be saved.

The flat heels I wore were a help. I tested the first piece of rock, and it held. Then I sought for the next. But it was too far away. If I tried to reach it, I could lose my balance. I scrambled to the top again, my fingers slipping on the wet stones, drips seeping through from cracks in the cave roof and spattering me with ice-cold water. I moved farther along the rim of the hole and found an easier place to climb down. I clung to hard jags of rock, hoping they would hold, and lowered myself. A dank green film covered some of the natural steps of stone, making the footing too slippery to be safe. But because of the gentle inward slope of the first ten feet of the hole, I clambered down until I was on a level with Ming. He stood, back arched, on his ledge emitting sounds no louder than a kitten's cry. I clung to the ledge coaxing, "Come on. You're more sure-footed than I. *Try*." Like many Siamese, Ming had a penchant for sudden leaps. If he leaped at me now in his wild relief at seeing me, even his light weight would certainly overbalance me. "Just try," I begged and sobbed aloud with fear for us both.

He made no effort at all. He pressed himself against the rock face and did not take his eyes off me. It was I who had to make the effort. Ming recognized the hideous danger; the onus was on me to be the foolhardy one. I moved, edging myself toward him, daring dangerous footholds, taking the blind risks of the fear-crazed.

I was nearer the black water now and I smelled it, sour and stifling like the hideous guardian of an underground treasure-house.

I clung to a sharp tooth of rock with one hand and held

197

out the other to Ming, shining the light a little way from him so that the dazzle would not frighten him. I even managed a step upward as if to tempt him to follow me, but he didn't.

"Ming."

"*M-i-n-g . . .*" The echo came. *But it had not been my voice.* Mine had been soft, in order not to frighten him. This voice was hoarse and was neither mine nor an echo. It had come quite clearly from above.

A distortion; a mockery. Then I heard the sound of a cat's bell. But it was not Ming's. It came, like the mocking repetition, from above me.

So Ming had not run before me into Mandrake. Someone else had done that—someone who knew I was searching for my cat and would follow the little bell.

Like some nightmare, relived in terror, I saw the picture. Ming had intelligence; nothing would have made him climb the Mandrake Hole. Someone had brought him here and tossed him down the gap—not too far down, only far enough for him to find a ledge. Someone used a cat's bell to lead me to him, and knowing that I would be crazy enough to try and move the whole damned rock face in order to save him, expected me to slip into the black swollen water of the lake.

I tried to curb my wild panic, because that way lay madness. No one was there watching me. The very sinister history of Mandrake was drawing me into its clutches. Holding on tightly to the jag of rock, I brought my flashlight up cautiously, my arm resting against the stone. When I could safely tilt it at the right angle, I flashed it on.

Someone stood in a deep cleft above me. I could see legs, the slight movement of arms. But the face was deep in shadow. A man—or a woman wearing slacks?

"Don't stand there. *Help* me." My voice was an angry scream that echoed around the cave.

The figure in the dripping shadow did not move. The crevice that hid him—her—was like an artist's palette, grass green and ocher red running into one another, gleaming with seeping water.

Then I heard the bell jingle again, mocking me. Ming yowled. I said, trying to keep the panic out of my voice, "It's all right. There's someone up there. He'll help. *He must help* ... Oh, for God's sake, don't just stand there ..."

The figure moved, bent down. The next moment a piece of rock came hurtling toward me. I felt the rush of disturbed air as I dodged down, crouching on my perilous ledge. The rock missed me, but ripped the flashlight out of my fingers. Some seconds later I heard the thud as both fell into the water.

Flattened against the rock, I had one wild thought. Perhaps if he couldn't see me, he might think I had fallen, that I was at this moment gasping and drowning in Mandrake waters.

I clung to a blind faith that someone would come and rescue us. I even turned my head, listening. No one came. Whoever stood above us, too concealed for recognition, had no intention of being my rescuer.

Then I heard the stage whisper. "Poor Suzanne ... Oh, poor Suzanne ... What are you thinking of down there?"

It was impossible to recognize the voice, for not only did the caves distort it, but the voice was obviously disguised as if someone spoke through the hollow of cupped hands.

Outside I heard the rumble of thunder as the storm came back. Lightning flashed across the mouth of the cave, illuminating it for a moment like an alchemist's chamber, turning the boulders to gold.

I had not moved after the rock had been flung at me; I had remained quite still, quite silent with the forlorn and terrified hope that the man would think I was dead. But of course, before he went, he would come to the edge and make sure.

Who knew I was here? Who knew I had gone to search for Ming?

Only Danielle. But I doubted if she would think I had come this far to look for my wandering cat. On the other hand, there was a chance that if I could only find the patience and the faith in my good stars, she would come to search for me. A chance, a faint one, for she had shown little interest in my comings and goings. Danielle ... or Sarne, again. Sarne who, on that first time, four years ago, had teased me into terror. This time threatening my life. For Wyncourt's, for Roseheath?

I clung, frozen, on my precarious ledge.

CHAPTER

24

THUNDER rolled nearer; lightning split the cave entrance. I heard the rain, like a torrent, pour onto the drowned earth outside. I looked upward, and water seeped through gaps in the cave roof, spattering my face.

Time seemed to stretch to an eternity. My body was cold right through to my soul. I gave an irrelevant passing thought to what I meant by that, and had no time to come to a conclusion. My fingers were so numb that they could scarcely feel the slimy green ledge of rock I clung to; my feet in their open sandals were soaked. What do I do next? What in the name of heaven *can* I do?

Ming's eyes, watching me all the time, changed from red in dark to startling blue in the intermittent flashes of lightning.

Move . . . do something, however desperate . . . To stay like this will be your certain death because your hands are beginning to feel numb. I leaned my head back and looked upward. I could no longer see anyone hiding in the crevice. I put one foot forward onto a small tooth of rock and, balancing myself above the black hole of Mandrake, waited for the next flash of lightning. When it came, I saw that the place that had concealed all but a pair of trousers and an arm was empty.

"Ming . . ." I called and waited.

No one mocked me; nobody laughed. I moved a little

toward the cat, and my left foot slipped. I gave a cry as I felt a sharp point of rock tear at my flesh. I clawed another narrow ledge, but my fingers slid over the green slime that covered it, and I just managed to regain my balance by flinging myself against the rock side. I remained there for a moment, gasping with panic.

I could feel the hot rawness where my leg bled. The thunder seemed now directly overhead. Had my assailant left the cave, certain that he had sent me to my death and that the thunder had drowned my cries?

But surely he would have made certain. Or would he? If I hadn't already been knocked off balance by the rock he threw, then sooner or later cramp would dislodge me. He had no need to remain. He knew my fate.

Quite suddenly my mind seemed to give a jerk like a muscle reminding one of a still animate arm or leg. I was sinking into an apathy that would be fatal to myself and Ming. I was doing just what had been expected of me by whoever had led me here. I had to snap out of it, take an immediate chance, and try to save myself. Time was not on my side.

I could see nothing in the darkness but the glitter of Ming's eyes guiding me to him. I began to move again, finding my way toward him with the help of the few lightning flashes. I had never in my life been so grateful for a stormy evening. Foot placed cautiously on ledges, testing, feeling the strength before my full weight landed on them, I came near enough to Ming to reach out and touch him.

And when I had got him, how in the world was I going to climb back with a cat in my arms?

"Suzanne . . . ?"

Oh no, things like this didn't happen . . .

I shut my eyes, feeling giddy, afraid of delirium.

"Suzanne?"

There was no reason on earth why anyone should come to find me in the Mandrake. I believed neither in miracles nor in coincidences. No one could have had such a hunch. Or perhaps this was my would-be killer trying another tactic—using her real voice. *Hers* . . .

Desperation led me to answer the second call.

"Here. We're here."

A powerful light flashed round the mouth of the cave and missed me. "Where? For heaven's sake . . ."

I said, "Oh God, Danielle! I'm down here in the Mandrake Hole."

The torch found me then. I saw her, wearing dark slacks and wrapped in a white raincoat, at the edge of the hole. *"Oh,"* she cried, and the brief word hung in layers of echoes over the cave. "I didn't come prepared to get you out of this! I haven't got a rope."

"Get—help—"

"You don't look to me as if you could hang on that long. I know. Your raincoat. I brought it with me when I realized you were out searching for Ming in that storm." While she talked, she began twisting the raincoat lengthwise into a kind of rope. "Do you think you could hold on to one end?"

It dangled near me, but not near enough. I didn't dare reach out too far for it in case I overbalanced. In the end she managed to hang it directly over me where it brushed my hair. I seized it.

"Don't pull so. Wait. I've got to find a purchase for myself or else you're going to drag me over, too." I watched her lie straddling a piece of rock. "Ugh, it's painful but I'll manage. Now be careful. I'm not at all certain the raincoat will take your weight. You must help yourself by getting a foothold before you pull on it. It'll keep you from falling, anyway."

"Ming . . ." I said.

"Oh, no. We'll try for him later. You first."

"I've gone through too much to risk losing him now. He's no extra weight, anyway." With the white nylon gripped in one hand I leaned forward. "Hold tight."

"Wait," she said and set her flashlight in a cleft in the rock shining down on me. Cautiously I pulled on the makeshift rope, steadying myself on a rock ledge, and reached for Ming.

I touched him, and the muscles quivered under his fur. "Ming, help me, you ass cat," I cried. Then I called to Danielle. "He's petrified with fright." My last word rose on a scream as Ming suddenly sprang. Tail flying, he leaped up the rock face, slithering, sliding, clawing.

I forgot to try to save myself. I remained frozen, watching his claws trying to grip the rocks with their slippery green ooze. I held my breath for too long and felt suddenly faint.

With a flying leap he landed on the top of the Mandrake Hole.

"Just like a cat," Danielle said. "You risk your neck. And there he goes under his own steam."

"Is he all right?"

"I don't know and for the moment I don't care. Hey, don't —pull—so—hard . . . I'm losing my grip. That's better. Ease your way up, try to find ledges that'll take your weight. If you hurry it, we'll both plunge to the bottom. So, go carefully."

By the light of the flashlight I crawled, panting, the nylon raincoat taking part of my weight between the ledges I so carefully looked for and tested before stepping on. Not once did I look down. If I had, I think the black water would have magnetized me.

The moment when I was heaved and then dragged over the top was too much. I lay numbed and shocked, my eyes closed, wondering whether I wanted to faint or be sick. My skin was grazed, my leg burned, and I could feel the warm trickle of blood from the cuts on my leg. But I was safe. I said weakly, "I feel—awful."

Danielle asked, "Can you walk?"

I thought resentfully, my eyes still closed: She might at least let me stay here for a while just to pull myself together. Aloud I said, "I . . . must . . . rest."

"Oh, no, you don't. You're wet through and exhausted, and if you lie on these icy stones you'll be ill. Come on, get up. Walk."

I tried to scramble to my feet, missed my footing, stumbled, and burst into tears.

She wrapped the wet nylon raincoat around me. Then she took off the scarf she wore and tied it over my hair. "I'm sorry. I know you're exhausted, and your leg must hurt you, but there's nothing we can do here. I didn't bring a first-aid kit with me—I didn't expect to find you here, anyway."

We came to the opening of the cave. I drew a long breath of clear air. It was still raining, but I didn't care. With Danielle's arm in mine, I half stumbled, half ran away from the demon place.

I said, "Where's Ming?"

"If he has gone back to the Mandrake, then he can stay there until we get a professional rescuer."

"He won't have gone back," I said. "He didn't go there in the first place."

"But you found him there. Or did you?"

"Someone took him."

"Suzanne, what *do* you mean?"

"Just that someone intended me to go and look for him in the cave. Someone meant me to find him down there—"

"I don't believe it."

"You weren't meant to. Everyone was meant to think that all the things that happened to me were just accidents. The fault lying in my stars," I added angrily and bitterly.

"But surely Ming slipped and managed to claw at a ledge?"

I said between chattering teeth, "Oh, that was planned. Someone probably tipped quite gently over the edge. I had to find him there, you see. I would try and save him and slip...my hands would go numb...I would grow giddy ...Oh, there were so many ways of my being killed at Mandrake."

"Suzanne, I don't think—"

I interrupted her. I was in a state where I couldn't stop talking. "And probably no one would ever have known what happened to me. At least, not for a very long time, until some potholers discovered my body in the underground lake. And Ming's. So, they would say at the inquest, 'Her cat strayed into the cave and she tried to save it and was killed.' There'd be no one to know the truth. Just Ming and I, and I'll bet our ghosts wouldn't have come back to tell them what really happened." I took a deep breath. "Do you know what really saved me?"

Danielle said dryly, "I suppose *I* did."

"I mean, gave me the strength to hang on until you came?"

"A healthy fight for survival."

"Oh, not even that. Just that I've suddenly found I have the sure-footedness of a mountain goat."

I laughed too loudly. My legs still shook so that I walked a little drunkenly over the black, uneven moorland. In the distance the gray mass of Roseheath was just visible. I said, staring at it, "How did you know where to find me? How *could* you?"

"When it began to rain I searched the grounds, calling you. When there was no answer, I went onto the moors. It was pouring with rain, and the lightning was brilliant. People have worn quite a path through the grass toward the caves. I took it because it's easier walking. I doubted if you had gone so far, but then I saw something shining on the ground. It was very small. I picked it up and saw that it was a cat's bell. That's when I realized that you must have come this way, and I was afraid a fox might have got Ming."

I said, "Don't you know that Siamese cats fight for their lives and their homes? The fox would have a bad time." I paused once again. "Listen."

Somewhere near us came the sound of his bell. Our eyes reflected the flashlight as we faced one another.

Danielle said with a gasp, "But Ming is wearing his bell, so—"

"So there was a second," I said. I was trembling so much that my teeth began to chatter again. Danielle took hold of my arm. "We'll talk as we walk. But what an extraordinary coincidence that I should find that cat's bell so that it led me to you."

"Oh, no, it wasn't. Someone used that to get me to the caves, jingling it just in front of me, darting from one clump of bushes to the other whenever my light shone the other way," I said. "Like a sort of ghastly will-o'-the-wisp. And then escaped along the path to the village when he thought it was all over with me, and threw the bell away."

"You know," Danielle said, "I feel I'm talking in a kind of dream. These things don't happen."

"I've said that ever since the curtain pole fell on me. The horrible thing is that every day, somewhere in the world, violence occurs because people hate. Who hates me? Danielle —who . . . ?" My knees were still melting under me. I clung to her arm to keep myself upright.

She said in her cool, remote voice, "We're nearly home. You're safe—"

"But for how long?" I demanded, my voice far stronger than my shaken, still numb body. "For how long am I going to be safe?"

The only answer I got was Ming's bell dancing merrily. I bent and picked him up, holding him close to me. His fur was wet, and the sable mask of his face nestled in my neck.

The blessed lights of Roseheath were nearer now. My legs gathered strength, and I began to run, and I didn't stop until I was in the living room with all the lights on as if I were preparing for a party.

Danielle said quietly, "First, get out of those wet things. I'm going to run a bath. Then you'll have a brandy."

"People are always suggesting brandy to me," I said irritably. "And I hate the stuff." Then I thought soberly: But something is always happening to bring me to a state of shock.

"Sit down and let me do something about those scratches on your legs. One is still bleeding."

"They're all right."

"Do what I tell you," she said. "Caves aren't famous for the purity of their water, and those rocks were oozing with a sort of green slime."

"It did look rather beautiful."

"So, I believe, does deadly nightshade and briony, or is it hemlock? Now, come on upstairs and we'll run your bath and clean up those cuts."

The water was soothingly warm, and Danielle had flung bath essence like roses, riotously. I even managed to take a superficial joy in the hot, scented water, though it stung the places where the rocks had jabbed at me.

When I was dry, I wrapped myself in a bathrobe and went back to the living room. Danielle had decided against brandy and made some coffee for us both. I found her looking at the little bell she had found. "It was all wet when I picked it up, and of course too small for fingerprints."

I sat down heavily in my grandmother's large armchair with the claw feet. "Fingerprints? Oh, no, you're not going to call the police?"

"Of course. If someone really was there in the cave and used this bell, then it could have been a deliberate attempt on your life."

"If? But someone *was* . . ."

"All right. If you say so."

" 'If I say so'! How right you are. It would be a waste of time to call the police, wouldn't it?" I said, bitterly. "For one thing, I have no proof. My story *is* just my story. And for another thing, between now and the time the police begin their enquiries, whoever hates me will be watching and will know that I am in touch with Inspector Reid. And he—or she—will make sure that I don't live to—" I gasped back the flood of words.

She gave me a long, doubtful look. "We'd better ring Sarne," she said.

"*No.*"

I sat looking down at my tightly locked hands. I was suspicious of everyone, even Danielle, certainly Sarne. I got up and looked at the bell she had laid on the table. It was the kind that could be bought in any pet shop and about as much of a clue as the rock that had flown past my head and hit the Mandrake lake thirty feet below.

Ming was watching me, making small throaty noises. "If you could talk my language," I said. "Or I could talk yours. If only . . ."

Ming began to purr.

I was now absolutely certain that every alarming thing that had happened to me in these past few weeks had been deliberately planned to oust me from Roseheath.

I held up the little bell. "Why was this thrown away?"

"I don't know. It could have been lying there for ages."

"It's very bright and new. Perhaps we could trace who bought it."

Danielle said, "Cat's bells can be bought anywhere."

So, it was no clue. I looked across at her. She reached up to pull the curtains over the window. She hadn't spoken to me again about telling the police. Perhaps she never seriously intended to persuade me. My suspicions were like spiders' webs; all those who came in contact with me were the flies I caught, and one of them was deadly.

"Would you like me to sleep in that empty room next to yours?"

I hesitated. And then said, "Thank you, if you would, I'd be grateful." (But I will lock my door, Mrs. Goddard, against someone whose face, as yet, I may not know—or may know too well . . .)

The hall clock chimed. I counted the strokes. It was incredible that it was only ten o'clock. I had lived through an eternity. Fear is an eon of time; happiness, a moment . . . I leaned my head back and saw Danielle watching me.

She smiled and said, "I'll go and make the bed up in that guestroom. You'll be all right while I collect my things, won't you?"

A car stopped outside. I heard the slam of a door and cried, "You rang for the police!"

"For Sarne. Someone in your family had to know," she protested as I pushed past her.

"I can open it myself perfectly well," I said. In my overwrought state there had to be some emotion to take the place of the past terror. It was not quite anger, but more than irritation. I flung open the door.

Magda swept past me. Her scent left a jasmine cloud over me; her white coat brushed against my arm, soft as swansdown.

I followed her into the sitting room and found that Danielle had disappeared. I was sorry. I wanted her there to substantiate my story. Magda came up close to me. "Danielle tells me that you had a bad shock tonight. What happened?"

"Didn't she give you details?"

"No. She asked first for Sarne. As he wasn't in, she said someone had better come and hear what happened."

I opened the cigarette box and handed it to her. She took one, lit it, and waited. "Suzanne, what happened to you?"

I slid my hands into the wide sleeves of my bathrobe and began walking up and down the room. "You'll think it too impossible to have happened; you'll think I've made it up."

"Try me."

I told my story standing by the table with the cat's bell on it. Halfway through I thought a little hysterically that I was collecting quite a volume of alarming tales about myself. If I went on at this rate, I might one day outdo Edgar Allan Poe.

Magda brought me to my senses. She said, "Do go on."

I took a hold on myself. I wasn't going to be hysterical, anyway. It was no more than an indulgence in my mind, a reaction.

"Well," I said. "And then I had to cling to the rock side and wait for the lightning to show me where my next move could be . . ." I continued my story without embroidery.

Magda listened quietly, and when I had finished she said, "You must tell the police."

I walked meaninglessly to the fireplace and back. Magda came toward me and put an arm on my shoulder. "You're in a daze. Snap out of it, and get to that telephone."

"They'll think it's a tall story."

"There are two of you to substantiate it. And it's up to you to convince them that it's true."

I said, "I suppose attempted murder usually does sound a tall story, except to the victim."

"So you'll have to tell them in plain, dull English."

"I'll be very calm," I promised and moved toward the telephone.

"But you'd better be prepared for their skepticism. The police are realists."

I stopped and turned. "Realistic to the point of disbelief? Oh no, they'll believe me. Danielle will help prove my story."

"That you went to the caves because that cat of yours strayed. Fair enough. The police will believe that part. Then

211

you found that Ming had fallen—that they'll believe, too. But the story of someone dumping the cat there and luring you with a cat's bell. Well—"

"And the voice?" I said.

"You could have—"

"Say it. I could have made it up, because I was just crazy with fear."

"Well, it's understandable. I'd be if I had to try and climb down even a few steps of the Mandrake Hole. I'd be terrified. One false step—"

"It happened, Magda, just as I told you. Someone threw a rock—"

"They get dislodged, you know, by heavy rain seeping through—and when thunder shakes the caves."

I said angrily, "You don't believe a word of what I've told you, do you?"

"Yes, I do. But will the police? Suzanne, listen." On the few occasions when she was really serious about something her voice dropped to a lower key. "I'm playing a kind of Devil's Advocate—arguing against your story just to show you how the police will see it. Please understand."

I did. I sat silent, picking at the sash of my bathrobe. Magda was right. The police might well argue that in the terror of the moments in the cave my imagination had flowed out as adrenalin flows through the body in anger; that the whole thing had been fantasy on my part. A wandering cat; an effort to save him; fear of a flooded hole from which, had I fallen, no one could have saved me ... echoes, slippery cave sides, storm-loosened stones ...

Again, someone had threatened my life but, as on those other occasions, the threat was so subtle as to have nothing for a rational mind to grasp. Yet each time, the act became that much closer to fatality. Next time ...

"Go on," Magda said. "Argue it out with me, find something that can be proof."

"As I told you, there *was* someone else there, pressed back into a cleft of the rock."

"Someone without a face."

"In the shadow."

"A trick of light; an uncanny rock formation. And don't look at me like that, I'm arguing matter-of-factly. Remember, I'm the Devil's Advocate. Go on."

I wondered suddenly whether Danielle had really believed my story, either. Perhaps she had only been playing at being the credulous friend; suppose when she faced Inspector Reid she would tell them that I went after my cat and climbed down the Mandrake Hole and panicked...

The devil could not have a more beautiful advocate...

Magda was saying, "You've lived near the caves all your life, and like everyone in the village you have a natural fear of them."

And no one had been there as a witness except one sapphire-eyes cat who didn't speak English.

"So what am I supposed to do? Wait until the final attempt? I've been scared enough times now. What's the reason? Did someone think I would manage to crawl to safety out of the Mandrake Hole—and do they hope to turn me into a shuddering neurotic whose only wish is to escape from Roseheath and leave it to ... to whom?"

To my next of kin? Now Oliver was dead, it became automatically my nearest relative, Magda. And, with Magda, Sarne.

I said, "Have you *never* hated me for owning Roseheath?"

She said in blank amazement, "When I have Amber Court? Oh, really, Suzanne."

"But someone does."

She was looking at her silver-pink nails and frowning. "I suppose you haven't seen Sarne?"

"No."

"We had our wildest quarrel yet, and he walked out in a

blazing fury. But he's taking longer than usual to cool off."

"I'm sorry."

"It wasn't a pleasant half-hour, but it has cleared the air. At least he knows with absolute certainty now that I'll never let him go. When he has adapted himself to the idea, we'll make it up. I'll tame my handsome Swedish tiger yet."

And hold him through his son . . . his daughter . . .

I wanted to ask if the quarrel was over Adrienne, or someone else. Someone new. But I stayed silent.

Magda turned and looked at herself in the mirror, touched her rich hair, and picked up her white coat. "You're tired and overwrought."

"I'm not—"

She patted my cheek. "Follow the example of your cat, Suzanne. Walk carefully."

"My cat," I said dryly, "nearly got himself killed at Mandrake."

She turned to the door. "If you should see Sarne—"

"Why should I? Why do you keep suggesting that I often see Sarne? I don't, and he's *not* here."

She smiled over her shoulder. "Oh, but he will be. He'll be here."

CHAPTER

25

BEFORE I got into bed that night, I went to the window. I could just see the moors in the rising moonlight, but not the caves.

Down below, something moved in the garden. Every nerve alerted, I watched, recognizing a man's walk, but unable to see his features sufficiently to identify him.

He walked on through the shadow of the trees into a patch of silver. And suddenly I knew without seeing his face that it was Sarne. Magda had said, "He'll be here." And he was. I should draw the curtains and see that every door was locked. I should weave a circle of magic around myself. Only I was neither wise nor fey. So, I stood and watched him.

I forgot that the bedside light was on in my room and that if he looked up he could see me silhouetted against it. And he did look up. For one moment, although I could not see his eyes, I knew that he was looking straight at me. I swung round, tore off my bathrobe and nightdress, dragged on slacks and a red sweater, and raced down the stairs.

When I opened the front door, I thought he had gone. If I had any sense, I should want him gone. Only, the trouble with reason was that it contained no emotion and so, in my case, it did not dominate. Idiotic, possibly courting danger, I had to see Sarne, to know why he walked in my gardens.

I peered into the darkness. I did not need to call him; the light pouring from the hall behind me illuminated me so that, if he were watching, he must know I was there.

The movement on the far side of the lawn came just as I was thinking that he had gone. I was going to close the door when I saw him leaning against the oak tree.

I ran down the steps and across the wet grass, calling his name.

As I neared him, he stepped sharply back. "What the devil are you doing here?"

It was worse than if he had slapped my face.

"It's my garden," I said, in sudden anger, "and if I choose to walk in it—"

"But it's not *my* garden and I have no right—of course I haven't. There are all those stretches of blasted moors where a man could walk and try to feel free."

He was in a black mood. I turned away. "By all means feel free to walk around the grounds here whenever you wish." My voice was haughty.

"Do you have to be so polite?"

"No. I can be more direct. You can damned well set up camp in the birch wood for all I care. I'm going to bed, and I'll leave you in peace."

"What's the matter with you? You used to be uncomplicated. Now, you're touchy; you spark with indignation—God knows why. Well," he demanded, "what's got into you?"

"Into both of us," I said despairingly. "You weren't exactly welcoming on my home ground."

"Pure unadulterated bad temper with me," he said without apology. "There's been a domestic crisis. Now what's *your* excuse?"

"Retaliation," I said. "I'm on the defensive. I'm frightened." I tried to see his face in the darkness.

"What has frightened you?"

Suddenly I didn't want to talk to Sarne about it. I had lost the power to trust. I said bleakly, "Never mind that. I'm sorry I gate-crashed into your solitude. I'll leave you in peace."

"Peace! You use the word so glibly."

"That shouldn't worry you. You're not a man of peace."

"Nor am I a man particularly enamored of hell. But that's where I am. Where Magda is, if only she'd acknowledge it."

"You married her. Why rant against fate because you've decided that you prefer to live with Adrienne—" I stopped and bit my lip so hard that the pain went right through me. I hadn't intended to say her name; I had meant to walk away and leave him to his angry despair.

"What the devil do you mean?"

"Magda told me."

"It would be interesting to know just what she told you."

"Oh, leave it, please. I shouldn't have said what I did. Only you—"

"I began it. Right. So what's this about Adrienne?" His eyes had the steel glint of anger.

"I only mentioned that Magda said . . . you saw a lot of one another."

"And if I do?" he waited. "What more do you want to know?"

"Nothing," I said, dreading that he might tell the truth about himself and Adrienne Wand. Yet the demon of bitter curiosity, the suicidal desire to be emotionally hurt, made me add, "By the way, when I was walking down your drive the other evening, I saw someone in the gardener's lodge. I think it . . . it could have been some tramp or—"

"I am the tramp," he said. "I use the lodge."

I stared at him, afraid of what he was going to say next, forming his words in my mind: *I told you I see Adrienne. That is where we meet.*

Sarne said, "Since the gardener left, I have used it in order to be alone. The house is always full of people and I need to breathe empty air. The lodge is my escape."

The quiet beat about us. I crossed my arms and rubbed my hands up and down the rough wool of my sweater.

I wanted to believe him. Like someone drowning, I clutched at his explanation like a piece of flotsam. I had made two attempts to leave him to his quiet walk. I tried again. "Whenever we meet, I seem to say all the wrong things. I'm sorry, but you did start it this time by telling me you had quarreled with Magda. Let . . . let's forget we said what we did. Good night, Sarne."

He stopped me as I turned away. His hand was on my arm and we faced one another, our faces hidden from one another by the thick black night. But something stronger than vision drew us toward one another. We moved simultaneously, obedient to a magnetic law. I felt Sarne's arms gripping me as if I were a lifeline.

He laid his face against mine. "I have a fury inside me that comes out when I'm balked. I didn't mean to shout at you when I saw you."

I was glad he had such a tight hold on me. I needed a prop.

I said softly, "It's all right."

"It was pain and pleasure, and I can't take paradoxes. They bewilder me."

"You are a paradox," I said. "So you must bewilder yourself sometimes."

He laughed very softly. "I do." Then his voice changed, became low, gentle, and urgent. "I have spent my leisure for so long wanting this and trying to hate you because I wanted you."

Time ceased. I could only lean against him and wonder at the powerful beating of a heart without knowing whether it was his or mine. Like someone hypnotized, I forgot my fear of him. To make matters worse, I asked the question I had vowed I would never ask.

"Why did you hide from me in the caves?"

"What in the world are you talking about?"

I had gone too far to retract. I said, "Four years ago—the evening after we met at the Mandrake Caves—you played a trick on me."

"I don't play tricks. And if you thought I had, why in the name of goodness not have mentioned it when we next met? That was the time, I remember, when you turned your back on me, walked out of the room, and didn't return, at least while I was in the house."

"Because of what happened in the caves," I said, and drew away from him. "It was such a horrible thing to have done that I couldn't bear to talk about it."

"All right, let's get something straight before we begin recriminations. What *is* this about going to meet me at the caves a second time?"

"You must remember. That first time, when Magda bent down to put the leash on her dog, I whispered, 'Can we meet here tomorrow, at the same time?' You didn't say 'No,' so I assumed you'd come but that you didn't say so because Magda had leashed her dog and moved closer to us."

"You must believe this," he said urgently. "I didn't hear you. Suzanne, before heaven as my witness, I didn't hear you! I couldn't have seen you the next day, anyway, because I was being taken to meet some people in the glass business."

I stared at him. "So if it wasn't you, who was it who was there, calling me farther and farther into the caves?"

"You must have known it wasn't my voice."

"In those caves sounds are distorted. You can't tell. Voices hit the walls, the damp places, the great hollows—they echo and change—"

"And all this time you believed I was there that evening playing some macabre game with you?"

"Yes."

"But, you little idiot, why didn't you tackle me with it when you next saw me?"

"I didn't want to embarrass us both."

He said, "The pride and sensitiveness and foolishness of youth!"

"I suppose so," I said, desperately wanting to believe. But then I remembered my fright just a few hours earlier. That time in the caves when someone had wanted to do more than just scare me. And Sarne . . . maybe I was being fooled again. My head dropped.

Sarne's fingers touched my hair. I was alive and vibrating with my paradox of joy and despair. I could not say, "Two hours ago I nearly died. Somebody tried to murder me or send me, terrified, away from Roseheath." If he didn't already know, he would, soon enough. When he got home, Magda would tell him. "Suzanne had a scare tonight. She thought someone tried to kill her. She had lost that cat of hers and found him at the Mandrake. She got stuck on a ledge trying to get to him, and then her imagination started playing her tricks." Something like that.

And what would he say? "The little idiot!" and pretend it didn't matter.

For someone who had just been whirled into the beginning of a love affair, I was behaving too reasonably. But that was it. For a tiny flash of time, I had lost myself in joy. But it hadn't lasted. There were questions and there were doubts.

He put his hand under my chin and tilted my face. After a moment he said, "For months now, I haven't stopped wanting you." Then he added violently, "And where will all this get you? Sitting alone and unhappy, thinking of me at Amber Court with a wife and a life of my own? Some women are born to be mistresses. But not you. Good God, Suzanne, not you. I couldn't bear it. I don't want to see you alone again."

A light flashed on with such suddenness that it dazzled me. I blinked and saw that it came from the spare room, which Danielle was using. I saw her come to the window. To close it? Open it farther? Or to look for me because she knew I wasn't in my room?

"For God's sake, go," Sarne said violently.

We broke away from one another with no more ceremony than if we had been strangers bumping into each other in the street. I started to run. I stumbled up the steps, closing the front door and falling helplessly onto the great settee that stood against the wall opposite the place where the Isabella had hung.

I lay panting and weeping for so long that I exhausted myself.

My last waking thought was: You've cried enough in one night to qualify for the role of Niobe.

When I was a child, my father had once said, "All right, cry if you want to, though don't do it too often, or it loses its effect."

I hadn't known what he meant, but instinct had told me that I wasn't going to get my own way by that method, and I had seldom tried it. So crying was a new and shattering phenomenon to me, and it eased nothing.

I must have slept in an uncomfortable position, lying with my face plunged into the yellow brocade cushion. Or perhaps it wasn't sleep so much as an unendurable longing that had rendered me unconscious of time and place. I only knew that I started suddenly as the clock across the hall from where I lay struck one. I stirred, and stretched my numbed limbs. Painfully, I blinked at the light and sat up.

From the shadows of the kitchen Ming crept toward me. I picked him up and carried him to my room. I undressed in a whirl of unreality, at one moment picturing myself dying in the Mandrake Caves with Sarne outside uncaring and at the next lying in Sarne's arms on dry moss under the silver birches.

CHAPTER

26

THE next morning a card came for me from London. On one side was a reproduction of a Gauguin, blazing with Tahitian color. On the other, Justin wrote, "I miss you. Will you marry me?"

And if the post boy had read it, as I suspected he had, the whole of Magnon Down would know that Suzanne Wyncourt had received a proposal on the back of a postcard.

Elbows on the breakfast table, chin on my hands, I spoke to Justin in my mind. "And if I sent a card back with 'Yes' on it, I wonder how you'd feel?" One of these days, on an impulse, he would say it to a girl who would hold him to his word. *Oh, you ass, Justin—you nice, huge, impetuous ass* . . .

Nevertheless, it was warming to know that I was not completely out of his thoughts. That would come later, among the monsters of Svenling's sculptural world.

Danielle and I had breakfasted together, and she had asked me whether I intended to see Inspector Reid. I told her of Magda's interrogation. I said, "I saw from that how the police were likely to view what had happened, so I'm prepared for their disbelief."

She pushed her cup away. She had finished half a piece of toast and drunk three cups of coffee. She looked so pale and her eyes had so completely lost their shining hazel light that I asked her if she had slept badly.

"A strange bed, that's all," she said.

"I'm sorry. I shouldn't have let you stay with me."

"Think nothing of it," she said vaguely. And then, "I've got to see the man from the insurance again today about the Isabella. I'm so tired of their repetitive questions. They're trying to trap me."

"I'm sure they aren't. How could they?"

She gave me a strange look. "Never mind," she said and got up and left me.

I saw her later walking in the garden. What was it, I wondered, that gave our relationship this strange quality of indecisiveness? So often our conversations broke at a crucial point, remaining unfinished. So often I had waited for her to answer me or explain a point, and she had just quietly left me as she had now. Her mind was an enigma. Had Oliver ever found the solution?

I debated whether to tell Mrs. Jo of my terror at Mandrake and decided against it. No, the person I really wanted to confront was Sarne. Away from the moonlight, without emotion, perhaps I could finally decide whether or not he was telling the truth.

But when I went to his office, his secretary, Tessa, told me that he had not been in that day.

The manager of the Accounts Department met me in the elevator that evening. "What do you know? Mr. Eskinholm played truant. His secretary says he had no particular appointments today."

"He may have called to see a client and forgotten to tell anyone."

"Maybe," he gave me a hint of a wink. He liked to think that the Wyncourts and the Eskinholms lived it up. He had such a dull life himself.

I was still determined to talk to Sarne about Mandrake before I saw the police. But where was he? After our parting by the oak tree, had he gone home? Had there been some sort of reconciliation?

I drove home through the village, bought some stamps at the post office, and called at the grocer's for sugar and salt and a few things I knew Mrs. Jo wanted and would probably defy me and get up and go out to buy if I didn't forestall her.

When I came out of the shop, Pauline was leaning against the window. There was a livid red streak across one cheek.

She saw me look at it and put up her hand to cover it.

I pulled her fingers away. "What happened?"

"Nothing."

I said again, more slowly this time, "What happened?"

She made as if to slip away from me, but I caught hold of her and bundled her unceremoniously into the car.

"I can't go home. Mum and I had a row, and she hit me."

"Why?"

"Because I said I wasn't going to Amber Court to pick up my things. Mrs. Chang let me have a drawer in the kitchen, and I keep make-up and on old mackintosh and a pair of shoes there because I won't do floors with my good shoes on."

"I'll run you to Amber Court to get them."

"I won't go. Never any more. I saw her and—and it was awful. I heard."

"Her?"

"Mrs. Eskinholm. She was screaming at him like she was mad. And he was yelling back. I ran."

So Sarne was home. "If they're having a quarrel, it's not for you to be scared," I said.

"I think they saw me," she said. "And they must've known what I heard. And—" She shot me a sideways glance. "It isn't just what I *heard*, it's what he said to me that night when you found me scared."

I asked carefully, " 'He'? You mean Mr. Eskinholm?

She cried instantly, "I didn't say that. I didn't say nothing to you." She was getting excited again. She had given away too much, and now she was frightened. I decided not to upset her any more for the moment. There was an obstinacy in her as tough as a steel wall.

Instead, I said as calmly as I could, "If you've really decided you can't work at Amber Court any more, then you're going to fetch the things that belong to you. No one will hurt you if I'm with you." My bravado was hollow, but Pauline was not discerning and we drove without protest, in silence, to Sarne's house.

When we arrived, I leaned across and opened the door on her side. Then I gave her a little push. "Out."

"But Miss Wyncourt . . ."

"Don't worry, I'm coming, too."

She was clinging to the car, her eyes wide, the weal across her left cheek livid in the brushed yellow and violet of the twilight.

I took her arm and we walked among the trees to the house. There was no sight of anyone, and the great picture windows were closed. We walked, making as little noise as possible, round the house and found the back door ajar.

"Go on in," I said. "Mai Chang is nice. She won't stop you collecting your own things."

Pauline strained back. "She's gone home. And . . . I . . . can't . . ."

I gave her a push. "I'm here," I hissed at her as if I were the bastion against all her dangers.

There was a yew tree between the house and the garage. I went and stood behind it, and the leaves pricked my face and arms like little teasing needles.

I looked up at the house and thought that in its way it was beautiful, all glass windows and white angles.

Beyond the hedge to the left of me, Sarne grew irises, the flowers he loved best of all; silver-bronze; peach-pink; proud, erect blooms with lovely names; Summer Song and Granada Gold and Beau Nash...

I jumped like a startled cat when I heard Magda's furious voice. "And what are you doing here?"

For a moment I thought she was speaking to me, angry with me for lurking like a conspirator in her garden. Then I saw Pauline with her arms full of her possessions brought up short as Magda stood in her way in the back door of the house.

"I...I was...getting my things. They're mine, anyway. I'm not pinching anything." Her voice was a whine.

"I told you never to come back. To get out of here, out of Magnon Down."

"I've done nothing wrong. Why should I?"

"Because if you don't, you'll get no reference from me. And then you won't have a job, will you?"

"You've no right not to give me a reference. I worked hard—"

"And hid in corners listening to conversations you had no right to hear."

"I couldn't help it if you were shouting—"

I held my breath, waiting for Magda's fury and poised for a rush to Pauline's defense.

Instead, after a long pause, Magda said very slowly as if she knew that Pauline needed time before she could assimilate every word, "Most of what you say you have heard here is untrue. Do you hear? You have cunning; you twist the truth. You are a great little liar, Pauline."

"I'm not. I'm not."

"If you try to make trouble, my child, then I shall be forced to tell the authorities of your thieving habits."

Pauline gave a loud gasp and dropped one of the shoes she was carrying. She bent to pick it up, fumbling with her load. We waited and watched—Magda standing in front of her. I hidden behind the great divided trunk of the yew tree.

226

The sky was darkening quickly. The lemon glow was gone, and night was crawling up from the east obliterating the evening star.

"Well?" Magda asked. "Are you going to give me your word to leave Magnon Down?"

"I'm leaving here, and don't think I'll ever come back."

"I said *leave Magnon Down.* If you don't, I warn you, it'll be the worse for you."

Pauline was casting terrified glances about her, looking for me.

Then she found a desperate courage. She faced Magda and shouted. Her voice was high and clear. "I saw him digging . . . down in the bluebell wood. It looked . . . like a grave . . ."

Magda drew a sharp breath. She cried, "So that's where he hid the painting. The Isabella, it's there—in the wood . . ."

I knew Pauline had shouted for my benefit. She still clung to the belief that I must be somewhere around, ready to guard her if things went too wrong.

"He said . . . he said it *was* . . . a grave . . . And that he'd dig one for me if . . . if I was . . . a . . . nosey girl . . ." Horror at her own words overcame her. She put her hand to her mouth. Shoes and raincoat and bits and pieces of make-up fell to the ground.

I darted from behind the trees, grabbed her hand, and said, "My car. Go on, Pauline. Get into my car."

As we raced down the drive, I saw Magda standing motionless. The painting, but why would Sarne care about that? I thought of last night and shivered. Then I made up my mind. It was time to go to the police.

CHAPTER

27

I BROKE every rule of the road; I speeded through built-up areas, I twisted in and out of the traffic, I honked at other drivers and behaved as if I were the only motorist on the road.

When we reached Amesdale I seemed to breathe for the first time. I drove to the police station, got out, and said to Pauline, "Lock yourself in and keep quiet. Do you hear?"

The Inspector was known familiarly as "Red Reid" because of his hair. He was about to go out when I entered the station.

I said, "I must talk to you. It's urgent. Someone at Amber Court knows where the stolen portrait—the Bernadino—is hidden." I still couldn't bring myself to name Sarne.

He turned, hung his hat up again on the peg, and took me into his office.

I had a lot to tell him, but now there was only time for the essentials. The Inspector did not waste time. He got up, took my arm and, with his sergeant, we made a brisk threesome to the police yard.

Pauline gave him a terrified look. He said, "You're going to be a good girl and help me, aren't you? Come along. We're going in my car, and then you and I can talk."

She reached out a hand to me. Reid said, "Miss Wyncourt will follow us in her car."

I knew that Pauline would tell the story as I had told it

because she hadn't sufficient imagination to lie, even if she dared try and deny everything through fright. I had often thought how thrilling it would be to follow a police car, but now I had a legitimate reason for doing so, I was outdistanced, and I lost them in the stream of traffic along the road to Bath.

Amber Court was in darkness; the living room windows were still closed, and the only lights were those that had been turned on at the swimming pool. They shone with a pink glow on the blue water, and the leaves of the trees that bordered the far side of the pool were like scattered gems.

The police car stood in the drive and I paused, looking around, listening for voices. The house stood in almost as much ground as Roseheath, and there were woods to the south and the north. Pauline could have led the police in either direction. The silent minutes crept by while I looked and listened for a clue as to where I would find them.

It was unusually still, as if Inspector Reid, his sergeant, and Pauline were stalking one another. And Sarne?

I walked round to the back of the house, and my footsteps on the gravel were the only sounds in that breathless silence.

I stepped off the path and crossed the lawn to the swimming pool. A deep ditch bordered what was once the boundary of Amber Court. Sarne, however, had bought an acre of ground on the far side of it. Here he had planted Christmas trees. Every year, on December 23rd, each member of Wyncourt's who had young children received a gift of a little tree.

The sides of the boundary ditch were covered with ferns. Sarne had had a little bridge built at the far end. The recent storms had made a stream down in the ditch and so I walked toward the bridge. It was humped like the little bridges you see in Chinese drawings, and I knew that from there I would get a clearer view of the whole of the grounds.

I was on the far side of the bridge, by the plantation, when I saw a moving light in the distance. The police were in the wood on the other side of the house.

"Hullo, Suzanne."

I swung round. Hugh came out of the shadows of the fir trees. He held out his hand to me. "I want to talk to you."

I said startled, "I didn't realize you were back at Lion's Hill.

"For several days. What's this about Pauline? Magda tells me she's been screaming that I threatened to bury her."

"*You* threatened to bury her?" A wave of relief swept over me. Hugh, not Sarne. So it was Hugh who had terrified Pauline. Hugh who had stolen the Isabella.

Something of what I was thinking must have showed on my face. Hugh grabbed my arm.

I pulled away. If I walked along the path by the side of the plantation, I would come to the wood where I had seen the beam of light.

"Do you know where Sarne is?" I asked.

He said disinterestedly, "For all I know, he could be on a plane heading for Bangkok. They had the row to end all rows last night. Why?"

"Never mind that. Did you know that the police are here?"

The hand on my arm jerked. "Good God, you didn't go and fetch them, did you?"

"I did, and brought them back here."

"What in heaven's name for?"

"To find the Isabella."

"It sounds like a game, doesn't it? 'Find Isabella.' Where are they?"

"Where Pauline saw you digging a hole in the bluebell wood, I suppose."

Hugh stopped walking, but his hand did not relax its grip on my arm. We had wandered a little way into the plantation. Because Sarne loved them, I put out my hand

and brushed the stiff little branches of the nearest trees. He loved me. He had told me last night. And now, even though Magda still held him, I felt an overwhelming happiness that he loved me.

Hugh followed me like a dog, saying nothing, walking a little behind me.

I was nervous of his padding footsteps, of his silence. It seemed that he didn't join me in order to talk to me, but just to shadow me until ... Until what? I was too far away from safety, and out of earshot of the police. I had also turned without realizing it and was walking away from the direction in which I had seen the light. It was difficult in an acre of small trees in the dark to keep to a planned direction— all the paths, all the little firs looked alike. I knew that I had to turn back, but Hugh's padding presence behind me unnerved me.

An unconsidered movement of mine might spark off what? Attack? Violence? But Hugh had always seemed to me the least violent person I had known.

I turned, "I'm not finding this walk very pleasant," I said.

He put out a hand. "Oh, come on," he said, then conversationally, "Sarne's precious plantation must look rather beautiful under snow. You know, I've never seen it like that."

"Well, it's not going to snow tonight, so you won't miss anything if we turn back. At least I'm going to ... Oh, do go ..."

He said with mock disappointment, "Don't you like my company, Suzanne? I thought you looked so lonely on your own."

"Well, I'm not. Let me pass."

I turned into the aisle at right angles to the main one.

Hugh dragged me back. "Not that way ..." To avoid him I side-stepped, trod on a piece of uneven ground, and slipped. I put out my hand and gripped the rough branches of the

231

nearest Christmas tree. It was not strong enough to support me and bent with my weight. I went sprawling.

Hugh sprang. I screamed, and he laughed and pulled me to my feet. "You little idiot. What did you think I was going to do, rape you among the fir trees?"

I stood shaken, feeling foolish and no less frightened. I rubbed the back of my hand across my forehead. "Let go of me. I'm all right."

"Then come along—*this* way."

"I'll go the way I want to."

He gave me no opportunity to do that, guiding me ungently away from the right-angled path which would have led me round the plantation and back to the little bridge over the ditch.

He was altogether too anxious for me not to escape him. Although I knew the police could not be far away, fear was curling up inside me. Where was Inspector Reid? Why could I no longer see lights? The grounds of Amber Court were too expansive, too full of turns and concealing hedges.

There was something uncanny about this companionship which I was certain was not prompted on Hugh's part by any desire to be with me. Was he playing for time? Or hiding from Magda? Was he trying to find out something he was afraid I knew?

I looked about me and in that moment I saw, in the distance, the yellow beams of torches. A tremendous relief broke over me. Hugh saw the lights, too. He flung back his head and burst into laughter. "They've found it. Great heaven, how marvelous ... they've found it!"

"Found—what—?"

"The thing Pauline found me burying in the woods," he said. "The *thing*, dear. Not the Isabella, but an outsize hare I found that must have died of old age. Oh, dear ... oh, dear ..." His laugh was too loud, too hysterical. But as he turned to look at the lights, I had my chance of freedom. I tore along the lines of little black trees. I thought I heard him calling me, but I didn't stop to make certain. I was aware only, with relief, that he wasn't following me.

I fled out of the plantation and across the lawn, skirting the swimming pool and plunging into the wood where the lights bobbed and swung.

Pauline, the Inspector, and his sergeant were looking down into the burial place of a very dead hare. Pauline was saying, "But he said ... if I told ... there'd be a ... grave for me, too. Why did he say that if it was only a hare? Why?"

Red Reid said, "Because it wasn't only a hare."

The sergeant leaned on the spade. "A hole that size to bury a small hare? Or made big, perhaps, to fool someone into thinking something else was there—something much more important."

The portrait.

I took two gulps of air, got a semblance of my breath back and said. "Hugh—Mr. Gayer—is in the plantation—" I pointed. "*He* told me it was he Pauline saw, but he was burying a hare."

"At some time, yesterday or today," said Red Reid, "someone dug this place up. My guess is that a second party was getting suspicious and was looking for the painting. And—well—the hare was indeed a red herring, if you'll pardon the metaphor."

"Then you really think the portrait was buried here?"

"As I pointed out, it's a large hole for a small wild animal," said Red Reid.

"So—?"

"A grave to fool Mrs. Eskinholm if she went looking for the painting." Inspector Reid said, "We'll go back to the car and wait. By the way, Miss Wyncourt, where have you been all this time? Or were you held up by traffic?"

"I was looking for you, and I wandered near the fir

plantation. Hugh—Mr. Gayer—came along. He seemed very amused when he told me about the dead hare."

"Did he, now?" said the Inspector gently.

Pauline was tagging along behind us, wailing. "I want to go home. Please let me go home."

"We'll take you, don't worry."

"I've told you everything I know . . ."

"And you've been very helpful. Now get in the car and sit quietly like a good girl until my driver can take you home."

As Pauline climbed reluctantly into the back of the car, Inspector Reid detained me. Leaning with deceptive idleness against the car, he said, "I wonder why Mr. Gayer followed you into the plantation?"

"Perhaps there was something he didn't want me to find, so he had to stay with me and steer me away from it." Immediately I had spoken, I knew that it had been quite unnecessary. Red Reid had already come to that conclusion.

He lit a cigarette. "It may be a long wait. Do you mind?"

It was all the same if I did mind, and I knew it. I said, "Someone has to come home eventually."

I stared out into the darkness. The windows of the house were like great pools of still water; on the two sun terraces I saw the tops of tubbed trees waving gently like black ostrich feathers in a growing breeze. My hair blew up and round my head and held it back, and I felt slight pricks on my wrist where the strong points of the little tree had needled me when I fell. I remembered how quickly I had been helped up and led away.

Red Reid's voice carried over the quiet gardens. "Forbes . . ."

There was an answering flash from a flashlight.

The Inspector turned to me. "Can you remember the way you took through the trees?"

"More or less. We walked in a straight line. Only when I

tried to turn off left toward the boundary wall and back along the edge of the plantation to the bridge, Hugh tried to stop me."

The Inspector pointed. "You went straight up in that direction?"

"Yes."

"*Then* tried to turn off left."

I said, "That was when—" and stopped. Something moved in the drawing room of the house. I caught a vague glimpse of a face, a whitened patch in the darkness. I cried, "Someone *is* in the house . . . in the dark . . ."

Again Red Reid had forestalled me. He was already walking to the window. He shouted, "It's Inspector Reid here, Mrs. Eskinholm. Will you please let me come in?"

The face had gone. The house looked abandoned again. The Inspector crossed to the door. He tilted the letter box and called. "Open this door, Mrs. Eskinholm!" He proceeded to hammer on the white paneling.

I had followed up the steps. I said, "You aren't surprised? You knew someone was there—"

He didn't answer my question. Instead, he shouted, "We're going down to the plantation, Mrs. Eskinholm. Perhaps you'll join us there."

He waved impatient fingers toward the long black mass of Christmas trees. The sergeant, who was coming toward us carrying the spade, understood and sprinted round the swimming pool.

Red Reid said to Pauline, "You stay in the car with my driver. Do you hear? Just don't move." Then he said to me, "Come on, Miss Wyncourt. Just take me for a little tour of the plantation—the way you went with Mr. Gayer."

"We'd better go by way of the bridge," I said. "There's a ditch dividing the plantation from the rest of the garden, and it's running with water."

"Where's the bridge?"

"At the far end—"

"Too much of a detour," said Red Reid. "I don't mind getting my feet wet in the course of duty." He put a light arm around my shoulders, guiding me across the lawn. "Now let's have a look at those Christmas trees."

"There are so many of them," I said helplessly. "You'll never be able to find anything suspicious, not in the dark."

"Lead the way, Miss Wyncourt."

We crossed the lawns toward the ditch. Twice I turned and glanced back at the house. The thought came, hard and bitter: Where is Sarne? And a picture flashed before me of Adrienne Wand's penthouse in Amesdale.

Last night under the oak tree could have been an illusion, a wishful thought fulfilled in a dream.

THE Inspector took his time about reaching the plantation. His powerful light flicked over flower beds and paths, pausing to examine a displaced paving, to brush a line of delphiniums beaten down by yesterday's storm.

He stopped when he came to the ditch, looked at the muddy water, and said, "Well, perhaps after all, the bridge . . ."

"Look!" I made my cry to the empty air.

Red Reid had seen it a split second before I had and plunged up to the top of his well-polished shoes into the ditch and the rain water.

I noticed only that he didn't use his flashlight. He splashed through the ditch and up the other side in total darkness.

There was only one light in that black evening. Someone had started a fire among the fir trees at the far end by the boundary wall.

I detoured, racing toward the little bridge. In the distance the burning patch had spanned out; I thought I saw flame forms. I debated whether to race back, break a window of the house if Magda wouldn't let me in, and dial for "Fire." But Red Reid's driver was in the police car with his own telephone communication. I ran on, over the bridge and between the neat rows of little trees. The firs were planted well away from one another to give them light and breathing space, but a sudden breeze might easily spread the flames. The police would know what to do; Sarne's charming plantation must not be destroyed.

The fire was very near the place where Hugh had forced me to turn back. I could now see the pile of red embers from which the flames rose. There was an acrid smell of oil, and even from a distance a faint heat touched me.

Sergeant Vale was beating at the flames with a broken broom he had found somewhere. I saw that he had made a mask of his handkerchief. It looked very wet, and I supposed he had dipped it in the stream as he, too, had waded through it.

The Inspector kept moving forward and then back. I saw, as I approached, that he had the spade in his hands and was trying to rake something out with it. They looked, in the darkness, like figures from some ritual dance in a black forest; to and fro, bending and swaying, with the flames dancing; dying down; becoming regenerated by a puff of wind; sinking again.

The place where they were standing was almost at the boundary wall. The last tree in the row was crackling merrily as if it enjoyed its cremation. In the heart of the fire, propped against the tree, I saw a lovely face and the blackened edge of a white gown; I saw carved and gilded wood.

The Isabella was burning its painted heart away. The sergeant was beating madly, but the fire was dying hard.

I heard my own voice, jerking out broken sentences. "The Isabella ... But if it's destroyed ..."

No one took any notice of me.

Red Reid must have had a sixth sense, for nobody could have heard footsteps in that roar and crackle of flames. But he swung around with a suddenness that rocked me as I stood behind him. His flashlight beamed on Magda, flying toward us, hands outstretched. "Get it out of that ... inferno. Save it, damn you, save it ... *It's mine ...*"

The Inspector held her back. "We'll save enough for identification."

She wrenched herself away from him, her hair loosening and falling wildly, itself like a flame, over her face. Her hands clawed at his restraining fingers.

"If you're too much of a coward, let me go. I'll do it. *Let—me—go* . . . Oh, save her face; for God's sake, save her face . . ."

"If you'll just let us get on . . ." he thrust her aside.

She turned furiously to the sergeant and tried to tear the broom from him. "Give it to me. I'll show you . . ."

He, too, pushed her away. She kicked at the red ashes, and her shoe scorched. Red Reid grabbed her.

She turned on him, screaming, "Go and find Hugh Gayer." She gave a wild look about her, and it seemed that she saw me for the first time. "You . . . you . . . and Roseheath. Sarne . . . Nothing stopped you trying to get him from me, did it? Dear God, how I worked on you . . . I bribed Hugh to frighten you . . . He stole the Isabella for me . . . But then he wouldn't let me have it till I paid . . ." The fire was, at that moment, secondary to her burning fury against me.

"All those things you said about Adrienne and Sarne; about his wanting my shares—about—"

The Inspector must have relaxed his hold for a moment, for she swung her hand at me. "I gave you lies to turn your obsession to hatred. But—oh, God—" She turned from me to the burning mass of the Isabella, and before anyone could stop her she sprang forward and plunged her hands into the fire. At the same moment the little tree against which the painting rested collapsed, its trunk burned through. Magda lost her balance.

I cried out. I saw the flames curl round her hair like some terrible lover's caress. I heard her scream and go on screaming, even when the Inspector and the sergeant pulled her out, beating at the flames. She collapsed on the ground, and another little tree broke as she fell against it.

I couldn't move. I leaned with sick horror against the wall.

Red Reid picked Magda up very gently. She was quite quiet now and I knew that she must be unconscious. The Inspector looked at me and said, "Quickly, call an ambulance!"

CHAPTER

29

THAT night I slept fitfully, waking, fidgeting, wondering if the police had located Sarne. At last the dawn chorus roused me, and I knew I would not sleep again. I flung the covers off me and went to the window, rubbing my arms, cold, stiff, and not in the least rested.

The morning light was just tingeing the eastern sky. The birds had now joined their songs into a choral symphony of thrush and blackbird, sparrow and swallow. They staked their claims on their few inches of leafy tree branch, bursting their throats with song.

I went to the bathroom and splashed cold water on my face, cleaned my teeth, and combed my hair. It was too early to call the hospital, so I made myself some strong coffee. I drank it while I watched the daffodil light spread over the eastern sky and the dark blue pale to aquamarine.

At breakfast I found Danielle. She had heard about the fire, and I told her as much as I could piece together of Hugh's part in the affair. After a few minutes she said, "The insurance company will have to know."

I had had the sensation before that Danielle had no resources with which to deal with crises. It surprised me in someone so self-contained. I reached out and touched her fingers. She swerved almost imperceptibly away from me as if she felt I had touched her by accident. "Nothing can bring back what is done, can it?"

"Nothing."

"That's why I said that there was nothing here at Rose-heath for me but the haunting." She dragged her eyes reluctantly from something she had been looking at over my shoulder and looked at me with a great sadness. "The evening that Oliver had his accident we had words—all right, a quarrel. What it was over is not important any longer, but I said things, and . . . he walked away from me up the stairs. He never spoke another word, Suzanne. It was only minutes after that that he fell."

It was hard to know what to say that might not, all unwittingly, hurt her more. I realized that this had been the barrier, this secret sense of guilt she carried. All I could do was to remind her that it was Oliver's weak heart that had really killed him.

She shook her head. "Don't you see, I shall never know now whether he was on his way down to me to make it up. I shall never know . . ."

I said, "We can all blame ourselves for something that we didn't do or say. We aren't angels, any of us." It was poor consolation, and I knew it, but I had to respond because at the back of the gray eyes was an emptiness.

She said, "I never loved him, and he didn't love me. We were two of a kind, we needed the normality of a man's and a woman's life together, but we had nothing deep to give. It's strange, isn't it? For Oliver, it wasn't important. Wyncourt's fulfilled his need. For me—I have no passion, either, no depth. Only the need. And Oliver knew it, and we satisfied one another." She turned away from me and left the dining room.

When the telephone bell rang, I jumped up, spilled coffee on the carpet, dropped my cup on a table, and went to answer it.

His voice was asking impatiently before I could speak. "Suzanne?"

Sarne. I said, "Yes, it's me . . ." Me—I—what was grammar at this moment?

He said, "I've been at the hospital all night. Magda died half an hour ago."

It was fortunate that there was a chair beside me, because otherwise I would have sunk to the floor. I sat clinging to the telephone, speechless.

Sarne understood. He said, "I saw a light through the trees, and I knew it was from your kitchen. Otherwise I wouldn't have phoned so early."

"Do you want to come around?"

"No. No, thank you."

"Oh, Sarne, what can I say?"

"What is there to say? The police found me at Adrienne's last night."

"Adrienne's!" In the midst of all the horror and dismay, I found a niche inside myself where I had space enough to hate him for telling me that.

He said, "She is taking over a shop in London, in Bond Street. She wanted advice."

He hadn't needed to give me any explanation. I was grateful to him. I said, "So now you know everything that happened here while you were away."

"Not everything. Nor do the police."

"You weren't at home at all yesterday?"

"I was in Bath, walking, trying to tire myself out. Then when I came back to Amesdale, I went to see Adrienne. Will you tell them at the office that of course I shan't be in today?"

Today. A work day. I would have to go to my desk and draw with a steady hand. Before I could reply to Sarne, he said, "Just give them my message," and rang off.

My chair swiveled round, and I was staring out of the small slit of window in the side wall at the oak tree.

A painting—a daub of flaming hair, a white gown, and a

ruby ring—had caused a death. I remembered how Magda as a young girl had stood in front of the portrait and cried, "It's me! It will be really me when I'm older."

And last night in the plantation of little Christmas trees, she has given her life for love of her own painted likeness.

A few birds hopped on the lawn. I got up, went into the kitchen, and found bread for them. It was cold in that early mauve-washed morning. I closed the garden door and went back to my room. Would I go to Wyncourt's today? Would I sit at my drawing board and dream up a design for a christening goblet for a rich child, or a set of crystal glasses for an Eastern millionaire?

In the end, I went because it was preferable to staying home alone. But halfway through the morning Red Reid sent for me.

Hugh had been traced to London, where he was in hiding at a friend's flat. No one told him that Magda was dead, and in his terror at whatever revelation she might make, he told everything on the assumption that honesty would exonerate them.

There were four of us in the Inspector's office when Hugh broke down, Sarne and I, Red Reid and Sergeant Vale. I had already told of the attempts on either my life or my sanity—I still had no idea which.

Sarne scarcely looked at me. He was as impassive as a statue, remote from us.

Hugh sat in a hard, upright chair, no longer immaculate, his hair untidy, his face disintegrated with terror.

"It makes a difference if I tell, doesn't it?" he asked as simply as a child trusting the adults to forgive. "It's called turning Queen's Evidence, isn't it?"

He waited. Red Reid said, "You tell me what I want to know, and we'll see."

"She wanted the Isabella. She also wanted Roseheath."

"Oh, no," I burst in. "She always said she disliked it. She once called it 'a monstrosity.'"

He said, pulling at his mouth with shaking fingers, "She didn't mean she hated the house—though she meant you to think she did. She meant the furniture—she always loathed antiques. But she wanted Roseheath, all right! She saw herself, when you had been scared into getting rid of it, as mistress there. It is one of the great houses of the county."

"Then what an actress she was to pretend it bored her."

He gave a bitter laugh. "It was a deal. I was to get the Isabella and scare you out of Roseheath. For that, she would hand over to me all the antiques in the house. But I didn't trust her. My part of the bargain had to come before hers, and Magda will always default if she can. So, I took the Isabella and hid it—she didn't know where. I dug up a bit of the wood as a kind of red herring. I planned to pretend, if she found the spot, that someone had discovered the painting there and taken it. I would promise to get it for her—and I would delay the giving of it until you were out of Roseheath and I had got the furniture—it'd have fetched a lot of money."

I said, "So you did everything you could to scare me out of my house because Magda wanted it. But—"

Hugh turned to the Inspector. "I've never harmed Suzanne; I never meant more than to give her some frights. But not violence. Never—"

"Not violence?" I asked. "Not in the Mandrake Caves? What I don't understand is why you tried to terrify me four years ago, before anyone ever knew I would inherit Roseheath."

"You'll have to ask your beautiful cousin about that," he said. His eyes slid around to Sarne and back to me. "Magda wanted something she thought you had."

I thought quickly. Of course, Magda had been bending down to put the leash on Jason. She could have heard my whisper, but the tall Sarne could not. At dinner at the Trents' on that night, Magda must have realized that Sarne could not possibly have been able to see me the next evening because of Maurice's plans for him. So, she had gone to the Mandrake Caves and waited, hoping that I would come. The caves had never scared her; she had enormous courage. But she was prepared to scare me into hysteria.

Hugh was continuing his wail. "I wasn't going to harm you, Suzanne."

"So you've said. But the other night, in the caves, what did you imagine would happen to me if no one came along to rescue me?"

"That you would climb to the top."

"As if I could, without help! Danielle saved my life. And if, before she came along, I'd lost my hold and fallen, nobody would ever have known that you had been there."

"I didn't intend—"

"To harm me. You'd better stop saying that. There's such a thing as mental harm. You mean *that;* just as Magda intended that Danielle should be suspected of the theft of the Isabella."

Inspector Reid broke in. "You buried the painting in the plantation, didn't you? Why did you set fire to it?"

"It—it was an accident..."

"Tell that to the children in a fairy tale," said Red Reid. "You thought you'd get rid of the evidence, didn't you? You were certain that by the time we arrived there would only be ashes. How were you going to explain them? That you had been asked to burn rubbish? But we arrived too soon. The ground was too wet after the recent storms for the fire to get a quick hold. So, you saw us coming and ran. Now, am I right?"

Hugh ground out his cigarette. "Get Magda here; ask her—"

"We can't."

"Why, has she gone suddenly dumb?"

"She is dead," said Inspector Reid.

Hugh dropped his hand and stared. His face was ashen. "You let me talk . . . talk and talk, when all the time you knew Magda was dead. You tricked me . . . you—"

He sat back in the chair and passed out.

CHAPTER

30

IN the end it was a casual remark of Pauline's that brought the action for manslaughter against Hugh.

I had called at her mother's cottage to take two of my dresses I thought Pauline would like. She was there. She was herself again, bright, contented, and very talkative.

She admitted that she was glad Hugh Gayer would never stay at Amber Court again. She said, "I don't suppose Mr. Eskinholm will keep that big house on, now his wife is dead. But if he does, he won't let *him* come."

"Mr. Gayer?"

"That's him."

She said, "He was always ordering me about as if he owned the house. 'Do this.' 'See to that.' 'Bring me the other.' It was like as if he paid my wages."

I murmured, "She liked having him around." It wasn't a question. I knew perfectly well why Magda had encouraged him to stay. With her sophisticated perception she recognized the potential criminal behind the graceful pose, and she had work for him to do.

Pauline was saying, "...and scaring me, like the night when Mum sent me to her friend Mrs. Jo at your house to ask her to come to tea the next day. It was nearly dark, but I see him—Mr. Gayer, I mean—down by the terrace. I had to pass him, but he was looking as if he was hiding, dodging behind the wall. And he said, 'If you dare say you've seen me here, you'll be a dead duck in the morning, do you hear?' I heard, all right. I thought he was after Miss Wyncourt, her being pretty and not married like Mrs. Eskinholm, so I said nothing. And then that same night Mr. Wyncourt fell down the stairs and died and—well—it was awful."

I grabbed her. "You're going to tell Inspector Reid about this."

"Oh, no. I've had enough of police."

"There's nothing more to be afraid of," I said.

Since the night of the burning of the Isabella she seemed to like me and trust me, so she let me drive her to see Red Reid.

At the Amesdale headquarters, Hugh was brought in again for questioning. Because he was alone now, and frightened, he admitted that he had gone to Roseheath on the night of Oliver's death. He had planned to hide in one of the unused rooms until we had all gone to bed and were safely asleep. Then he would take the Isabella.

But the house was strange to him. Neither Grandmother nor Oliver had ever invited him there. Magda had described the geography of Roseheath to him, and his first visit had been when he had come to look for the Isabella and had taken the precaution of loosening the curtain bracket to facilitate a quick get-away if he should need it. (The foresight of a natural criminal, I thought when I heard.)

What terrified him most of all was that he might be accused of Oliver's murder. "I didn't kill him . . . I'm not a killer. You've got to believe that."

Only, unwittingly, he had caused Oliver's death. Knowing, at the time, only the hall where the portrait hung, Hugh had entered the house by the back door to look for a room in which he could hide until the house slept.

He had intended to hide in one of the south-wing rooms,

but he heard Mrs. Jo moving about and escaped her by slipping up the back stairs. What he did not realize was that this staircase had not been divided like the main one, for it was so seldom used. He had no idea that he had strayed into the west wing. When he reached the first-floor landing he turned the wrong way and found himself face to face with Oliver. Overtaken by fright, Hugh had pushed past him. Oliver had stepped back, lost his balance, and fallen.

Sitting in the Inspector's office, Hugh had told all as if, like in the confessional, admission would wipe out his sins —and his punishment.

"You see, I didn't kill him. It was an accident . . . I don't want to die . . ."

"You aren't going to, sonny boy," said Red Reid calmly. "You've got one hell of a time in front of you here on earth."

It was over. As if Roseheath knew that its shadows were lifted, it seemed to blossom in the spun gold of early autumn.

Letters came from Justin with snapshots of himself taken on the hillside of Svenling's world.

"This is the life. Every day has its mixture of hard work, good food, and marvelous companionship. One day I want you to come over here for a holiday. I want to show you my world . . ."

For some weeks, I saw little of Sarne. Occasionally I caught sight of him turning a corridor at the Works or getting into his car. After Magda's funeral he did not come near me, nor was I asked to Amber Court.

I breathed freely and did not fear the darkness. And while I laughed and met my friends and put the world to rights over coffee and danced at the Martinelle in Amesdale, deep inside me, where it didn't show, was the ache of limbo.

A month later came the one hour of the day of the week that I would remember for the rest of my life. Three o'clock on a honey-gold afternoon in September.

I was trying, very belatedly, to cope with the pile of letters from friends and acquaintances who had written to me since the two sudden deaths of comparatively young people—Magda and Oliver—had hit the headlines.

I sat at the desk that used to be Grandmother's, which stood at right angles to one of the windows looking out over the garden. There were certain letters in the pile that tempted me to write more fully and personally than the usual ones in the circumstances of death. These were from Wyncourt people—the aunts and uncles in Australia and South America. But in every case, the family, so partially united, so generally alienated, had written only very formal letters of sympathy, and I felt that an acknowledgment was all they wanted from me in reply. They had obviously no desire for us to meet or correspond.

I had lost two families, my own and my adopted one. Now it was up to me to make my life, and I would. I would make Roseheath what it once had been, a place of people and living and laughter. I would divide it into apartments. There would be no more great closed rooms, no more sweep of grounds with only the birds' songs and Ming's bell to break the stillness.

All this was a happy thought, full and positive and rich. But until the planning and the conversions were done, until the families came that I chose to have apartments at Roseheath, there was a time of emptiness that I could not seem to fill.

I signed the sixth letter of my pile and reached for an envelope. As I did so, I glanced into the garden. A gilded haze hung over earth and sky. The grass was brushed with it; the trees stood against the sky as if painted on an apricot background.

I leaned forward, blinked, and brushed my hand across my eyes. I was not dreaming a dream.

Sarne stood under the oak tree.

As on the night when I had escaped death at the Mandrake Cave, he did not move. But I guessed he had been watching me for some time.

I thought: He has come to tell me something, but his courage is failing him ...

I knew that I had to go to him, for he would not come to me. The oak tree was the very boundary of his approach to Roseheath. He had not been inside the house since he had come to give me Adrienne's check for my ring.

I pushed back my chair with such a force that it overturned. I left it where it was, went to the front door and out into the misty sunlight. Warm air sweetened by late flower scents closed around me. I walked slowly over the grass, afraid to meet him.

I don't know at what moment the miracle happened, but at some time during my approach, Sarne must have lifted his arms for, as I reached him, they enclosed me and held me.

"Suzanne—"

"Oh, Sarne, I've wanted to see you, to talk to you ..."

He said on laughter, "You are like your Siamese. You like talk too much."

And a long time later we walked, hands locked, toward the silver birch wood where the birds sang.